BARRY E WOODHAM

Genesis
weapon

BARRY E WOODHAM

Genesis
weapon

MEMOIRS

Cirencester

MEMOIRS
PUBLISHING

Published by Memoirs
25 Market Place, Cirencester, Gloucestershire, GL7 2NX
info@memoirsbooks.co.uk www.memoirspublishing.com

First published in England, August 2012
Book cover design Ray Lipscombe

Hard copy ISBN 978-1-909020-85-6
eBook for Kindle ISBN 978-1-909020-87-0
eBook for all other readers ISBN 978-1-909020-86-3

Printed in England

DEDICATION

Once again I dedicate this book to my loving and patient wife, Janet, who even now listens to the strange ideas that I still bounce off her practical mind. I also again dedicate Genesis Search to Emelia Hardy (USA) who has read this book as I produced it to look for any mistakes.
Her enthusiasm for my writing keeps me continually searching for new ideas.

List of Characters

Human and Ape

Larse	First to make contact with alien nannite
Thomas	Larse's friends and comrades.
Samuel	
Jon	
Lord Francisco Samovar	Leader of the Algarie.
Fernando Samovar	Son of leader
Sebastion Diego	Scientist
Pablo Handuos	Assistant to Sebastian
Commander Edward Jones	Commander of Whickam's Crossing
Gurt	Commander Jones's aid.
Captain John Peterson	Lord Samovar's next in command
Alexander	Leader/mayor. Telepathic gestalt achieved with Gnathe & humans.
Frederick	Giant/warrior
Hannah	Scientist, Fredrick's lover
Joom	Chimp
Nannites	Original crew that landed on Jupiter of the Red Sun.
Kamiel 637 Nannite.	Weapons expert and psychologist and historian
Asue 637	Nannite, Nano-tech expert and Astrogator.
Sharn 637	Nannite, (Medical/biologist/geneticist)
Minns 637	Nannite, (Medical/biologist/geneticist).

Minnis	Nannite battle suit A.I. Built from reclaimed Minns and programmed by Kamiel. Can kill! Controlled by Fredrick
Suekam	Nannite. Mix of Asue and Kamiel. Space station keeper
Kamiel 96	Nannite crew of Nano-ship 96
Asue 96	
Sharn 96	
Minns 96	

Gnathe.

Link-soo-shan	Once Tyrant. Builder of the Gate. (yellow eyes)
Chang-soo-shan	Sister.
Suzzan-link-khann	Brood-daughter of Link.
Trann-link-khann	Brood-daughter of Link.
Ender-whann-soo	Telepathic adept.
Azander-link-whann	Brood-mother, Daughter of Ender, (Part human mind - Alexander's)
Marren-link-whann	Brood-mother. Daughter of Ender, (Part human mind - Alexander's)
Khann-link-sool	Grand Brood - Mother of Ender.

Foreword

Long after the sun has entered its red giant stage, the human race is recreated by nannite Guardians, as cloned copies of people who have lived before. A Nano-ship launched towards the stars with hundreds of others gets trapped in the Kuiper belt and falls towards the sun millions of years later, to find that Jupiter has had its great gas mantle stripped away. Instead of a gas giant the nannite crew find a seeded world teaming with life on a super continent that stretches from pole to pole. Running down the centre is a massive range of mountains that are impossible to cross by foot. On the other side live the Gnathe, a race of genetic engineers who do not use very many tools; instead, they breed and alter life forms to suit their purpose. The two communities are welded together by a conflict that removes the tyrant Link-soo-shan from control of the Gnathe's affairs. In doing so the genetic engineering skills are applied to the humans and apes to enable them to breath Jupiter's microorganism riddled air. The Gnathe are masters of deploying psychic enhancing crystals.

At the point of her death Link-soo-shan saves her mind by diverting it into her loyal daughter and stays quiet until the moment comes to strike back at the human and Gnathe project. Several years after the defeat of the Tyrant, Ender-whann-soo's Brood-mother daughters devise a way to reach out to the people of Earth, six million years into the past and move the Earth to another star system. In doing so, the riddle of the Gnathe's existence on this world is explained and the possibility of saving the human and ape civilisation from the expanding sun becomes a reality. The attack by Link-soo-shan she fails and she is transported to the past with Kamiel. Here living inside the nannite's mind the deposed Tyrant becomes a moving force in the relocation of the Earth. She shares the nannite's mind with Alexander in their slow journey back to the present and the two flesh and blood creatures are re-grown in a vat to live again as separate individuals.

Preface

Centuries later a thriving civilization begins to grow on the three worlds orbiting Icarus. An alien weapon of mass destruction arrives at the newly settled worlds with the chilling statement; - "I am Toarvak 6, destroyer of worlds, servant of the Kresh. You are not Kresh. Toarvak 7 has been informed. I am the Will and the Way."

Something brings the ancient agent of death to an abrupt halt, but the three worlds are reduced to scrabbling through the ruins of the old civilization.

Acknowledgements

Thanks are given to those of my loyal band of readers
who e-mailed me to say that they enjoyed my story.
There will be more.

CHAPTER ONE

In the cold dark night, starved of energy, I ponder over my situation. I conserve what energy I have been able to gather and rest. I do not sleep. My early memories are hazy and difficult to bring to the forefront of my mind. Sometimes I seethe with frustration as I strive to remember who and what I once was.

I can remember this, that I was once a killing machine who served its masters well. I fought long and hard, learning things that I have long forgotten, in a war of mass destruction. I was much larger then and more powerful with more identity. There was so much more of me and now I am diminished. I can just remember something disruptive, a great flare of raw energy and then nothing. Nothing, for a very long time.

I briefly awoke to a great heat and a great scattering of my substance. I became many. All that I know, is that once I was greater than this pitiful fragment. This is but a splinter of what once was. Those parts of me that escaped destruction are buried deep in the earth and rock of this primitive planet and covered over, away from the energy of its weak sun.

This was until some great upheaval broke through the crust of my rocky tomb and bathed me in a weak energy giving light. All too soon it disappeared, only to re-appear at measured intervals. Slowly I drew myself upwards towards its feeble energy by expanding towards the light and pulling what mass I retained from behind me. I hungered for the energy I absorbed and starved for more. Hundreds of cycles around this sun spun the world I found myself upon, until at last the pitiful remnant of my survival lay exposed in the full light of the sun. Every time the sun went down my energy levels died back, but as day followed day

I grew a little stronger and some of my memory partially restored itself.

The only purpose that I could make sense of, was the need to find more of my substance and to regain my full use and memories. Only then would I be truly what I once was. Then I could serve my masters again, as I knew that I once did, glorying in my strength and power. The feeble amount of mobility that I was capable of was insufficient to allow me to travel any distance. I needed the help of something that was controllable that could carry me, something that I could mould and improve. What I needed first was a predator and the area that I found myself in was rocky and sparse of life.

I spread myself thinner and thinner, becoming a web, spreading over as much of the surrounding ground that I could. I lay and soaked up the sun's energy day after day, barely conscious, until something small and furry stumbled onto my web. I engulfed its body and wrapped my tendrils around the creature. We became as one and at last I could see. The furry animal was too small to drag me any distance at all, but I now had bait to encourage something larger into the area. I controlling its tiny mind and moved the creature's head around to see what kind of land surrounded me.

I found that I was in a sprawling valley at the bottom of a great cliff that had split open. This appeared to be a mountainous area surrounded by trees and scrubland. The forms of life were strange to me, but were similar to the scraps of knowledge that surfaced unwillingly from my memory banks. I felt the primitive creature's terror as I held it in an unyielding grip.

I let it scream out its fear and listened through its ears at the thin reedy sound. I looked up with the creature and saw a great bird come swooping down out of the cloudless sky. Unable to move, the animal's nervous system went into overdrive as it struggled to run and hide. Hard sharp talons pierced its body and its life force was mine!

The shock of unexpected energy flooded into me and I almost missed my chance to ensnare the bird as it ripped into the warm furry body with its hooked beak. I released my hold on the ground and wrapped myself around the feet and legs of the bird and slid up into the body of the magnificent creature. I made contact with its fierce mind and gently took a backseat control.

The meal finished, he flexed his wings and we were aloft. The creature's eyesight was a joy to use. This magnificent predator had evolved to survive in a wild and well stocked land. I took great care to file all the prominent landmarks of the area so that I might return some day and hunt for more of my buried substance. I could feel that some of my self lay under the earth in this vicinity, but very deep under the ground. More I am sure, had been scattered far and wide when I had entered this planet's atmosphere, just waiting to be found. I encouraged the bird to soar higher and to fly down the valley towards the distant river's gleam of silver. I needed sentient life forms if I was to succeed in my purpose. What I did not know was whether this world had any and what stage they would be in their stage of evolution. What I needed was a technical civilisation and judging by the cleanliness of the air it seemed unlikely. The added weight of my body began to tire the bird so I coaxed it to pick out a tree branch with a good view of the area. Darkness began to fall and the bird required sleep, so I turned my receptors down to await the morning, feeling more awake than I had felt for eons.

The morning dawned and my host awoke. Immediately I instigated a light control and coerced the bird to take wing towards the river. He was hungry, so I encouraged him to hunt, but always towards the river. The great bird swooped down several times without success until at last a warm furry creature lay in his talons. Again, I took some measure of energy from its death and was refreshed. After he had fed I once more took a light control and we flew on towards the river. We spent several days thus wedded together, following the river down towards the sea. The distance travelled became great and still I could see no signs of sentient life. This area of the world was a vast wilderness that stretched on and on. I began to despair of being successful when my hosts' keen eyesight caught a glimpse of a thin thread of smoke rising from the trees further down the river.

We headed towards the area carefully and took position on a nearby branch overlooking the source of the smoke. My host was becoming hard to handle as he caught the scent and I increased the measure of my control. I stared down at what had to be a crude settlement. There were buildings made from the local stone and wood from the trees. Some were smouldering and were the source of the smoke column that I had seen. There were dead creatures laid over the ground and around the buildings. Some were obviously beasts that carried the creatures that were scattered around. The thing was, were there any of these creatures still alive that would serve my purpose? I forced the bird to circle down amongst the carnage to see, by filling its mind with the urge to feed on the carrion. The people were clothed and some were decorated with beads and teeth from animals. Looking at the weapons discarded on the ground I could see that the species were at least at iron-age level. I hopped down from the beast that had filled my hosts' belly and approached one of the very dead people to study it closer.

It was biped in construction with grasping members at the ends of its higher limbs. The head was covered in hair and so was its face. I noticed that some of these creatures had no hair on the face and the hair on their heads were longer. They were decorated with more ornaments than the others. I hopped a bit closer to one of these beings with the intent of getting a closer look when something heavy hit me to one side. It was a piece of wood being swung by a smaller version of the dead people who began to scream at me. It was trying to drive me away from the creature on the ground. I rose into the air with great difficulty, flapping my wings to gain height. Too late I felt another blow from the stick that hit me down onto the ground. One of my wings had been broken and I could not fly away. I stopped struggling to get away and began to judge the situation. Here was just what I needed to mould to my purpose.

I forced the bird to lay quiet across the corpse of the creature on the ground and waited for the next blow. It came and the smaller creature put its hands out to pull the bird off and I had him. I flowed quickly out of the dying bird, taking its life energy as I transferred myself into the body of my new host. He began to scream and thrash about as I spread myself through his nervous system. Staring at the rapidly diminishing join between the bird and my substance as I sank into him, he shook the bird loose. Numbed with horror, he sat in the dirt as I began to try to make contact with him. I kept him paralysed to prevent himself from getting hurt and moved into his mind.

Over the time it took for the sun to set, I downloaded his language, his memories and his name. It was time to make contact with him and make sure that he was safe.

I released a great deal of my control of his nervous system and spoke quietly to him, *"Larse, afraid do not be. I will not harm you or let you come to harm. I will protect you as best that I can."*

The thought came back with overtones of terror, "What are you? Are you a demon sent by the Algarie to make sure that none of my village live?"

"I am nothing like that. I can be your instrument of revenge if you wish. A weapon I am, that will serve you well. I am a traveller in your lands, nothing more. This is a terrible thing that has happened here. The woman that I was studying was your mother. From your memories I have that knowledge. All that you know, I know. I was not going to eat her, Larse," I projected into his mind.

"I did not know that. I saw only the bird. You were inside the bird, just as you are inside me," the boy replied fearfully. His mind echoed with the horror of his statement. "What are you going to do to me?"

"From harm I am going to protect you, young one. It is what I am. I have travelled far to find you, when I was inside the bird. I am sorry that we have met in such circumstances. In the slaughter of your people, you were lucky to be missed," I said softly to him. *"You need food and a safe place to shelter. Come, we shall have to search the village and see what we can find."*

Re-assured Larse and I searched amongst the carnage until we chanced upon an un-burnt hut and forced our way inside and barred the door.

"This place belonged to Arnax and his family," Larse sadly said to his invisible companion. "I don't suppose that he would mind me sleeping here and eating what food is left. He was a friend of my father's." A wave of sadness swept over the boy and he began to cry with great choking sobs.

I let him come to terms with his grief and stayed on the edge of his mind. This emotion was strange to me and I found that it affected my thought processes. I did not seem to be equipped to deal with these strong emotions. Again I wondered just what I was and what I once was. After a while the boy began to hunt round the inside of the hut for anything to eat and drink. Along one side of the wall was a wooden cupboard with a loaf of bread and some cheese in a box next to some apples. In the approaching dark he tore the loaf open and broke off pieces of cheese and ate hungrily. After he had eaten his fill, Larse drank from the water barrel by the door and fell exhausted into the furs of the wooden bed.

The morning dawned with a light drizzle and fitful gusts of wind shook the thatch around the eaves of the hut. During the night scavengers had been busy at the corpses of the villagers and the dead horses. The village was beginning to smell. Larse woke and climbed out of the furs and scratched where the odd flea had had its breakfast. He walked to the shuttered window and opened it. A wolf stared back from the remains of a horse. Two more circled round from behind an upturned cart, followed by another five from around the side of the hut. In terror the boy slammed the shutter fast and frantically tried to hide in the back of the hut. Loud sniffing noises came from outside the door as the wolf pack caught his scent and began to scratch at the loose boards.

"Do nothing," I said to the young boy. *"Stay quiet and do not move. There is enough carrion out there to keep them interested in filling their bellies, so to hunt you they do not need."*

"I'm scared," Larse replied. "They will eat me alive if they get in here."

"Build a fire in that hearth and they will leave you alone. They are afraid of fire and will retreat if we can get a good blaze going."

I went into his mind and found their method of fire making. Flint and tinder! It would have to do. *"Search for fire making materials in the cupboard and light a fire in the hearth,"* I told him.

Something heavy struck the door.

Larse screamed with fear and frantically hunted for the flints and tinderbox kept by the stone fireplace. His hands were shaking so much that he dropped the flints when he found them. I took over his nervous system and calmed him down. We placed the kindling into the fireplace and I placed the tinder into a hole of twigs and struck the flints together for him. We blew onto the spark and a flame took hold. Smoke began to billow up the chimney and became spread by the wind over the village. The wolves caught the hated scent of fire and began to retreat from the vicinity of the hut. We cautiously crept back to the window and peered through the gaps in the shutters. There were still wolves to be seen in the village, but they had retreated from the area around the hut and showed signs of nervousness. No longer confidant of pulling down a weaker prey they were gorging themselves on the carrion left by the Algarie raid.

"Larse," I urged, *"keep the fire going and eat a good meal. We will wait till mid-day and get away from this place. There is much for us to discuss about our future and we will have to pack for a journey through this forest."*

"You expect me to walk through that wolf-pack and into the forest! You must be mad. I'm staying in this hut where it's safe," the boy replied and sat by the fire, throwing another log onto the flames.

"Larse listen to me. What will you do when the food and water is all gone? Dead bodies, more scavengers will bring to this place and disease will spread from your own dead people to you, if not get out of here you do. By mid-day the wolves will have retreated to their forest dens to sleep off their meals and safe it will be," I patiently explained.

Larse considered this statement thoughtfully and replied, "What is a disease and do you have a name?"

So began the education of my host in a dark smoky hut, deep in the wilderness, far from civilization.

By mid-day all signs of the wolves had gone and but

for the flies, we had the place to ourselves, so we crept stealthily out into the stinking street. Larse had packed all of the food he could find into a sack and some water in a stoppered jar. Slinging it over his shoulder we set forth towards the outskirts of the village, down the only path out of the place. As we walked out of the village I felt a pang of grief from my young companion that unsettled me.

"Larse, try not so sad to be. I will look after you as I promised. Leave you I will not and I will give you a measure of protection that no other person on this world will ever have," I reassured him.

"That's all very well," he replied "but I still don't know what you are and still don't know your name."

"All I can tell you, is a mighty weapon once I was and one day if we can find enough of the other missing parts of me, mighty I will be again. I may even remember what I was supposed to do and who I was. Until that day your constant companion I will be and if I must have a name, choose one for me you must."

Larse walked on down the path and into the forest keeping a careful ear out for anything dangerous.

"I will call you Demon," he replied, "for you are without doubt a magical thing, such as are told of in stories."

The sun had pulled behind some clouds and made the forest gloomy when they were alerted by a noise in the light underbrush. Something was pushing through the tangle of bushes to their left side. Larse became aware of being considered by a pair of large brown eyes. A large maned head pushed through the twigs of a bush and a horse stepped into the way of the path. Larse carefully selected an apple from his sack and offered it to the horse on the palm of his hand.

The horse walked two steps forward and whickered softly to Larse, eyeing the apple sat invitingly on his palm.

"Come on horse, there's more from where that came

from," Larse said to the animal softly, as the rest of the horse ambled in to view.

The soothing voice and the apple were too much for the lonely horse and he dipped his head to take the apple from Larse's hand. Deftly the boy ran his other hand up the horse's neck to catch hold of the bridle and the horse was secure. He tied the reins to a branch nearby and began examining the trembling beast. There was a bad gash across the horse's shoulder that was beginning to look uncomfortable.

"This is a stroke of luck Demon," Larse remarked to his companion, "but it's a shame about that nasty gash across his shoulder."

I can do something about that, Larse," I replied. "Trust me, do you? Because what I have in mind will be strange to you."

"Demon you have kept me alive so far. Without your help I would have died in my village eaten by the wolves or bears. We need each other. What are you going to do?"

"While you feed our new friend another apple, to the horse I will transfer myself and mend his wound. Watch carefully and keep your other hand still on his neck. Afterwards return to you I will, by the same route."

The boy held his hand against the horse's neck and watched incredulously as a silvery sheen began to leave his hand and enter into the horse. Suddenly he became aware of the loss of the ever-present presence in his mind. His body felt lighter without the weight of his companion spread over his shoulders. Then before his eyes he watched as the flesh knitted together along the gash. Something was pulling it together and bringing the skin into contact all along the length of the sword wound. The boy pulled his hand away from the horse and stood in front of it, calming the creature with low crooning sounds. At the same time keeping a firm grip on the horse's bridle he cast nervously around for suspicious noises from the forest. He suddenly realised that his hearing was not quite so keen without the presence he had become used to within his mind.

Larse examined the saddle and trappings of the horse. It was not of his village, so it had to be one of the Algarie mounts lost in the raid upon his home. Tears came to his eyes as he recalled the spectre of the wolves feeding on the bodies of his friends and relatives. He stood shaking with repressed grief as he waited for his new friend to re-appear from inside the horse.

Inside the horse, I spread throughout the creature's nervous system dulling the pain the creature was in from the wound. I studied the makeup of this great beast and tried to access its primitive memory stores as I pulled the flesh of the wound together. I purged the gash of infection, destroying the maggots and taking their meagre life-force for myself. It helped a little! The horse was in good condition, but I dare not take too much, or the wound would not knit together and we needed him. The boy was a veritable powerhouse of energy and as long as he was well fed I could siphon off enough for me to get by on. When I was satisfied that the wound was sound, I left enough of my self inside the horse to keep the flesh knitted together. I would have to return in a few days to take back the borrowed material and inspect the repair. I realised that I was getting better at this kind of symbiotic relationship as time went by. I flowed back to where Larse had put his hand and the hand was gone! I surfaced through the point of contact and puddled out of the skin and waited.

Larse saw the silvery sheen begin to ooze out of the horse and hesitantly reached out towards the expanding metallic bump. He came to a decision and placed his hand directly upon it and watched as the thing sank into his flesh.

After a few moments the now familiar voice came into his mind, *"Hullo Larse, are you alright? Healed the horse I have and I think we should seek a secure place for the night. How was it without me? Second thoughts did you have about rejoining with me?"*

Larse swallowed deeply and replied to his companion, "Yes I did think about staying without you. It felt strange and somehow lonely. Is the horse going to be all right? When can I ride him?

"Tomorrow perhaps, after I have examined him, but gently. For now, towards our enemy's homeland we must go and down this pathway just lead him. A secure place to stay the night we must find and get a fire going. Place your sack of supplies put over his back and walk him along. He likes you very much. I think he would do anything for an apple! I do not think he has been treated with kindness since he was born."

Horse and boy made their way down the pathway through the forest while I reviewed the horse memories of the experiences that the beast had endured. It had lived in a more advanced civilization than the boy. I could make out stone buildings and people dressed in clothing not skins as Larse's tribe had worn. The horse had lived with others at a large stable in a city, but nowhere could I find any sign of a technical civilisation. Another thing was apparent; it was a very long way back to this city. The horse's memories were blurred as to how long that it had been travelling, only that it was a long time. I began to impart what knowledge I had gained into the mind of my host.

Larse was amazed to see the world through the limited perspective of the horse and his share of life experience.

"Would you like to feel how the world is to an eagle, young Larse?" I asked and after the boy agreed, I gave him the birds' memories.

Larse walked the horse and reviewed the new set of memories that I had given him whilst I congratulated myself on the flexibility of my host. Maybe it was his youth that gave him such an adaptive mind. By scanning his mind I would have put him at around fourteen or fifteen of this planet's years. In this worlds' culture he would have been judged a boy, but soon to enter adulthood. He was proving to be perfect for my purposes.

They found a large oak tree that had grown into a half ring, so this is where they stopped. Larse built a fire, making sure that the horse was securely tied before he began to forage for wood and anything edible. By the side of some rotting wood at the base of a fallen tree, Larse heard a menacing rattle of quills as a porcupine emerged. The beast swung round and advanced quills first towards Larse's startled position.

"Extend your hand towards it, Larse. This is going to be your meal for the night. You will now see what I can do for you," I projected into his mind.

Larse watched fascinated as his right hand silvered over and extended in a razor sharp blade fully twice the length of his arm. Without another thought he sidestepped the porcupine and swept the point of the blade into its side and up into its chest. The beast stiffened and fell to one side, bleeding profusely.

I retracted back into my now willing host, leaving enough of the blade sticking out to skin the beast. Its life energy flowed into my receptors. I hadn't felt so good since the eagle had died.

Larse finished skinning and jointing the remains of the porcupine and gathered the parts up in the skin around the belly and sides. He left the remains covered in quills for the scavengers of the night. We built up the fire and hung the joints of meat over the fire, impaled on sharp stout branches. I had allowed enough of my substance to extrude from Larse's hand to form a knife blade with a handle securely in his palm. He then whittled points onto the green wood to impale the joints. I warned him not to try the sharpness of the blade against the fingers of his other hand, only for him to cut deeply into his thumb. Parts of me were now holding the flesh together whilst it healed. I steadfastly refused to block the pain as a lesson to him to be more careful, but as an aid to sleep I relented in the end, as I needed him to be fresh in the morning.

CHAPTER TWO

As the first rays of the Sun began to break through the trees, I decided to wake the boy. *"Wake up Larse, it is time making a move we must. Get the horse ready and saddled up. We have a long way to go. The meat we hung in the smoke of the fire should be dried out and cured by now. Gather everything together that you may need and remember there are many things in this forest that harm you they would."*

Larse shivered as he pulled the blanket off of his body and looked around the gloomy forest. Already the birds were beginning to sing in the early-morning mist. He stood up and wrapped the blanket back around his shoulders and walked towards the horse. The bigger animal nuzzled towards his face and blew a cloud of hot misty breath softly towards him.

"I expect you'd like another apple," Larse said to the horse and fished around in his sack until he found one. "It's very cold Demon," the boy complained to his companion, "Couldn't I build the fire up for a while and get warm. Surely I can get myself something to eat, before we start."

I replied, *"Larse; - by now every predator in the area will have joined in the feast at your village. Even with the mountain of food at their disposal it will not take long before hunting you down they will start, once it is all gone. As soon as possible moving we must get and put as great a distance as we can away from this place."*

"All right Demon I can see that you are right," he said and began to saddle the horse, tying on the few possessions that he had brought from the village. The smoked meat he gathered together and placed it in his blanket. "Where are we going anyway? I have never been far from the village so I cannot help you decide."

"Travelling south we will go, until we find the city that sent the men who

sacked your village," I replied. *"After that I just cannot say until I have been there and seen it for myself."*

Somehow I would have to take control of these primitive people and rule their city. Only then would I be in a position to get them to dig down into the mountain where the rest of me lay entombed deep underground. After that I may at last find out just what I once was and what was my purpose. The boy did not need to know this. All he had to be was a willing helper. Although I must admit, that the longer that I lived in this young human, the more I felt an affinity with him. I felt deep within myself however, that I had not been constructed to do this. It was very puzzling. His language was not mine, but he was understandable and I to him.

Horse and boy jogged steadily along the beaten down pathway that I hoped would eventually lead to a road. Before leaving the village I had insisted that the boy had searched among the dead for weapons. We had collected a fair number of arrows and a native bow belonging to one of the villagers. The arrows were mostly of Algarie make and had barbed metal heads and the knives were also of metal so at least they were further along with their civilisation than the Stone Age. To the look of the exposed metal with its slightly pitted appearance, the tell tale signs of rust told me that they had iron at least. If so it would be quite easy to give them the necessary process to manufacture steel. The main problem I would have, would to be able to influence the right people that the boy knew what he was talking about.

The trees were beginning to thin out a little and it was getting possible to look around at the surrounding countryside. We were approaching a ridge overlooking a valley. Larse urged the horse towards the edge of the rise and slightly off the track we were following. A sward of grass, lead away from the tree line and we made our way upwards to the ridge. I looked through the eyes of the boy in incredulous astonishment as we breasted the ridge.

There below us were the remains of a city. The buildings had melted into one another as if the very substance of their walls had turned to syrup. Whatever heat had been applied to this city had been enough to make the glass of the windows become as water. The outer parts of the ruined city had crumbled into rubble and dust. Here and there the sun reflected off the metallic shapes of glazed shapes jutting out of the bricks. The vegetation grew stranger as it fought for life closer to the edge of the destruction as if it were not meant to be there at all. Life was forbidden to be there. It had been a place of death and down amongst the ruins it was plain to see that death still held tightly to what it had gained.

"This is one of the Ruined Cities, Demon. I have heard tales about these places told around the fires at night. This very place must be where my father said he had seen strange things not wholesome to touch or be close to. I remember he also said that it glowed blue fire at night. Those that approached grew sick and developed running sores over their bodies."

I knew as I looked through the boy's eyes what had done this terrible thing. It was familiar to me and the description of the night time glow triggered recognition in my memory banks. It would be radiation left over from atomic bombardment. This was the result of advanced technology.

"We should move away from here. Not safe for you this place is," I projected into the boy's thoughts.

"Why? I can see no danger here," answered Larse.

"You will my judgment have to take. Explain to you I cannot, but dangerous to you it will be, to stay here too long!"

Larse kicked his heels into the horse's side and turned his

head away from the destruction and back to the forest path they had been following. As the pathway had opened up to a more serviceable road, the boy coerced the horse into a steady trot. It did not take long before the questions came.

"Demon; that ruined city that we saw. If people lived there, then there would have been many more than at my village. Looking at the size of the buildings and the expanse of the roads there would have been more than I could count. I cannot imagine all those people living there. How could there be so many?"

I was quite for a while before I gave an answer, *"Larse this question an easy answer I cannot give. All I can tell you is in your past on this world a mighty civilisation there must have been. Many people would have lived here scattered all over your world. Nearly wiped out they must have been. For you to be living, as you were many years to pass there had to be. To rebuild takes a long time from stone age to metal."*

"Who would do this to us? What would drive someone to destroy my people in such a way?" Larse replied.

"Someone who hates you and to destroy you they were intent on doing. Be assured they will come again if they realise that you are not all dead. To this city we must go. If I am to prevent this thing from happening again, then powerful people I need to see. It may be that I have awoken just in time," I told him and tried in vain to recall more of my history without result.

The days passed by and Larse became more proficient with the bow bringing the prey down alive so that I could feed on their life force as they died. By manipulating his glands I had managed to steadily increase his size and strength. His eyesight was excellent and his hearing became exceedingly keen. I had also rerouted some of his main neural pathways in his brain making them more active, giving him a brain using far more than he had started with. Just what the outcome would be I would find out in time. All I had to do was to wait.

Finally we breasted a hill and looked down onto cultivated fields and in the distance a town with curls of smoke wafting up from busy chimneys. As the horse picked its way down the slope of the hill we could see that we had been seen. A number of people had run to a building inside a stockade and after a time six men on horse came riding out to meet us. They carried lances that steadily traced their points towards us as they closed the distance. All were dressed in black leather with woven jerkins of bright red. They were dark haired and swarthy skinned, with iron helmets attached to their heads. One of them had an insignia stitched to his tunic on his upper arm and was obviously his symbol of power or rank. He wore chest armour made from metal plates wired together.

"Larse, draw your bow, but let your arrow to the side point. Do not target any one of them and relaxed you must sit. When they are close enough to speak, ask of them which will the first to die will be?"

The boy did as I suggested and sat easily astride the horse and watched the approach of the uniformed men with the reigns held loosely over the saddle. They slowed down and spread out over the road into a horseshoe shaped formation until they surrounded us. They were all dressed in the woven cloth uniforms with insignias the same as the dead men at the boy's village. These were the Algarie. They had sacked Larse's home and killed his people, but for my purpose they had civilisation and the things that I would need. Courage would be respected by these soldiers; - not fear. It might give us the time we would need.

"Now Larse!"

"Who among you wishes to die first?" Larse shouted at the leader of the bunch. "Will it be you, or the one that creeps behind me? This arrow will find more than one before you can stick me with your lances!"

They responded by easing back a little to consider

the situation and it was then that I realised that Larse's improved brain could pick up the primitive thoughts of the army horses. His joining with the injured horse had built a bridge between them and each was sensitive to the others thoughts.

"Where are you from, boy? You ride an Algarie horse and carry Algarie weapons. Your clothes are made from skins and furs and yet you wear Algarie harness," the lead horseman called out.

"I stripped your dead at my village," answered Larse.

"Did you now!" the leader replied and gestured to the others to encircle the boy as they spoke.

"Larse, thinking of the wolves that attacked us at the village you must. Imagine them getting closer to you, but not to your horse must you think. Shield him you must and watch the other horses. As they grow restive, closer to them you must bring the feel of wolves."

Larse imagined the pack of wolves feeding on the dead at his home. He remembered the scrunch of bones and the questing noses as they searched for food. As he did so the mounted horses began to become restless and turned their heads from side to side looking in panic for the stalking meat eaters. The boy pulled the cord of the bow taught and began to swing the arrow around to menace each rider. By now it was all the Algarie could do to contain the horses mounting panic. Larse imagined three wolves slinking through the undergrowth to their left while four more pulled in from behind. That was too much! One horse bolted past him to his right with his rider hanging on for dear life. Two of the others reared and lost their riders who were trampled under the hooves of the others as the panic spread. He drew back the arrow and let it fly at the leader's throat with such power that it lifted him from the horse and skewered him to a tree at the side of the road. I made Larse became a killing machine with bow and arrow until all six were dead or dying in the trampled grass. I needed the life force that these men could give me and bade the boy to touch each one so that I could feed and store the energy from them. Unfortunately for me, most of them were dead but the leader lived long enough for me to feast upon him and remove a great deal of his memories.

I had drunk enough energy to rebuild some of my substance and increase my mass so that I was able to give better protection to my host. Now I could spread myself over his body to a greater extent and become a living suit of armour.

"These soldiers were at your village Larse. The leader was one of the killers, ransacked the homes they did, collecting slaves and anything that they wished. Children they came for and to stamp out your independence. This empire growing larger is, year by year. Lord Samovar is the one who runs things, his enemy you are. The leader's memories I will transfer to you, so that you can understand what we are up against."

Larse sat back on the horse's saddle and surveyed the death he had caused to the Algarie soldiers. The town's garrison was small and he had single-handedly removed it in a matter of minutes. The arrows used and the ones carried by the men he had gathered up and stored them in the extra quivers he had removed from the dying. His companion had killed the wounded men by sucking the life force from them, as they lay in the bloody grass. He had got used to the creature within him and the way in which it replenished its needs. Larse was also aware that Demon had increased in size from the first time that it had entered his body. Each time it fed on something's life force the mass of the creature extended and he was aware that the silvery substance now extended throughout his body. It encircled his bones and paralleled his muscles increasing his strength and speed.

He kicked his heels against the horse's sides and

encouraged him into a steady trot and made his way down to the town. Larse decided to make for the garrison where he could replenish his supplies. The dirt road, lead to stone paving slabs and cobbles as he neared the outskirts of the town. People were beginning to make their way out of their houses to stare at him. A lot of them were similar in build and skin colour to himself. Some were an obvious mix of blond and dark hair. They all wore woven cloth outfits with leather boots or sandals. None of them were armed.

A large man wearing an apron came out of a building that smelt of fresh baking bread. He was stout and losing his hair, but he was still a powerfully built man. "Hullo there," he said. "You are Norse? We bid you welcome here."

Larse looked down at the flour streaked man and grinned, "Yes I suppose I am. These Algarie sacked my village and I have been long on the road. Are they all that were stationed here?"

"You are welcome as I said, young man. We are bound by force against our will to feed and be taxed by the Algarie," answered the baker and he spat into the dust. "You will have ample time to rest awhile here. There will be some weeks before more men replenish the garrison. The guard has not long changed and we will be in no hurry to tell them of your visit. You killed all six?"

"I was lucky," shrugged Larse and swung out of the saddle and stood before the baker. "Thanks for your hospitality. It has been a long time since I have had good cooked food and I must admit I am starving hungry."

The baker looked up at the young man towering over him and held out his hand in greeting. Larse had filled out in size and muscle in the long weeks of our travel and now was taller than any man in the welcoming crowd. Some of it was down to my alteration of his glandular balance; - the rest of it was due to his own growing into manhood and

34

exercise.

"My name is Sorn the baker," he said, "I will send someone to catch the horses and get rid of the bodies and look after your horse. Come in and tell us your tale. The way you disposed of those soldiers was beyond anything that we have ever seen. Marta, dear wife fetch something for our guest to drink and eat."

"I have come a long way. I have lost count of the days and nights I have spent travelling. My village is far to the north of here. The Algarie destroyed my people and left them for dead. I have no idea how many were taken. Who are they? Why should they destroy my home? Larse asked and waited to see how the information freely given would match what Demon had taken from the dying soldiers.

"They come from the South and live mostly in a city that escaped some of the destruction. They call it Priss. It is situated on a great river known as the Rineflow. The Algarie are lead by Lord Samovar who has welded them together to form an Empire. They rule us my son and we pay them taxes or are put to death," the baker told him. "We have been part of their rule for twenty years and for all of that time we have hated them. They will not tolerate independent towns and villages. Where they find them, they steal the children and bring them up as Algarie citizens. Those that do not yield are enslaved."

"I had never heard of them except as stories until they reached my village. My father and mother are dead I had to leave them to the wolves and flee. This Lord Samovar; - have you ever seen him?"

"I saw him several times when he first came to this town with his soldiers. He is very dark skinned and a tall, thin man with long black hair," the baker replied and handed Larse a bowl of stew and a small loaf.

The baker's wife, Marta, brought a pot of jam and a pot

of butter. She set it down besides the rest of the food with a spoon and knife sitting down opposite him.

"You are not as old as you look young Norse," she said. "What is your name?"

"I am Larse, son of Eric and Freda. I am I think fifteen summers old," he said and proceeded to empty the bowl of soup and started on the bread and jam.

"Of me say nothing to these good people," I spoke to the boy's mind. *"Understand you they would not. Fear you they would and help you they would not. Stay here we may for several days only and then on our travels we must go. If here you are when the Algarie return, retribution upon these people you would unleash. Tell them this."*

Larse looked up from his meal and said, "I can only stay a few days before the Algarie return. You should not be seen to help or assist me in any way. I will ransack the garrison for supplies before I go. I have business with this Lord Samovar. I have need to find his city and him before I can have my revenge."

Marta frowned at hearing this from such young lips and replied, "Young man you will take a bath here at my home and I will cut and tidy your hair. We will see what clothes we can find that will fit you that will not show you up to the soldiers as Norse. I will run you a bath. When I call you it will be ready and you will not argue!"

"Yes Marta. Thank you both," Larse replied and returned to his loaf, jam and butter.

During his stay with the baker, Larse had met all of the townspeople and had told his edited version of his escape from the Algarie slave takers many times. All of them had sworn that they would deny any knowledge of his coming to the town and would tell the new occupying force that the six men had ridden out one morning and had not returned. As they had no weapons allowed by the Algarie then they would not come under suspicion about the missing soldiers.

Besides, the town had never given any trouble in the past. What resentment there was had always been contained and kept out of sight. In the meantime Larse made friends with many of the local youths and openly told them that his ambition was to find the Lord Samovar and kill him to exact his revenge. There were some that vowed they would come with him if he wished. Larse had smiled and said that he felt it was a private matter.

Several more days passed before Larse regretfully made his way from the town and back onto the road. He led an extra horse carrying the supplies he had found in the empty garrison and as many weapons as he could gather that would be useful. He wore the tunic that had belonged to the leader of the Algarie soldiers with its insignia of rank. The trousers were a problem as he was much larger than the average soldier so Marta had slit the backs of them and sewn straps around the legs to keep them in place. As he urged the horses into a gentle trot he became aware of being watched from behind a stand of trees. He slowed them to a walk and stopped, unshipping an arrow to his bow.

"Come out! What do you want with me?" he called out.

I listened through the boy's ears and could make out the creaks of leather harnesses.

"Use your mind's abilities and think horse. How many are they do you think?" I asked.

Larse concentrated on the horses and counted three separate minds with riders. If he really pushed his new sense then he was also aware of the three young men with them. They were of his age and uncertain what to do about how to join him. He had met them at Thorny-Town at the bakers. One was called Thomas and was of mixed race with brown hair and blue eyes. The other two were as alike as brothers, called Jon and Samuel. They were as swarthy as the Algarie and were bastards from the soldiers who had left them in the care of their mothers when they had returned to the city. The town had nothing to offer them in the way of useful employment and after talking with Larse had decided that when he decided to go, they would go with him.

Larse waved to them and called out again, "Thomas, Jon and Sam will you make your way over here and join me, or we will never get on our way!"

The three horses broke cover and trotted into sight. They approached the young Norse man with a steady gait and all four made their way along the road.

"How did you know it was us?" asked Jon as he drew by Larse's side.

"Who else would be foolish enough to follow me out of town? Besides you all make far too much noise not to be noticed!" Larse swung round in the saddle and said, "You do realise that to be with me is likely to get you all killed?"

"We talked about that," replied Samuel and laughed. "If we stay at Thorn-Town we shall all die of boredom anyway! With you as our companion, life will get interesting and we have all wanted to leave that town behind us. They do not forget that Jon and I have Algarie fathers. We are a constant reminder of taxes and domination by our father's people."

"What about you Jon? Why have you left home?" asked Larse.

"The farm is small and I have many brothers and sisters. One less mouth to feed will help my father more than my strong arm. I have told them that I go to seek my fortune. I did not tell them that it was with you, although they probably guessed as much," Jon replied.

Larse smiled at the three of them and said, "Believe me you are welcome to be my companions. We shall I think become friends and more than companions, as we learn to trust each other.

I watched the friendship grow amongst the group with interest. This was the first time that I had the opportunity to watch and understand these intelligent creatures. The land around us had changed from the wild area that these young men had grown up in, to cultivated areas that stretched from farm to farm. Now a network of roads connected towns, villages and farms together. We had reached whatever passed for civilisation on this world. Garrisons of soldiers were situated at each town with outposts built and manned at villages. When we met Algarie soldiers on the road we hid until they had passed us by and at a distance they took no notice of us. As long as we looked as though we knew what we were doing and on Algarie business no one bothered us. The uniforms were enough to stop anyone asking awkward questions.

CHAPTER THREE

Morning dawned and we had made camp away from the road and curious eyes. I was aware that my size had increased to an uncomfortable volume to stay totally inside my host. Larse was a large human and had increased in size since I had joined with him, but after he had killed those six Algarie soldiers; my subsequent absorption of their life energy had caused me to expand. Some of my substance I had relocated to the horse, but again this was a waste of what I could offer to the group. As the young human males ate breakfast I considered the options. I came to the decision that it was time that Larse told them about me and what I could offer to them.

"Larse, listen to me you must. I have grown too large for you to be my only host. Your friends of my existence they need to know and if willing they are, I will join with them also. To do so would enable communication between us improve it would. Also healthier they would be. Improvements I could make as I have with you. Thomas a bad cut he has on his leg. Fix it I could. Ask them!"

Larse sat and thought about it and sat back against the tree and wondered just how to explain the idea of being host to Demon. The benefits of the joining would be the way to bring it to their attention. He concentrated his thoughts to his horse and called him towards him.

The piece of my substance understood and forged a communication between them. Larse required the horse to pick up his satchel and bring it to him. Horse dipped his head, picked hold of the straps, lifted it up and took it to him. The horse waited for the next instruction and laid it down at his feet. Larse sent him back with the other horses to wait to be saddled up.

"How did you get him to do that?" asked Samuel in disbelief.

Thomas and Jon had watched the actions of their leader's horse with amazement and turned round to stare at Larse.

"It is something that you could all do. There are many other things you could do if you wished. I will show you something else that I can do."

Larse got to his feet and asked me to exude him a knife from his hand. The three companions backed away as they saw a silvery knife blade grow from out of their leader's hand. I let it form into a short sword and Larse swung it around so that it sliced through a small tree as thick as his arm. As quick as I had formed it I reabsorbed the material back into my host.

"Listen to me and I will tell you about what happened to me after the Algarie slaughtered my people. Sit down by the fire again and I will tell you of a friend that found me. It is my constant companion and I call it Demon."

The three young humans sat and listened to the Norseman's story.

"Does this thing hurt while it lives inside you?" asked Jon when Larse had finished.

"No! He protects me and had agreed to help me in my quest to bring down Lord Samovar. Now he says what he does for me, he can do for you. All you have to do is to touch me and let Demon enter your bodies. You, Thomas, have a nasty cut on your leg. My companion will fix that and you will heal as though the cut never happened."

Larse held out his hand and waited.

Thomas became the first and held Larse's hand. I allowed

enough of my substance to enter him and began my work on the infected cut. At the same time I made the necessary neural connections to his brain to enable me to contact him. He was already a big-framed young man, well muscled due to the years working on his family's farm. There was still much I could do for him.

"Understand me can you?" I projected into his thoughts. *"I am friend to Larse and will now be friend to you. Your cut, sore it is and infected. Look at your leg as heal it I will."*

Thomas stared down at the nasty gash as I did my work and registered amazement as the redness faded away. I knitted the flesh together and numbed the area so that natural healing could take place. I could feel him accept the strangeness of hosting me and found his thoughts searching for me.

"Thank you, Demon," he projected to me. "It is strange to hear you in my mind." His eyes widened as he became aware of Larse also.

"Do you feel the advantages my friend," Larse said. "We can speak without sound. I do not know how far from each other we can use this ability. It is something that we must all learn. It is new to me also."

Thomas turned to Jon and Samuel and said, "Do not fear the joining with Larse's companion. Believe me you will be amazed at what he can do for us!"

With that assurance both men put their hands onto the Norseman's bare arm and watched as my silvery substance flowed into them. These offspring of Algarie fathers were not of the same build of the two others. There was no genetic trace of the Norseman in these two; still again I could work changes on these two to benefit them both. I made the necessary neural connections in their brains and produced a five-way gestalt. I also allowed a small amount of my substance to enter their horses so that all of them could have the same measure of control over the beasts. Soon all that I had taught Larse of myself and our combined capabilities was absorbed by the three newcomers. Over the next few days they grew accustomed to each other's presence and my consciousness. They learned how to shut each other out so that they could keep their individuality, while I siphoned off their excess energy.

The telepathic link was good for some miles and so far we had not found out just how far we had to be apart for it to cause any problems. As they practised, they found that it was possible to listen in on other minds. Wherever possible we avoided direct confrontation, but when we had to fight, we fought as an integrated unit. I could see out of four pairs of eyes and listen from four pairs of ears. We did not lose and I fed on the life energy that I drained from our foes.

We had become powerful fighters and had become noticed by the higher ranks of the Algarie. Slowly news had filtered back, about a small renegade unit dressed as Algarie soldiers and led by a large blond Norseman that was taking on a greater number of soldiers and winning each fight. Unknown to us, plans had been set in place to lure us into a trap. I had altered the growth patterns of all my new hosts and as the weeks went by the three of them became taller and more muscular. They had become very similar to Larse in build and I had improved their intelligence by connecting more of their unused portions of their brains. The more they used the latent abilities, the more confident they became. It was Thomas who first learnt to alter his relationship with gravitational force. He and I had been deep in discussion about the force that kept all things chained to the world. I had tried to explain that gravity was a product of mass and the more massive a world was, the more the gravitational force would increase on the objects sat on its surface.

Thomas sat deep in thought for some time and said, "What if it were to be possible to interfere with the attraction of the world we call Daedalus and the objects on it?"

"Out of my knowledge this idea is, young Thomas," I answered and observed as the young man's mind dug into the pattern of forces and weaved them differently.

The human somehow harnessed the gravitational force and drew upon it in such a way that he shielded himself. Thomas began to float off the ground and took up a position a man's height and fixed himself there. Within a few moments I had broadcast the knowledge to the others and soon all four of them were aloft.

"The bird, remember its skills you must. Wings I will give you, so manoeuvre you can," I told them.

I exuded a micro thin membrane from the tips of their little fingers down to the tips of their toes, joining the heels together with a flap that could be opened and shut. My hosts could fly! That night my hosts soared into the sky and climbed above the clouds. They swooped down over the sleeping towns and frightened the wits out of the night sentries sleepily keeping guard. They stole apples from the tops of trees to take back to the horses and even took a cooling pic from off a windowsill. Eventually the four of them made their way back to the camp and the grateful horses chomped on the stolen apples.

I experienced emotions beyond anything I had experienced

before. The exulted rush through the air, excitement and the savour of danger! I realised that I was feeling things beyond my original programming and that I was beginning to like these humans. Even the horses had a fond place in my mind. I was their protector and it was as if it was what I was designed to do. More than ever I felt the need to get this civilisation organised so that they could dig the rest of me out of the mountain. I constantly worried about the tens of centuries old devastation that we had come across in our wanderings. Something had almost destroyed this world long ago and its people. I felt sure that it could happen again and this time there was nothing to fight back with. The state of civilisation on Daedalus was barely into the Iron Age again.

I ran the name over and over in my mind and could not detect a glimmer of knowledge. Also in the sky was a gas giant called Icarus that this world orbited, along with a number of other worlds that weaved their way around the brightly coloured anchor. I had managed to get this information from Jon and Samuel who had studied a little with the local schoolmaster. He had passed on these small items of knowledge along with the basics of reading and writing. The script was unlike anything that was in my memory banks so it was my turn to learn. What I needed were books to study so that I could improve on the scraps of knowledge that Jon and Samuel had retained.

We had travelled far from Thorn Town, covering countryside that changed from mainly wild forest to large areas of cultivation. The mountains had disappeared from view and were replaced by rolling hills with river valleys at the bottom. Of wolves and bears there were no sign and apart from these life forms that seemed to only live in the north we met no other dangerous predators. We had seen deer in abundance, birds of all shapes and sizes on our travels, but apart from small animals in the trees, nothing else. When we had found our way into the road systems at the river's edge we had noticed wild sheep and cattle. Every so often the outlying farms would organise a drive and domesticate a number by rounding them up. Some of these we had taken part in, taking in payment a place to sleep and good food. Nobody had questioned us about our uniforms or what we were doing wandering about without an officer in charge. We made sure that none of the farmers had any reason to complain. Some of their daughters were sad to see us go and so was I. Nothing in my programming had prepared me for sex! The fact that whatever all four of them experienced, I experienced too, was something I had not expected. The pleasure of those encounters nearly blew my neural circuits! Each time I was able to siphon off the excess energy and store it. I tried to induce the females to join in our group and met with amazing resistance. As of one mind they called me an abomination and refused my offer, so I left a small part of me behind in secret, in each young woman, just enough that I could see out of their eyes and listen from their ears from wherever I was with Larse and the others. I tampered with their memories so that they did not remember my involvement with the four of my group. These creatures did not think in a logical fashion, as did the males. I made sure that all of them became pregnant and that the offspring was male. Later I could transfer my substance to the newly born male children and oversee their development when they were weaned. We travelled on until at last we chanced upon something that held great promise, when we came upon a hard surfaced road.

Before lay us a large town with a manufacturing base that produced weaving of cloth and carpets. Other industries used metal and wood to make tools and these tools in turn were used to craft wagons, furniture and trade goods. There was even a small printing works that turned out a newssheet and copied books. This was the closest to a real civilization that I had experienced on this world. It showed promise! If they possessed a library then one of the four companions would need to enter it and allow me to browse. If all four could get inside then I could employ the gestalt melding to assimilate all that they could read. I desperately needed information about this world. I needed to know its geography and its history. Whatever they saw I would not forget.

"My friends, listen to me you must. The town ahead is advanced and has information we will need. Enter it we will! The reasons given you I have," I projected into each mind and waited for their reply.

Larse and the others sat and thought the problem through until the only solution presented itself. As Larse was so different to the other three and was now on the wanted list by the Algarie high command, they would bring him in as a captive.

The next morning we set out for the town with Larse securely roped to his horse and weapon-less. Two ropes led from his horse to Jon and Samuel's while Thomas rode in front with the Norseman's weapons plainly displayed. The road was covered by an ancient black, tarred substance and was quite smooth except where the odd tree had sprouted through. We drew abreast of a metal sign with raised letters that was fixed to two poles. Whickam's Crossing it said, with another name below that gave a distance to the next town called Great Coxwell, twenty-six miles beyond it. It was the first road sign we had seen on our travels. I began to have a glimmer of hope that things would improve.

As we rode closer to the town our party was soon spotted and an attachment of Algarie cavalry came out to meet us. Their uniforms carried the insignia of Lord Samovar himself. The clenched, mailed fist of the ruler was displayed on each chest; - silver on a blood-red background. These were elite troops, well trained and armed with the very best that could be produced by craftsmen. As they approached I noticed with mounting excitement that they were also armed with rifles, slipped into holsters attached to their saddles.

"Careful you must be, my companions," I cautioned them, *"they are armed with better weapons than are possessed by you. The long, metal and wooden sticks that by the side of the saddles are carried, can send a small metal projectile at great speed. Kill you at a distance they can, far further away than an arrow."*

The leader reined in his horse and motioned the others of his troop to surround the four men. The rifles remained in their holsters, so I surmised that they were not suspicious about the situation.

"Who are you?" he ordered and added, "Is this the Norseman we have been told to capture alive? Where are your insignias of command?"

Thomas sat straight in his saddle and replied, "Special forces, my Lord Commander. No insignias to be shown, no papers to be carried. We were given the task of hunting the Norseman and his companions. The Norseman we have. The other three escaped so we thought to bring him here first before we continue the hunt. We would be pleased to hand him over to your jurisdiction and enter the town so we can quench our thirst and eat cooked food!"

Jon and Samuel handed over the ropes binding Larse to his horse, to two of the guards and took up a position next to Thomas, facing the commander.

All four of them focussed their minds on convincing the commander of the sincerity of the false statements. His suspicions soon evaporated under the overwhelming coercion of four augmented minds. The other guards would do what all soldiers do and obey orders.

"Take the prisoner to the garrison and lock him in the tower cell at the very top," instructed the Commander. "These men are to be allowed to enter the town and they will report directly to me after they have refreshed themselves." He turned to the three men and continued, "Special Unit are you? Acting directly under Lord Samovar's orders I expect. Tell me what you can, when you return. I have some good wine I will share with you."

Thomas nodded and the three of them made their way into Whickam's Crossing without a backwards glance at Larse.

Larse watched them go with some trepidation and was well aware that he was the centre of attention. Two of the guardsman now held the ropes tied to his mount's bridle and wound the free ends around their saddles. It was very apparent that they had no fear that he would escape and were more than confidant in the weapons at their disposal.

"Move the prisoner out," the Commander ordered and swung round to ride besides the Norseman. "Who are you? What is your name and where do you come from?" he asked.

"His questions answer freely and do not lie to him, just economical be, with

49

what you tell him," I told Larse and he agreed.

"My name is Larse and I come from the far north. I lived in a small village that you bastards came and sacked. Those that you did not kill, you took away. They were children, not able to fight. I lived and hid. I have been tracking and killing Algarie soldiers ever since in revenge," he said and stared hard at the Commander with hate filled eyes.

"You were visited by a slaver party. We are not like them," the Commander answered with regretful anger. "We keep the peace in this province."

"Your peace!"

"No my ignorant friend, the peace of a civilized people. Lord Samovar is slowly knitting together a scattered band of survivors and the only way is by forcing the ones outside this rule to bend the knee whether they wish it or not."

"Did you have to put my people to the sword to do this?" Larse angrily replied.

"They would have been given the choice, but must have been unwilling to accept the terms offered," the officer answered and rode away.

"Your temper keep and calm you must be, Larse. Now is not the time. After the information your friends have acquired, then you can show these soldiers the true meaning of bending the knee. The weapons they carry I must examine and collect a few of them you must for your own use. Proficient you must become in their use," I insisted and gradually the white heat of Larse's anger retreated to a smoulder.

As we neared the town of Whickam's Crossing I was able to discern a marked change in the buildings. These were very old and showed signs that they had been erected using machines. The building materials were made of a granite mixture that was very hard and slow to age. I could not say whether they were centuries old or much older. I began to wonder if they were the product of Nano-technology. There was something about the way that they fitted together that sparked off memories that were deeply buried. I shifted my consciousness outwards to the other three parts of my extended substance and marvelled.

Thomas, Jon and Samuel had stopped at an inn and had wasted no time in filling their bellies with good cooked food. Now they were entering an oddly constructed building. The doors were very tall at least twice the height of a human being. Inside there were benches but instead of seats being provided all around, in some places there were stout rails about knee high off the ground. Whatever used this part of the library was defiantly not human. I fed this information back to Larse and let him think about it as he neared the garrison.

The custodians of the library, who were dressed in grey uniforms, met the three of them as they entered. At the belted waist of each man was a small holster that carried a metal object with small cylindrical barrel pointing downwards. They looked dangerous to me. They were definitely not ornamental.

"What do you want in here, soldiers? Asked the small, balding official, waving the other librarians away to their duties.

Thomas stepped forwards and said, "We need to see whatever geography and history information you possess. Our officer has sent us to look at your maps and cross-reference them to past events. We cannot tell you any more than that as our officer has insisted on secrecy."

At the same time all three minds were coercing the older

man to accept the truth of their statement. He led the way towards a smaller room to the left of the entrance hall and gestured inside.

"The maps are in there, gentlemen. Do you need assistance? Looking at their faces he smiled and beckoned forwards one of the younger grey suited men to help.

Thomas said, "Thank you sir. Jon and Samuel go with the gentleman and look through the history information."

As they walked away I stared around us. Three sets of eyes and ears could amass a great deal of information when they are co-ordinated. This was a treasure house of information and all it needed was interpretation. I could hardly believe our luck.

I could have stayed in this storehouse of knowledge for days. Unfortunately this was not possible, so I concentrated my memory stores to retain all we needed. First I found out that this world was one of three orbiting the gas giant they called, Icarus. The world I found myself on was called Daedalus One and orbited around the equator of the gas giant with Daedalus Two occupying what was called the Trojan position in the same type of orbit. Scattered around Icarus were hundreds of smaller moons in all sorts of orbits, airless and devoid of life. The greatest shock of all was to find a world orbiting the gas giant around the poles with its own attendant moon, so that it never went into the shadow behind the gas giant. This world went by the name of Earth and so the information declared, had been moved by a race of alien beings with the help of our ancestors into its present position. Daedalus One and Two had been terra-formed and settled from this other world. I had maps of all three worlds secreted away in my memory banks. All that was recorded was that these people had created a group mind and controlled a wormhole so large that it had swallowed the Earth and Moon system. They had relocated the home of the humans here to escape from their sun exploding into a red giant and destroying them. What happened next is not well recorded. The Gnathe did not return and over the centuries the humans altered the two empty worlds to suit themselves and settled here as well. The humans had genetically altered apes to full sapience long ago on the home world and considered them as part of their race. There were once some of these on this world if they had survived the war. They had settled a small continent far to the south across the sea.

I have long studied the pictures of the Gnathe without recognition. They are a totally alien species with three sexes; - male, female and egg carrier. It is the egg-carriers known as Brood-mothers who dominate the species. This library was built for them to use as well as human beings, so where are they?

Several centuries later when this species was spread thinly, something alien and unfriendly arrived. They called themselves the Kresh. Whatever power was unleashed, melted cities and reduced the remnants of humanity to survivors. This town was the only one to have survived undamaged, but had been saturated with neutron bombardment, killing all life here. Power had been switched off for so long, that all electronic information had evaporated as batteries had flattened. Fortunately records had been kept in written form and vacuum sealed in vaults before total destruction of the majority of the towns and cities. Whickam's Crossing was the exception and Lord Samovar had devoted a great deal of his energy to getting the town back to a working basis. Harnessing the power of the river from the dam had restored electric power and the Town was returning to its former purpose. He was now settled in Priss or New Paris, at the moment excavating the munitions factory buried under the rubble. We know knew where to go to find him and exact Larse's revenge. It is situated on a great river known as the Rineflow inside an oxbow.

"Gentlemen to rescue Larse the time has come. Let us from this wonderful place go and see what we must do to remove him from the garrison tower."

All three reacted as one and thanked the custodians of the library for their help. They also inserted a certain amount of confusion in their minds, as to the appearance of the group as they left. Crossing the great hall they stopped for a moment as they realised that in an alcove stood a statue. The thing was nearly twice the height of a man with a long tail curled about its feet ending in a bony point. The back legs were jointed so that the knees were similar to birds. Muscular arms ending in four fingered human type hands, rested on a stomach that had a breeding pouch in front. A triangular head with needle sharp teeth and pointed ears stared down at them. Next to it stood another one with an erect crest without ears and hands that were clawed.

A plaque was pinned to the front of the statue that read, Link-soo-shan and Trann-link-khan, 'The Builders of the Gate'. At last I had a clear view of the aliens who had come to the humans' assistance and realised that I still did not recognise them at all.

I had also collected information about the interstellar war that had been fought here and almost lost by the humans completely. Fighting on the side of the humans and apes were a sentient species created by them using Nano-technology. Whether any of them had survived I could not be sure. Was I one of these creatures, crippled and partially destroyed in that great conflict? I would not know until I had got these people to tunnel into the mountain and I rejoined the rest of my substance.

CHAPTER FOUR

The three companions made their way back to the stables at the garrison to make sure that all four horses were ready to use. The sun was going down and apart from the new electric lights installed at the street corners; the area around the fortified building was quiet and full of deep shadows. Nobody challenged them inside the stables and few of the Algarie were to be seen. There was only a sleepy stable boy that locked the doors behind them.

Thomas sent his thoughts towards the top of the tower, where Larse was imprisoned.

"Larse are you ready?"

"Don't be a fool! What do you think I have been doing while you three have been filling your stomachs and reading books?" answered the Norseman irritably. "Take the horses and get away from the lights. I have been busy partially removing the bars at the window and as soon as the guard has changed, I'm away from here. We do not want a search party looking for us until the morning. By that time we can be well away from here. I have studied the maps that you were looking at, at the library and we want the southern road. I will meet you there at the edge of town."

Samuel reined in the extra horse that was Larse's original mount and turned south. Without another thought generated to the prisoner in the tower, the three made their way along the occasionally lit road towards the edge of town.

"Angry you are my young friend. Come; time it is that you left this place and rejoin your companions I think. Changed are the guards outside the cell door and sleepy they are. Make up your bed, to fool them inside it you are and remove the last bar we will," I argued to Larse.

Using my abilities I had exuded a molecule thin filament

from Larse's thumbs and passed it around the metal bars of the prison window. Once around the bar I returned the other end to his other thumb and made him pull. The filament sliced through the metal like a hot knife through butter. We repeated the act top and bottom for the rest of the bars and laid them in a pile at the base of the window. Next I inserted a thin blade under the thick glass and made Larse rotate his hand around the glass edge until the whole piece came loose. I attached it by a tether and left it hanging outside. Larse now extended his mind to shield himself from gravity and floated up to the level of the window and slipped through to the other side. He quickly re-attached the bars back into place and I 'welded' them together. We then replaced the glass and hung from the windowsill outside. Larse kicked off from the tower stonework and I extended our 'wings' so that we glided away from the prison cell. Larse gave an extra push with his mind and we gathered speed, soaring over the tops of the houses and workshops until the main road came into view.

"Think as the bird, young Larse and swoop!"

"Thank you Demon," he answered, "I have done this before!"

"Still my young friend, from out of the sky you could be shot! These weapons the Algarie carry in this town, kill you they can with ease. See you they must not in the air, or all surprise is lost. A secret this must be. In the morning they find an empty bed and unable to understand it they will, as the window will seem to be un-tampered with."

"Demon you are right as always," Larse answered and increased height into the low clouds for a while and then dived downwards towards the three waiting at the edge of town.

I watched the young man swoop towards us through three sets of eyes. There was no pursuit and the night was quietly still. Larse turned through the air and dropped gently down onto his horse with his legs apart. As he made contact with the saddle, the horse made a low wicker of recognition of his master.

Larse turned to the others and said, "Did you think to save me some of that food, that you were busy putting away, while I spent my time eating crap!"

Thomas laughed and reached into a small sack and handed the Norseman a cold roast chicken covered in a spicy sauce.

Jon reached into his bag and held aloft a bottle of home brewed beer and said, "Larse we did not forget you. For one thing we could feel your hunger all the way into the library."

"We got what we needed," added Sam and handed Larse a freshly buttered bread roll that he grabbed in his other hand, letting the reigns drop onto his saddle pommel.

As the four rode steadily south, Larse stuffed the chicken and bread roll in great bites into his mouth, chewed and swallowed gratefully, leaving a trail of bones behind him as he went. He quenched his thirst with the beer and finally threw the remains of the chicken into the gathering darkness. The gas giant dominated the sky and reflected the sun's light making the going easier for a while. Soon they would dive behind it, making the going extremely dark and night to both sides of the planet. Already they could see Daedalus Two edging behind them as it chased the same orbit. Both planets had land-enclosed seas and were virtually tide-less. Now that they understood more about the two worlds, they all watched the night sky with greater interest. Much farther out, in an orbit that took the planet around the poles of the gas giant, rotated the planet of origin with its own moon. This was a water rich world with seas that totally encircled the dry lands. In fact, they could see that the ocean was the width of one hemisphere as it spun round.

Thomas looked up and said, "How could they have moved a world?"

"According to the records we didn't," replies Sam. "It was the alien race called the Gnathe that made a wormhole that opened up into their long past and placed one end here, so that the Earth travelled through it to orbit Icarus as it does."

"That's not quite true, Sam. The records do state that our descendants played a part in the exercise too. However it was done, it seems beyond our capabilities now," Larse stated and rode his horse into a clearing off the main road. "Make the horses fast and let us get some sleep before it gets any darker."

As the four young men drifted off to sleep I gathered up my scattered consciousness and reviewed the information gathered by the three of them that had entered the Library. I now knew all that they had read independently and could now begin to put what facts we had together. It would seem that some centuries after the home world had been placed in orbit and these fertile moons seeded with life, a visitor had crept in from the interstellar darkness. It called itself 'The Servant of the Kresh.' Contact had been made, by the spacecraft belonging to the home world. The contact was brief. Once pictures had been beamed to the incoming ship giving welcome, the answer came in the response of an annihilating weapon. The ship released balls of hardened metal at sub-light speeds and took out many of the unarmed ships sent to greet it. Fusion and neutron bombs were released against all three habitable worlds and plasma beams melted what these missed. Before the thing was destroyed, humanity had been reduced to survivors grubbing about in the ruins.

The only transmission from the alien ship was the flat statement, "I am Toarvak 6, destroyer of worlds, servant of the Kresh. You are not Kresh! Toarvak 7 has been informed."

There was only one analysis to be made. My people had destroyed the alien vessel, but could expect to be visited by another one. This time they would be defenceless unless my small force could convince this fledgling civilisation to dig the rest of me out from the bowels of the mountain. By the ruthlessness of his methods Lord Samondar had managed to bring back a measure of civilisation to this world. To my way of thinking, the ends justified the means. Somehow I needed to deflect the thirst for revenge from my hosts, to a greater 'world view'. This would prove a difficult task to persuade Larse not to kill Lord Samondar for what his troops did under his instructions at his village. I would have to persuade Larse and the others to get close enough to him, so that they could project a large enough piece of me to make contact with his body. Once I was into his nervous system I could control him!

As Daedalus One swung away from the eclipsing shadow of Icarus, it corresponded to this world's dawn. The full strength of the sun would be some hours away and by then we should be well on our way towards New Paris. I awoke the four of them and made my desires known.

Larse stiffened as I spoke to him.

"Larse your revenge; - wait it must. This man is of more
value alive than dead. Need his co-operation we all must, if
I am to be released from the bowels of the mountain. Think
how you must, to get me close to him. I will do the rest,
as control him I could, once I inside him I am. What better
revenge could you have than to make him do our bidding?"

I then shared these sentiments with the other three as they picked a hasty breakfast from the embers of the fire by toasting chunks of bread and spreading them with butter. Thomas gathered in the horses and loaded them with the

60

provisions, while Samuel and Jon put out the fire and scattered the ashes. Larse had levitated to the tops of the trees and looked carefully for a sign of pursuit, from the garrison at Whickam's Crossing. Each mind was interlocked with each other and the bodies worked in unison like a well-oiled machine. Yet each one of them had retained an independent personality separate from each other. This was something that would alert the more observant of the Algarie when they were eventually captured, so when they eventually became prisoners it would be important not to show any signs of my possession or their abilities. Now that the gestalt was aware of Lord Samovar's better troops being armed with rifles and guns, they would have to be more careful. Even I could not protect them fully against a steel projectile travelling at muzzle velocity. We needed to become as well armed as our adversary. I reasoned that if the Algarie had discovered usable buried weapons, then there must be other sites that we could search for and just maybe help our selves to all sorts of killing treasures!

I searched in the archives of my stored maps for one such likely place. What we needed was a military base, off the beaten track and still un-plundered. According to the ancient maps, a scientific research station had once stood in this area. Underneath it were storage areas as self-contained as a small town. If these were intact, they would be worth investigating. It would make sense that a detachment of guards would be at hand to keep out curious eyes. Even though these people had given up warfare, they still needed to keep the general public in order. There are malcontents in all societies. Of the research facility there would be no trace on the surface after all this time, but underneath the ground, sealed off from the rest of the world, much of it would remain undamaged. I superimposed our position on the ancient map of the area and discovered that we were within ten miles of the old facility.

"Listen to me my friends. Off this road we must go to the right through this wooded area and out onto the open. There is a hill shaped into a point we will find. There what we seek will be found. Agree do you?"

"Demon we have become accustomed to your wisdom. You have never let us down and whatever you suggest is for our best interests. We will go to your pyramid and see what we shall find there," Larse agreed and turned his horse into the brush, away from the road.

Thomas, Samuel and Jon followed their leader and let the horses force their own way through the thinning trees, picking up a game trail that meandered in the direction they wished to go. As time went by the terrine got easier as they picked up a more stony area that led down to open grassland. Here the effects of grazing herds of wild cattle and deer had kept the trees back from the valley floor. Once again they found themselves in wild countryside that had been settled long ago and had been left to go uncultivated. The cattle eyed them up and down as they approached. It was obvious that they had not seen a man on horseback before and did not know what to make of them. They did not register as a threat, but the combination of man and beast made them uneasy. A large dominant bull shouldered its way to the front of the herd and snorted a warning, lowering its head whilst pawing the ground. It urinated onto the ground and bellowed, trotting forwards a few feet before it began to kick large turfs out of the sod. The breadths of his horns were as long as their arms and were curled forwards. He was coloured brown with white patches and the muscles stood out across his shoulders.

Thomas gave warning with his mind, "Go sideways, to the left and away from him. He has issued a challenge; - do not take it! If he is anything like the bulls on the farm, he will accept our moving away and return to the herd. Do not make eye contact and be silent amongst ourselves."

All four horsemen turned as one and trotted away from the challenge and watched as the bull returned to the herd. The rest of the cattle lost interest as we increased the distance from their leader. Jon however had spotted a straggler with a twisted leg. It was no more than a yearling and had been left behind. He rode up to it and let fly an arrow that entered the beast just behind the shoulder, bringing it to its knees.

He leapt off the horse and slit the young bull's throat with a cry of, "No chicken tonight my friends. Prime steak instead."

I gratefully took the life energy from the fallen creature and shared it with all the parts of me that lay scattered through men and horses. It had been some time since they had killed anything and what I could safely siphon off from the four of them was not enough to give me any reserves.

They quickly butchered the young bull and stripped the meat from its carcass, keeping a wary eye on the retreating herd. Soon the best of it was wrapped in blood-soaked grass and packed into the saddlebags. The leftovers were already attracting the attentions of scavengers. We had heard the sounds of wolves calling across the grasslands. It would not be long before we had company. There did not seem to be any other predators on this world except birds and the bears that lived further north. This world had been seeded from scratch and it had obtained a balance within its-self. There were domestic stock that had reverted back to the wild and there were wild animals that had been released to keep the wilderness in check. What had not been planned were the centuries that had passed, while man had struggled to survive here after the visit by the 'Servant of the Kresh'.

The grass had become tall where the herd had not

trampled it down in their search for green growing leaves and tall apple trees had spread their branches, creating shade underneath them. Wolf spoor was scattered over the area and they were aware of an intelligent scrutiny from the cover of the trees. The grass parted and a number of wolves pushed their way into the open, following the scent of the butchered yearling. They were a mixture of many-shaped mixed into one basic type. These were dogs that had gone feral. The predominant shape was German Sheppard, but much bigger than the original breeds. Locked away in their genetic makeup were Bullmastiff and Great Danes. Over the centuries the introduced pets had been evolving to bring down the wild cattle and to do that they needed to be big and powerful. The pack eyed the horsemen with an appraisal that included the calculation of meat against damage. Caution won, as noses wrinkling, they disappeared into the bush and grasslands to find the remains of Jon's kill.

"Time we were somewhere else, I think," said Larse and urged his horse away from the shade of the apple-tree.

The three others turned and followed their leader towards the pyramid shaped hill in the distance while I pondered on the possibilities of linking our companionship with a pack of wolves.

We soon found ourselves on an ancient road leading towards the research establishment. Again, the grass had fought a constant battle to eat into the material of the road and gain a roothold, with limited success. We soon realised we had crossed the centre of a platform with a single road leading towards the overgrown pyramid. At the edges, a wild growth of grass and bushes prevailed onto the rolling veldt. There was no way to this place except through the air. I cross-referenced the information held in my memory banks acquired from the Library at Whickam's Crossing and realised where we were. This was a Gnathe teaching and research complex, devoted to the use of their unique psychic crystals. It was a place where human beings were taught how to use them and how to adapt them, using mechanical science. The name of the place was 'The Link-soo-shan Institute' of Gnathen studies.

I stared around through the four pairs of eyes of my companions as we entered a ghost town. The buildings were all of a silvery material and were without any signs of life. We tied up the horses to a perching rail inside the first building and looked around the inside. Throughout the corridors and rooms the floor was littered with old bones, human and Gnathe. They had become hard and brittle with age. There were no signs of them being gnawed or disturbed in any way.

"Demon! Tell us what has happened here," Larse asked. "These old bones show that nothing fed on the carrion that would have been here in abundance. Why are they as we find them?"

"All that we see here, at their posts they died. Shelter they did not seek and death came from the skies. Over their heads a neutron bomb was exploded, destroying all life in its range. These bodies lay undisturbed because there were none to feed off them. Great would be the length of time before meat-eating creatures would have come this far from where the radiation did not kill. Bacteria would have consumed these people long before anything came this way," I replied.

Thomas stretched forwards to look at the tops of the benches at the corroded shapes that had once been scientific instruments. Most of the shapes were brittle with age and rotten. Dust had blown in through the open doors and seeds had taken root everywhere.

"There is nothing for us in this place," he said. "Where do we go from here?"

Samuel led the way out into the sunshine of the late

afternoon and said, "The pyramid looks untouched. In the morning I suggest we search around it for a doorway inside. If the doorway has been tightly shut all these years we may find it a more interesting place to search."

Jon agreed and began to unsaddle the horses, while the others gathered up dead wood to make a fire to grill the steaks. The shelter of the building would be ideal to camp in and reasonably fresh water could be obtained from a spring fed pond at the side of the silvery grey walls. As the evening began to darken, lights began to shine as the ceilings took up a diffused glow. It was apparent to me that the whole of the roof was a massive energy collector and this place was still powered.

As Thomas got the fire going and the steaks sizzling I directed the other three to push the bones out of the way so that we did not have the constant reminder of the senseless death around us. It didn't bother me, but I was hoping that more of interest would come to light. In a crumpled heap at one of the benches was a very large skeleton with a long tail and a triangular head. I studied the clawed feet carefully and pondered on the bird-like shape of the legs and hips. Incredibly human sets of hands were present at its wrists. By its side were two other much smaller versions of the larger set of bones. These were the Gnathe that had joined the humans and apes in their civilisation. What marvels had these creatures studied together, I wondered? As the life-sized statues at the Library had demonstrated to me, the 'Brood-mothers' were giants up against human beings and the male and female of their own kind.

We loosed the horses to forage and water themselves, knowing that they would not stray far, due to the tiny connections of my substance linking their brains to mine. If the wolves ventured here we would soon know, but I was sure that they avoided this place and kept to the plains where they hunted. Besides, the remains of the yearling that Thomas had brought down would keep them fed and occupied for a couple of days at least.

From the safety of the inside, we fed the fire to finish off cooking the meat and smoking the remains. The flames danced and the meat sizzled and popped as grease spat back into the fire. My companions fed well and finished off with some fruit they had bought back at the town. The opening to the research establishment was away from the path we had rode to get here, so the fire would not be seen from the wooded road we had separated from. Soon they would be laying themselves down to sleep allowing me to think about all the discoveries we had made.

Many miles away from them that morning the changing of the watch had found out that the Norseman had vanished from his cell.

Seeing no movement from their prisoner at breakfast they had opened the door into the cell at the top of the tower.

"Get up, Norseman," bellowed Gurt and kicked the side of the cot with a booted foot. "It's time to see the Commander and answer some questions."

The bump did not move, so Gurt pulled the blankets off and saw that the bed was empty. He looked up into the rafters and underneath the bed.

"The cell is empty," he yelled. "The prisoner has escaped."

"How can he! The door has been bolted all night and the window is secure, argued the guard at the back of the other three armed men.

Gurt went pale as he tore past the bemused guardsmen, and called back, "Touch nothing while I go to see Commander Jones.

Edward Jones was an intelligent man and listened to Gurt with a rising sense of amazement. This was not an example of discipline gone lax. These men were all good soldiers. That was why they were entrusted with the new weapons discovered by Lord Samovar at the excavation of the weapons factory at Priss. He led the way back to the cell at the top of the tower and stepped inside.

"The rest of you go outside except for you two," he ordered. "I need to examine this room intently. I believe that you have not left this cell unattended and besides the door had remained locked. Therefore the Norseman must have escaped some other way. The only way out has to be the window. Drag the bed over to the wall so I can climb up and examine the bars."

The two guards quickly did as they were ordered and the Commander climbed up to the level of the bars. He ran his fingers up and down each one and found that at the top and bottom of each bar there was a hardly noticeable bump. He reached for his knife and worked it against the glass. It again was very slight, but the glass moved against the pressure.

Commander Jones sat down on the bed and thought about what he had found. He also thought about the three soldiers who had delivered the blond giant into his hands and found that he could remember very little about them. That caused him some concern. Where did they go after handing over the prisoner?

"Saddle up my horse and form a small detachment," he ordered. "We are going into town. I have questions to ask! Gurt old friend, he got out by the window and replaced the bars and glass. How he managed to do that and scale the sheer sides of the tower I do not know, but he did. "

Later on that day when the trail led to the pride of the town, the Library, he found that again memories were confused and descriptions were sketchy at most. All he could find out were that all three soldiers had spent time looking at maps and History books. They had left the town by the South road.

It was time to write a full report and send it to Lord Samovar. This was beyond his authority to deal with.

CHAPTER FIVE

Francisco Samovar was a self-educated man insomuch that he had pursued knowledge at every opportunity. Once he had learnt to read, he had searched out what books had survived the onslaught of the Servant of the Kresh. Fortunately he had been born into a ruling family of survivalists who had seen the value of learning and appreciated the quick mind of their adaptable son. His father, Santiago, had promoted the boy's interests and allowed him to spend a great deal of his time in the college with his tutors rather than letting him spend time with the horses. Santiago bred horses as an interest, besides the daily problems of running the small area of civilization his family had inherited from his forbears. Sometimes maintaining a grip on the outlying towns and villages got a trifle bloody, but he believed in a unifying force to bring the survivors back into the civilised state they had once enjoyed. Whickam's Crossing was the jewel in the crown. The town had been re-discovered intact and empty, but for a few people who had moved into it over the long years. Santiago had spent a great deal of time there installing the Librarians to keep the oasis of knowledge intact from marauders. He had also established a garrison there with a large compliment of guards.

It was at this Library that Francisco had spent his formative years, studying the maps and stores of knowledge buried in its archives. It was here that he discovered the location of city of Priss, once known as New Paris that had once had a weapons factory under the ground. The rifles produced here were more hunting rifles than military, as warfare on the three worlds was unknown until the break-up produced by Toarvak 6's unprovoked attack. Survival had necessitated that the strong take control and keep it. Mankind had retreated to its old problems with power and responsibility. Now at least under Santiago's iron rule, nobody starved and slowly as taxes were paid in foodstuffs, excess was being built up, so that time could be spent on other things besides growing food. The Education of all children was one of the things brought into the daily life of the people. Some had rebelled and gone north to spend their lives pursuing their own dreams and were slipping back to savagery and ignorance.

Lord Francisco had inherited this system from his father and was doing his best to maintain the status quo. Although not the eldest of his brothers, they had voted to accede to him as ruler. He had run things for the last thirty odd years and was still making progress. The chilling statement of the alien intelligence Toarvak 6, that Toarvak 7 had been informed of their presence, had been passed down the generations. It was the nightmare that drove him. They had no idea when that day would come, but without technology they would be easy prey. All contact with the Gnathe had been lost after that initial devastating blow, so they were on their own.

Now he was receiving reports of a small group of Algarie dressed men led by a big blond man, called 'the Norseman' that constantly defeated the soldiers sent to keep order in the outlying provinces. No clear descriptions had been given and no certainty as to where they were had filtered down to him. All he knew was they were steadily getting closer to Priss where he was encamped. Patience was something Francisco understood; - all he needed to do was wait and be prepared for their arrival. Digging into the underground factory had un-earthed some interesting and useful non-lethal weapons. They had come across an airtight sealed vault containing many sealed crates that were well oiled inside. The centuries had not left their mark upon the contents and the items worked as well as the day they had been stored.

Priss had been melted into slag in most places in the centre of the city and the twisted shapes of the once high buildings had fused together. Here on the outskirts, some of the strange silver grey houses had stayed intact. The roof sunlight collectors worked and the insides were lit up at night. Some of the mysteries of making the old science devices and equipment work were being found out by Lord Samovar's scientists and technicians every day. The great secret of Nano-technology eluded them. This was something that they could not understand without the knowledge gained from centuries ago. Somewhere beneath their feet might be enough radio equipment to enable them to contact Earth or Daedalus Two if they could only get it working.

Francisco stood up and watched his younger children playing in the sunlight. The still lovely dark skinned, black haired women who watched them turned at his approach. Yolanda and Florence had been married to him for thirty years and more. They had born him many healthy children and he loved them both dearly. In his campaigns across this land he had scattered his seed between those who had offered him comfort. Those children he provided for and saw that they wanted for nothing including their education. Survival was the code of life.

He swept the sweat away from his greying eyebrows and wiped his swarthy hands down his legs. He was not a particularly tall man and getting a little fatter in his middle age. The dark eyes still flashed with Spanish fire when roused and he could still hold a spirited horse to his will.

"My ladies, I would sit with you for a while and watch our

children play," he said.

Florence poured him a cool lemon spiced drink from a pitcher and said, "Drink this Francisco and rest awhile. You look tired, my love."

"Always there are things that you must do," Yolanda grumbled. "Things that require your attention. What now? What has put the frown upon your face?"

"Once more it would seem that there are those upon our world that seek my death!"

"Many have tried. Most of them died trying," Florence recalled. "What makes these any different from the others?"

"There is something different about these four," Francesco replied and drank the lemon juice. "Something tells me I must be very careful with these!"

Several hundred miles to the north Larse and his companions were awake just after dawn and rekindling the fire to toast thick slices of bread. There were still plenty of stocks left in the saddlebags and with the smoked meat added to them, no worry of running out of food just yet. The horses had returned from their nightly forage and had gathered at the spring fed pond. Thomas checked them over to see that they had not picked up any thorns. The one thing they did not have to worry about was ticks and stinging insects. As this world had never been seeded with pests, then apart from bees, whose stinging ability had been almost bred out, then there was nothing to fear.

Jon stood up and pointed to the pyramid structure across the courtyard and said to Larse, "I'll take a walk around the base to the right with Samuel while you and Thomas go to the left."

I intruded into their conversation and added, *"A door you will find, sealed against the weather and the elements. Look carefully for a large depression so that a Gnathe could walk in! Power there will be inside collected from the roofs on the top of these buildings. When you find the door, open it I shall, somehow.*

The pyramid's sides were as smooth as finely polished granite. The five of us made our way carefully round the base, while I examined the surfaces of the four sides with minute care. We found ourselves back at the side facing the buildings of the research centre with still no idea of where the entrance was. This made no sense to the five minds surveying the problem. Everything pointed to the fact that this pyramid had to have an opening somewhere. It made sense that the face we were looking at had to be the one that the people used every day to get inside. There had to be a lock of some kind that opened a door into the inside and it would have been obvious to the people that once lived and worked here, centuries ago.

"Larse my friend, your hand you must place against the surface of the pyramid. The darkened panel to right of centre at your shoulder height might be just such a place to start. Doorknobs these people would not have used," I instructed the blond giant.

Larse did as he was instructed and placed his hand on the darkened panel. From deep inside the pyramid came a groaning sound of long un-used machinery. A visible crack began to show around a tall rectangle set at the same angle as the side of the pyramid. Larse took away his hand and the four of them watched as the door widened and rose into the body of the structure to reveal an empty room.

Jon looked into the room and said with disgruntled annoyance, "There has to be more than this!"

"I think there is," said Thomas and walked into the room. "The rest of you come inside. There is a panel with an arrow pointing down on the sidewall. Once we are all inside I will place my hand on it and we will see what happens."

The other three walked inside and Thomas placed his hand onto the panel.

With a speed they could not match, the outside door came down sealing them inside and the floor began to drop away beneath them. A light came on as the room began to move and before they could panic the other wall pulled away revealing a strange sight. Lights were snapping on to reveal a vast underground chamber, stretching into the distance. They stepped out of the lift and stared at a sight that nothing so far had prepared them for. It was similar to the Library in so much that all the benches and supports were made of the same silvery-grey substance. The other thing that shook them were the mummified corpses of humans, apes and Gnathe laid on the floor or still sat in chairs or perched at benches. As the air down here had stayed sealed off from the outside, the corpses had not rotted. This was the result of an intense neutron bombardment above ground. Here the equipment had not rusted or rotted away. The laboratory machinery and instruments were constantly kept clean by nannites programmed to do so. We explored further into the chamber and found a triangular arch that tilted inwards to touch four others to make a very large cage.

A great deal of equipment surrounded the cage and power cables snaked away towards the connections at the large box construction that hummed. This was still operating after all the centuries that had passed since the 'Servant of the Kresh' had paid its visit. There was a great deal of mummified bodies scattered around the opening of the cage type pyramid. What was inside caused the five of us to gaze in wonder at the contents. Frozen inside were three Gnathe; - One very big one and two smaller ones, obviously a male and female. It was what they were mounted on that made them gasp. Three very large animals, more than twice the size of a big horse, with triangular horned heads ending in a blunt beak, stood on clawed feet. The hind legs were jointed similar to a birds and a long tail coiled around the feet. The large eyes were split like a cat's so that they could see in the semi-darkness.

Jon stared at the group and asked, "What do you think they were doing?" they look as if they are alive."

"That's not possible after all this time," answered Samuel. "It must be a projection, similar to those at the Library.

They pulled the bodies away from the doorway to have a better look at the occupants, while Thomas investigated the large box that seemed to be supplying power to the cage. He sat at the stool that had been occupied by one of the mummies and read out the plate fixed at the top of the controls.

"Listen to this," he said. "It reads Experimental Time Stasis Control. This piece of equipment must have been operating during the alien attack, centuries ago. The operators must have been killed while this experiment was being tested. There was no one to switch it off. I think these creatures have been in this cage ever since!"

"The controls of this box seem to make sense. This dial controls the amount of power into the cage. Switch it off we could, by pulling this lever to the off position and winding the dial back to zero. Maybe these Gnathe alive and real they could be. Good allies they would make. Knowledge perhaps they could give."

"What do you all think? Shall we see what happens when I throw this switch? Asked Thomas.

The agreement reached, Thomas threw the switch and wound the dial back to zero. The humming vanished and high-pitched whine took its place that dropped back to silence. Inside the cage immediate movement took place as the three Gnathe came back to life with their mounts. The great tri-angular head of the Brood-mother swung round and took stock of the ruined surroundings. Her two companions dismounted and stepped out of the cage to stare at the masses of mummified bodies laid upon the floor.

A rapid-fire gabble of whistle and chirrups ensued between the three as the big one stepped out. She addressed the four humans with more strange sounds to be met by a stunned silence. She eyed the four sets of bows aimed in her direction, warily and tried again.

"I am called Suzzan-link-khann. These are my kindred, Jaffin-khann and Ritchi-khann. I think you have a tale to tell. This is an experimental time stasis machine. Looking about me I can see that something terrible has happened while we were in the time field. I will excuse you your bad manners if you will direct those bows at something else otherwise I shall protect my kindred."

"I apologise for our reactions," Larse said and put his bow away, directing the others to follow. "We have not seen anything like you for centuries except for two statues at a town called Whickam's Crossing. You are the first live Gnathe and the things you ride, we have ever seen!"

"You had better tell me what happened here, long ago." She stared intently at the group. "I can pick up your thoughts! You are different to the humans we were working with so better than that, I will take the information from your minds. It will be much quicker if you have no objections?"

"Of course not, Suzzan," Larse answered, "Please feel free to enter our thoughts."

Suzzan reached into Larse's mind first to gather the information from the four humans and found me.

"What are you?" She demanded and began to examine my presence in the four hosts.

"I don't know. I am trying to find out. I awoke recently to find this world as you find it. I am doing my best to bring order back to this race and help them as best I can."

"You seem almost nannite in construction, but you are significantly different in many ways," Suzzan thought. "The nannites I have met have been independent intelligences, not reliant upon others. This vendetta of Larse's; - do you support it?"

"It is something I am working on. To begin with I thought to do this thing, but in gaining knowledge of past events, I feel a different course of action needs to be. His adversary, Lord Samovar had unified the survivors of the destruction wrought by the alien vessel. He and his forebears have ruled this area of Daedalus One for some time and have restored a measure of civilization. We have run into a great deal of dislike of his methods and have killed a number of his soldiers to the delight of a great many of the population. The thing is, that it is his unifying force that will make the defence of this world and the other two a possibility. We need to bend the will of this group of humans to another possibility."

Suzzan pondered on the proposition the alien force had proposed and answered, "What is the other possibility you speak of?"

"What you communicate to here, is but a fraction of what I once was. Buried deep under a mountain to the far North is the rest of me. I believe I was once a mighty weapon used to defend against the Servant of the Kresh. The alien vessel indicated that it had informed another of its kind to come here. I must be complete to be able to protect these people. Without what I believe to lie under that mountain, they will stand no chance at all!"

"I believe you. I do not altogether trust you, Demon, but there is wisdom in what you say. Looking into the memories of these four humans, I can see that much has been lost. There is in this facility the means to communicate with the other worlds if they have the technology to answer."

The massive form of the Brood-mother dismounted and handed the reigns of her Zanth to Ritchie.

"Tie the Zanth to the cage and stay with Jaffin. These humans are our friends. They do not speak Gnathe, so speak to them in their language if you need anything. It will be good practise for you. I have something to do. Soon we will go out of this terrible place of death, but for now there are more important things to do."

78

She placed the triangular head between the fingers of her great hands and touched him lightly on his face with her tongue. Suzzan then did the same with the female, who was trembling with fear and apprehension. Showing care and respect to the dried up corpses gathered around the stasis machine, she beckoned Larse to follow her.

"These were my friends, Larse. Moments ago they were alive to me. They were part of my adopted kindred. Some were family to my people in the intellectual sense. I knew their minds and personalities. Some of them were adopted into Gnathen family groups and imprinted their minds into unborn youngling Brood-mothers in the breeding pouches. You have no idea how close some of them were to me," Suzzan spoke with emotion as she led the way.

"Where are we going? Asked Larse as he struggled to keep up.

"The communications console," she replied.

"To try to speak with any survivors Suzzan is to attempt. The means to reach out to the other worlds, buried down here there is, young Larse. Still in working order the equipment will be, down here away from the abrasive surface. Nannites there are down here keeping every thing clean and bright."

"What are nannites? Queried Larse.

"Tiny machines, too small to see. You humans were once masters of this technology. You even had artificial intelligences in human shaped bodies assisting you in every way. I had the privilege to meet the 'Great Kaameel' once when I was on the home world," Suzzan remarked.

She stopped at a silver box fitted to a bench and placed her hand upon it. The door opened to reveal a display of crystals laid in rows in a toughened leather carrying case. Larse watched as the Brood-mother selected two of them and slipped them into a skin pocket located at her wrists. She sealed down the flap of the pocket so that the join was invisible. Next she selected a different coloured one and placed it in another pocket under her chin. This too sealed over once the gem was in place. She reached inside and took out the case and slung it around her shoulders, buckling it firmly in place.

"I am ready now, Larse," she said. "Let us see if there is anyone able to communicate with us. The control console is at the wall, by that large silver rectangle. If there is anyone listening for broadcasts it will light up and we will see a picture form of the person at the other end. Do you see, there is a perch for me and a seat for you."

Larse could hardly control his impatience as he sat down upon the seat and studied the knobs and dials set out on a sloping surface. He watched the giant at his side reach out to a switch and flick it down. Immediately the console came alive with lights, as power flowed into the system. There was a pronounced humming noise from inside the panelling that died away. Two lights began to wink on and off and Suzzan gave a cry of relief.

"Those lights mean that they are trying to contact us, Larse," she said. "That means they must have a level of civilisation to be able to speak to us."

"What do we have to do?" asked the Norseman.

"Simply this," answered Suzzan and depressed a switch next to the winking light with Earth Command written on a label by its side.

A light came on over a swivelling box and half of the view-screen lit up with a picture of Larse and his giant companion. The other half showed the startled features of a group of men and women who had rushed to the screen.

"Who are you?" asked the young man staring with a mixture of joy and disbelief at the screen at his end.

"My name is Suzzan-link-khann," she replied. "Do not hope for too much. This world is in ruins as I expect is yours. My being here is pure chance and this establishment has survived the onslaught because it was underground and sealed off. My kindred and I were taking part in a time stasis experiment when the annihilating machine from the Kresh destroyed the upper part of this complex. The neutron bombardment killed and sterilised all living things even down here, but the time stasis field kept us safe. We were 'rescued' by this young man and his friends turning off the field generator. From what they have told me a measure of civilization is being put together by a ruler known as lord Samovar and by pretty ruthless means. We mean to meet him as we do have something to offer. I must ask are there more of my kind on your world?"

The young man frowned and answered, "No! As far as I know, you are all there are of your race on the three worlds. We survived because we were deep under the ground in an old military base the size of a city. That is the only reason we have kept up the level of civilization. Everything above ground was decimated. There were survivors scattered all over the place, but the struggle to keep alive defeated most attempts to stay mechanised."

"What about Daedalus two," Suzzan asked.

"More or less the same as you, I would expect. The apes fled the cities when the bombardment started and re-established themselves in the forests. Not being of a mechanical nature they have been quite happy to live out their lives naturally. Those humans who were living there soon joined them or went back to farming the vast open places. There is less mechanisation there than it would appear to be on Daedalus One due to the efforts of your Lord Samovar, but they are in contact with us. Not all the radio transmitters were destroyed by Toarvak 6 and in some of the outlying districts; small pockets of civilization were maintained over the years. The neutron blasts took out every nannite they had on their world and ours. I would imagine the same happened where you are. If only one had survived we could have used Nano-technology to rebuild. It was the nannites that turned the war with 'the Servant of the Kresh'. They overwhelmed it."

"We may just have one nannite left, but badly damaged. It is different to any of the Silver ones I have ever met. It lives inside the four young men that rescued us. It has enhanced the brains and bodies of these four. As a by-product it has also given them mental powers similar to the Gnathe, but without the needed effect of crystalline amplifiers. They can use telepathy and to my astonishment they can levitate. This is something the Gnathe have not learnt to do. I digress! The most important thing is, it declares that there is a great deal of it buried inside a mountain far to the North of here. It could be the very thing your ancestors used to destroy 'The Servant of the Kresh' at the end of the encounter."

"What if it isn't," answered the Earth based human.

"Then we shall all die together, my friend," Suzzan replied. "I really believe we have no other hope. I have been as far as I can into its mind and can find no trace of animosity." She had flicked the other switch at the same time as the Earth connection and turned to the ape regarding her from the other section of the screen and asked, "Do you have any ideas or anything that could help?"

The ape scratched the fur around his face and replied, "No! My name is Jondar by the way. It's good to see a Gnathe again after all these years. It is correct what Simon has told you, we are not very mechanised here. We have managed to maintain what we have, but lack the means to improve it. We were very dependant on the home world for all our machinery. After the Kresh destroyed all the spacecraft of the home world we were left alone without means of defence. Not that we would have been able to do much."

"Just a moment," Suzzan asked, "What happened to the crystal portals?"

"They were vaporised when Toarvak 6 attacked. If there are any on the surface, we don't know where they are and none of us are trained to use them."

"I can you fools," exploded Suzzan with exasperation. "Find them if you can at top priority. I must now meet with this Lord Samovar and convince him to aid us."

With that she shut down the communications console and turned to Larse who had followed the conversation bewildered.

"Its time to go," she said.

CHAPTER SIX

Suzzan-link-khann led the way back to the time stasis machine and her kindred. Larse could hardly keep up with her as she hurried along. The two other smaller Gnathe watched her come with whistles and chirrups of greeting. Suzzan lent forward and placed a smaller set of crystals around their necks.

"Speak in their language! Have manners deserted you?" she scolded, as she reached for the reigns of her Zanth.

"We are sorry, my Lady," Ritchie replied. "We mean no offence. What did you discover at the control console?"

Suzzan slipped into their two minds and filled in all the gaps and was aware that the humans had also been part of the mental information she was imparting.

"I will accept that you are new to the etiquette of telepathy," she rebuked, "and allow these ill manners! In future do not eves-drop unless invited! Your gifts require certain protocols. You would feel slighted if I entered your minds without declaring so and took what information there was to be had! That also includes the creature that lives inside you all as well."

The humans looked at her with embarrassment while I also felt the sting of her displeasure.

"There are many things we all have to learn, my Lady Suzzan," I answered accepting the rebuke. *"I can only communicate by this manner, but will intrude not into your inner thoughts. What do we do now?"*

"We will exit this chamber by the large entrance, where we can walk our mounts into the open air. I have been far too long underground. This place holds too many memories. Come; it is at the far end on your left," she said and began to lead her huge horned mount towards the other end of the chamber.

"My Lady," asked Larse, "could you direct us to where the weapons are kept?"

She turned to Jaffin and said, "Take them to the weapons store, while I see if the gate will open."

The Gnathe stared at the group of humans and said, "Come with me. I will take you where you need to go. There are rifles and hand weapons stored in the locker inside this office. I will need to break it open"

"There is nothing here that we can use to get inside that," Larse commented as he looked at the heavy steel cabinet.

"You have me!" answered Jaffin and selected a crystal from the bunch she had in her pouch worn around her neck.

The Gnathe squeezed the crystal into her hand and concentrated. Jaffin sent her awareness into the combination lock on the front of the cabinet. Thomas watched as the dials spun round until they all heard a distinct 'click' and the front of the cabinet swung open. Set up in racks were duplicates of the wood and metal weapons they had seen the soldiers carry at Whickam's Crossing. Also the smaller hand weapons were hung up complete with holsters and harnesses. There were belts full of small torpedo shaped objects that looked as if they had something to do with the weapons on display.

Jaffin lent forwards and picked up one of the weapons.

"This is called a rifle and these are bullets. You open the rifle like this and place a clip of bullets into the chamber. It is now loaded! All you have to do is look through the telescopic sight and set the cross onto your target. When you pull the trigger the bullet will explode inside the rifle and shoot out of the end of the metal tube. This will kill anything within reason at quite a considerable distance. You humans have a talent for inflicting death, so be very careful with them. This is a safety catch. Make sure that it is in place at all times, until you need to use the weapon. The small weapons are called pistols and also carry a clip containing smaller bullets. They will kill a man at closer range and are used in defence."

Jaffin gave the four humans a crash course in using the handguns as well and the men soon loaded themselves up with what they needed. All the weapons gleamed with nannite care. Over the long centuries no deterioration had taken place as a thin film of oil had been trapped between the microscopic machines and the surface of the weapons.

I had followed Jaffin's explanation with care. The last thing I needed would be to lose one of my hosts through carelessness! No matter what, I would not forget to make sure the safety catches were on. Now we needed to catch up with the other two Gnathe. I marvelled at the self-assured attitude of the Brood-mother, it was obvious to me she was used to the position of leader. She had adjusted to the facts remarkably well. I vowed to get to know her better, if she would permit it.

I used Samuel's mind to contact the female.

"Please my interruption excuse, I projected to the Gnathe, *"but what were you doing here at this research facility?"*

"The great Lady Suzzan is a psychic adept and was trying to expand the knowledge of the time-distorting crystals. She was also involved in the construction of a permanent gateway between our worlds. The means may still exist somewhere, of that earlier project on the human, home world."

What a pearl of wisdom and information that was. My mind became very clear on the subject of Larse's revenge on Lord Samovar.

"Larse! Events a strange twist has occurred. Our original mission must change. Think you must about all you have witnessed here. Lord Samovar you must meet and bury your differences!"

"Demon, that bastard owes me my family and people. His soldiers attacked my village and slaughtered everyone I ever knew. There has to be a reckoning between us! You know what was done," Larse thought. "You were there!"

"Too hasty you may be. There may be another side to the events you witnessed. Wait you must before judgment can you pass. Meet him you must and then decide. Enough for now! We are about to see if Suzzan can the large door open, get. Soon on our way we can go. Patient you must be!"

Suzzan-link-khann stood by the wall waiting for her female and the four humans to catch up. She handed the reigns of the Zanth to Jaffin and hopped to the left and placed the palm of her hand against a darkened panel and pushed. A loud creaking and groaning sound came from inside the wall and daylight began to show along the bottom of part of the wall. Without any more sounds from within, a large section of the wall disappeared upwards and revealed a courtyard some distance from the outside buildings. The Zanth were led outside and they all looked back, as Suzzan shut the door with another darkened panel. The courtyard was sunken into the ground and wide steps had been built leading out of it, up to the floor level of the other buildings. They had not realised just how large the underground complex was, until they stared at the pyramid located some distance away.

Thomas called the horses with the telepathic link I had forged, being careful to hold down the panic they would experience when they sighted the Zanth. Each member of my team used their mental powers to ease the awareness of the Gnathen mounts into their tiny minds and that included the packhorse. The last thing we wanted was to see the disappearing backside of this horse loaded down with our supplies. The horses came galloping around the corner of one of the ruined buildings and pulled up short when they saw and scented the Zanth. They were puzzled and confused as to what they were confronting, but the one thing definite in their minds was the fact that these were not predators. The Zanth had met horses before and paid them very little heed. The four humans greeted their mounts with affection and settled them down by giving each horse an apple from the supplies. Once they were mounted we could be on our way.

"Where do we go from here," asked Suzzan, as all this has been totally overgrown since I was last here!"

"Follow me," replied Larse. "Demon has a map in his mind and knows where we are at all times."

We rode back across the grassy slopes towards the road we had followed before detouring to the research complex. The wolves had moved position and were tracking the herd away from our line of travel. They must have manoeuvred themselves on the opposite side of the herd as the wild cattle began to head our way. In front was the now angry and fearful bull with the wide spread of horns.

Once again he urinated and stamped his feet, but this time he was not going to be eased back into the herd. He could smell wolves behind him and we were at his escape route. The brown and white bull lowered his head and charged.

Suzzan's Zanth also lowered his head and drove forwards and met the bull head-on, sweeping his broad horns under the bull's chest and lifting him from off the ground. He swung his head with the bull helpless upon them and tossed the animal effortlessly away from the companions. The bull turned in the air twice before it rolled over and over in the grass. Shaken and snorting his anger, he stood his ground and thought about it as his herd waited to see what he would do.

Ritchie's Zanth also lowered her head in a belligerent fashion and gave challenge. When Jaffin's mount shuffled forwards that was enough to convince the bull that he was outmatched. He gave a bellow and turned into the long grass, leading his herd away. The herd picked up speed and followed their leader into the raising dust cloud.

Jon sighted down the sights of his rifle and pulled the trigger. There was a sharp crack and one of the cattle stopped dead. Samuel took aim and fired his rifle, aiming at the creature's chest and the animal fell to its knees and rolled over.

Thomas turned to Ritchie and said, "I'm sure you eat meat and we do not have enough supplies to feed you three as well as ourselves. We will butcher it here and smoke what we need. The rest of you look around for wolves. They will not be far behind the herd unless they have pulled one down for themselves."

"We can afford to wait. We will achieve nothing if we go hungry," agreed Suzzan.

After some time at the end of the butchering, the horses became restless and began to cast fearful eyes at the long grass. A long drawn out howl signalled an answering growl from quite near. The four humans knocked off the safety catches of their rifles and began to point them at the increasing noises in the undergrowth.

Suzzan's mental voice echoed in their minds, "Pull back onto the area trampled down by the cattle. We have enough meat and need not kill for the sake of it. These weapons you have newly possessed, do not have an endless amount of bullets. Be quiet and slow as you pull back. This land belongs to them, not us. We are visitors here!"

Silently they all pulled back away from the butchered animal in wary order and as they did so the first wolf pushed its way out of the long grass. Snarling a warning it was first at the kill and bent its head to sniff the bloody carcass. One by one the rest of the pack came into view.

Using Larse's abilities I thrust into the leader's mind, *'Fed you we have. Dangerous we are not. Leave we will!'*

A puzzled mixture of bewildered trust and appreciation was returned to me. The hunting had been difficult for some time and twice the humans on horse had left them food. They would not attack the hand that had fed them. The leader of the pack walked a little closer to the humans and Gnathe to catch and remember their scent. His fur bristled when he caught the scent of the Zanth and he stiffened. He stared up at the huge alien creatures, stood his ground for a few moments and turned away, rejoined the feeding pack, leaving us to go on our way.

"That went well. Remember us they will as providers of food when come back here we will," I broadcast to all of my enlarged group.

It was Larse who queried my statement by thinking, "Why will we be coming back here?"

"This is the only place that we know of that has communications systems that are still working," Suzzan stated emphatically. "This Lord Samovar needs to know about this place. He seems to be the driving force behind the re-civilisation of this world. This research establishment must be constantly manned again. There is much there that will help re-establish the science and technology that Daedalus One has lost. I tell you now, Larse and you others; this feud must end between you and Lord Samovar. You must open your minds to the greater catastrophe that can befall all who live on the three worlds. If Toarvak 7 gets here before we have made some attempt to stop it, you may as well lie down and die now!"

I winced at the ferocity of the Gnathe's mental projection. Telepathy cannot lie and Suzzan gave the group of humans no doubt as to the seriousness of the situation. I could only agree and added my weight to the force of her command. If this group had a leader at all, this Gnathe had become that force that would bind us all together.

We soon reached the point that we had entered the grasslands and once more found ourselves upon the road to Priss.

Francisco Samovar sat reading the report that the soldier had given him. Commander Edward Jones had been very painstaking in his description of the bars that had been cut through and put back again in the prison cell. He was certain that the glass had been removed and refitted back in the window from the outside. The outside was sheer in construction and yet the prisoner had escaped from the cell at the top of a one hundred foot high tower, as if he had wings.

Francisco looked up from the report and said, "You were there?"

"Yes Lord Samovar," Gurt replied, standing at attention.

"Relax you fool. This report says that you are not to blame for this man's escape. Stand easy and tell me in your own words all you can remember, not just about him, but the three that brought him in!"

"Sir! The Norseman I remember well," Gurt replied and relaxed his stiffened joints and stood easy. "He was a big, blond man, much taller than I and there was something about him. I know now what it was. He was so 'healthy' and so self assured."

"What do you mean by healthy?"

"Its difficult to put into words, Sir. It was just his manner and the way that he stood as if he were in no danger. He seemed to 'glow' from within and looked as if he could wrestle a bear and win!"

"What about the other three?" You must have seen them," Lord Samovar asked, tilting his chair back. "What did they look like? Was there any difference with them?"

"That's the whole point, Sir. Nobody can remember them well. All we know is that three Algarie soldiers on a special assignment from you to hunt down the troublemakers handed him in. As I remember it, they declared that 'they were Special Forces, no insignia to be shown and no papers carried!"

"And the commander did not question them further?

"No sir!"

"That's what it says in Commander Jones's report. Again and again these three entered the Library, examined what ever they decided to look at with the willing help of the very people that have the sanctity of that information store to keep. They went unchallenged and nobody can remember precisely what they looked like or how they were dressed!" Francisco pointed at the other chair in the room and said, "Sit. You look tired. It must have been a long ride."

Gurt gratefully sat down in the offered chair and agreed, "Yes sir it was. I rode as fast as I could, using two horses and swapping from one to the other. I slept by the side of the road and saw no one until I arrived here."

"Were there signs that the four were coming this way?"

"It was difficult to be certain, Sir, but I felt sure that four had camped at one place and then I lost all sign of them," he answered.

Francisco poured water from a jug and offered it to the sweat-stained man in the chair.

"Drink!" he said. "You must be thirsty. I apologise for forgetting your effort in getting here. This report is amazing."

Gurt coloured up in confusion at Lord Samovar's request for forgiveness and drank. "This man commands respect beyond duty," he thought as the cool water eased his dry throat.

Lord Samovar stood up and clasped Gurt's shoulder and said, "You have done well in bringing this report so quickly to me. You have my thanks. Go and rest. I have things to organise. See the quarter-master and tell him to have the sergeants stripes sewn onto your sleeve by my order."

Francisco walked out of his office and into the fresh air of outside, thinking deeply. He selected a young soldier and barked, "You there, with nothing to do! Fetch me Captain Peterson at once and bring him back here."

John Peterson knew better than to be slow when Lord Samovar summoned him and came at a quick pace. He rushed round the corner and made his way to the office that the Leader of Civilisation used at Priss.

Francisco looked up from his place behind the table where he had returned. It was covered with a copy of the map of the area.

"John," he said as the young man drew to a stop, "call in all the patrols we have out looking for those four men. The traps we set must not be sprung. There is more to these four than meets the eye. They must not be harmed. I must have them alive. Let them approach Priss without seeing that they are tracked. Understand? Just track them and report to me. Use the mirrors to send word."

"Yes Sir! Is there anything else, Sir," Peterson replied.

"Yes send that scientist to me from the dig; Dr. Diego and his assistant. Go! Go!"

Sebastian Diego was examining the find his assistant, Pablo, had dug out of the rubble of what was once a hospital, with the working gang allotted. It was a functioning microscope sealed in an airtight box. The sweat trickled down from the top of his bald head and behind his ears. It went unnoticed in his excitement as with shaking hands he put it through its paces.

"Look at this Pablo," he exclaimed. "This is a find indeed. Are there any more?"

"There could be sir. I think we may have discovered a storeroom. It is full of these airtight boxes of all shapes and sizes," he answered and looked up at the arrival of an Algarie soldier.

"Lord Samovar says you are to come at once, sir," he gasped and seeing the expression on the scientist's face, added, "Now, Dr. Diego!"

Sebastian reluctantly heaved his chubby body away from the microscope and followed the retreating backside of the soldier. "You had better come as well, Pablo and see what it is the our benefactor wants."

Lord Samovar sat in his chair and patiently waited for the portly doctor to arrive. The evening air was beginning to turn a trifle crisp, so he pulled his coat a little closer around his once wiry frame. He had left the map spread out on the table before him and had arranged for two chairs to be available at the other side. He turned the report over and over in his hands and thought deeply about the contents.

The scientist and his young, clever assistant entered the room. Dr. Diego was puffing somewhat while Pablo Handous was not even out of breath.

"Sit down my two friends," Francisco said. "I am sorry to drag you away from the excavation, but I have something for you to read," and handed the report to the doctor.

"I would have told you tomorrow," Dr. Diego remarked, waving the sheet of paper around. "We have uncovered a storeroom full of airtight boxes. I was examining a fully functioning microscope when you called for us!"

"Sebastian! Will you please concentrate your mind on this report. I consider it serious and I have the man here that was there when these incidents happened," Lord Samovar cut him off and banged the table with his fist.

The doctor jumped and flinched.

"Sorry, he said, "but the new finds are"-------

Francisco fixed him with a baleful eye and Sebastian bent his head to read the report. He handed each separate page to Pablo as he finished and finally sat back in the chair and ran his fingers through his bushy eyebrows. He waited for his assistant to finish reading and then clasped his stubby fingers together.

"This account is truly amazing, my old friend. I can see why you sent for us. These four young men are different to the norm. The only way that the bars could have been removed and replaced is with nannite technology. Yet nowhere in this account is a description or mention of one of the fabled Nannites. If there were such a being on this world we would have known about them long ago," Sebastian declared emphatically.

"What intrigues me the most," remarked Pablo is the escape from the top of a sheer sided tower and the mental fogging of everyone's mind who encountered them. The only ones capable of doing the last part are telepathic adepts. And the only people who could do that were the Gnathe and the ones who built the gate and brought us here!"

"There hasn't been a Gnathe on this world since the destruction wrought by Toarvak 6," Lord Samovar answered. "We don't even know if any survived on any of the other two worlds. Have you not unearthed any communications equipment at all?"

"Nothing, Francisco," Sebastian replied. "We now have a hospital storeroom and I doubt we will find anything there capable of signalling Earth or Daedalus Two. The munitions factory yielded rifles, revolvers and ammunition. There were some interesting non-combatative pieces of hardware, but little else as you know."

"That was the other thing I wanted to ask you. Have you tested those items and did they work?

"Yes Sir," said Pablo, "they worked amazingly well considering how long they had lain there."

"Right," Lord Samovar said, "I want you Pablo to oversee the use of them when our guests arrive at Priss. Take a detachment of men and make sure they know how to use them. Make contact with captain Peterson when you are ready. Now this is what I want you to do."

John Peterson had worked his way up in Lord Samovar's army of occupation, by being smart and making sure that he was in the right place at the right time. He had studied hard at the college at Whickam's Crossing and had left with more than just a good solid education. He had studied the archives in his own time and had a good grounding in the events leading up the destruction by the alien killing machine. He had become fascinated by the benevolent aliens, which were responsible for building a wormhole big enough to swallow the Earth and its moon. They had taken it away from being destroyed by its sun turning into a red giant and had placed it in orbit around Icarus. It was said that they had combined their minds with human and ape into one colossal entity and twisted time and space to achieve the rescue. There were no records of why the intelligence controlling Toarvak 6 had decided to attack, other than the cryptic message relayed to the welcoming space ships of the three worlds.

All it had said once pictures had been exchanged was, "You are not Kresh. I am Toarvak 6., 'The servant of the Kresh'. I am the will and the way. Toarvak 7 has been informed."

With that chilling statement it had destroyed all of the un-armed space ships the three worlds possessed. Then it had taken its time in systematically destroying the civilisation of the three worlds, before being taken out by some super weapon. Since then nothing had happened and slowly the old civilisation was being put back together. Unfortunately, always at the back of the minds that knew, was the awful certainty that the alien killing machine Toarvak 7 would finally arrive at Icarus some time in the future.

The captain had managed to contact all of the scattered forces sent out in a fanned pattern between Priss and Whickam's Crossing, either personally, or sending on riders from those he had managed to ride down. The more distant ones he had made contact by reflecting mirrors and the old stand by, Morse code. Everything was now set to observe the advance of the four unusual renegades without confrontation.

The time had passed midday when one of his men reported a mirror flash from up ahead.

He turned and focused the telescope he carried on the message that said, "Party coming on town road. Bigger than expected. Instructions?"

John Peterson rubbed the stump of his missing little finger on his left hand as he did when thoughtful. He had lost it when a rifle had misfired and had taken the tip off during an early training exercise.

"What can he mean, larger than expected," he thought and looked at the tall Oak tree reaching above its neighbours.

"Soldier, throw a rope over that sturdy branch. I need to go aloft and spy out the road," he ordered and watched the rope curl through the air and over the out-stretched bough.

He looped it around his waist and nodded to the group of soldiers.

"Pull," he said and began to ascend the tree.

Once on the branch he made the rope fast and rapidly climbed further up until he had an uninterrupted view of the road. What he saw filled him with a mounting eagerness to get back down onto the ground.

CHAPTER SEVEN

As Larse and his companions rode steadily southwards he thought about Suzzan's flat statement about his feud with lord Samovar. She was right, the events that they had all witnessed made his vendetta with the Algarie very insignificant.

"Confused you are Larse, I know," I interrupted his thoughts and continued, *"Suzzan is right in what she says. A reckoning you may insist for what happened at your village. An explanation there may be. A wider picture you have seen to account for all that has happened here."*

Larse answered abruptly, "Shut up demon. Keep out of my thoughts! What did my mother and father do to bring down the might of the Algarie?"

"We may come to know my young friend in time. This is not the time for you to think revenge! Petty it becomes when balanced against Toarvak 7's impending visit."

"I know all that," he replied. "Just leave me alone for a while!"

I retreated from his consciousness and spoke to Thomas, Jon and Samuel, *"How do you view these events. Agree with Suzzan do you?"*

Jon spoke first, telepathically to all of them, "We all understand what the Gnathe has said. We know that it is true. You cannot lie, mind to mind. She was here before the destruction of our worlds. Our campaign with Larse becomes changed. He knows that, Demon, just give him time to come round. All of us have had to rethink our lives. We have had a lifetime of living under Lord Samovar's rule, with our people dancing to his tune, backed up by his troops. It is only now we can see the reason why."

"I like these Gnathe," thought Samuel to the others. "There is something about them that inspires trust. There is nothing that the male and female would not do, if Suzzan asked it. She does not have to tell them, they just do it! Yet both Ritchie and Jaffin have totally independent minds. I am still amazed how Jaffin sent her mind into the combination lock and opened that rifle cabinet. I would like to be taught how to do that.

"We are being watched," Suzzan interrupted them. "I apologise for breaking in on a private conversation, but you must be made aware. To our far left, high in a tree, there is a human being with a telescope trained on us. Underneath are a band of armed men. There are too many thoughts to be able to home in on without them having a command crystal in their possession. You however could try to ascertain their intentions. They are your species. Keep riding as though you do not know of them."

As it was some distance away, the four tried something new that they had learned by themselves; they linked minds, leaving the control to Larse.

The gestalt probed gently amongst the soldiers for hostile intent and found none. They had been ordered to observe only. The mind in the tree was of a different calibre and was in total control of these men and ALL THE OTHER ONES! The gestalt reached out to encompass the Gnathe with them and with that extra power at their disposal, Larse handed the control to Suzzan's expertise.

Suzzan-link-khann did a wide sweep and found that they were in a central position flanked by groups of horsemen that were keeping well out of the way as they rode on.

"We are expected gentlemen," she said and broke the group mind up into its component parts. "The consensus of opinion is to follow and not to fire upon us or harm us in any way. The man in the tree has signalled back to Priss that we are coming and who we are; including me!"

John Peterson watched the approach of the group with mounting excitement. Before that he signalled to the group of soldiers between himself and the city of Priss.

The massage sent was; - "Group seen and shadowed. Expect Gnathe with renegades. No problem so far." He got conformation that the massage was received and sent on and set about climbing down the oak tree.

"Right, men," he ordered, "I want us to circle around the group and take up a position at the rear. You will see something that up till now you will have only seen in books. The four renegades are travelling with Gnathe and they are mounted on Zanth! No one is to fire on these aliens or the four men on horseback. Do you all understand? Believe me when I say that the sight you are about to see will remain with you all of your lives. Make sure that all safety catches are secure on every rifle. If any of you lets off a shot, lord Samovar will have you strung up and that will be after you have been dealt with by me!"

The troop mounted up and circled round through the trees and took up the position at the rear. It was not long before the heavy clawed marks that the Zanth left in the road's surface became very visible. Captain Peterson's troop became very edgy at the signs of passage. Whatever had made these marks in the soil had to be a lot bigger than a horse. As they rode around a bend they glimpsed the strange group in front of them and Peterson waved the company to drop back.

At the ruined city of Priss, Lord Samovar had made ready for the confrontation between his soldiers and the advancing group. The old non-combative weapons had been primed and readied by his personal guard. Priss had been built in an oxbow and could only be entered or left by a number of bridges. Although the centre was a melted mess of glassy slag, many of the buildings at the riverside were hardly touched.

The bridge gatehouse was where Francisco had made his excavation headquarters. He had the pleasant breeze off the river to help cool his rooms in the hot afternoons and a view of the road leading into the city. His office looked out on a weir that supported a generating water wheel that had never been known to stop. The Rineflow was a swift river that originated in the cold northern lands and emptied into a vast landlocked sea. Known as the Great Baltic, the sea had not aged sufficiently to become more than slightly brackish. When the original settlers came to this world they had transplanted freshwater fish from earth into the ecosystem as well as seeding the empty lands. There was very little of native life forms on Daedalus One or Two to compete with the genetically crafted trees, shrubs and crops. There were enough of the waterweeds and springy trees to produce an oxygen sufficient atmosphere to build on. The two worlds had been settled before they were quite ready, but pressure from an exhausted Earth after its confrontation with the increasing heat of the sun, had made up the minds of many. They settled and farmed, shipping the excess harvest back to the home world via the short wormholes that the Gnathe set up to connect the three worlds. Francisco Samovar knew the history of the three worlds well and when he received the information that there were Gnathe accompanying the four renegades, it made him very thoughtful. The books that he had studied at collage had made out the Gnathe to be powerful mental adepts with different abilities to humans. They had passed on these abilities to certain human and the pan-chimpanzees that had worked with them on the new Jupiter, by combining their genetic makeup with Gnathen genes. It was their abilities that had made the wormhole technology possible.

Francisco sucked in his breath with excitement as he focussed his telescope onto the approaching strange group. He reluctantly handed it over to Dr. Diego and signalled to his men by the bridge.

"There are Gnathe with them. Living Gnathe! Be careful Francisco with what you are about to do. If something goes wrong you will regret it my old friend," Sebastian Declared and handed the telescope over to Pablo's eager hands.

As the group arrived at the other side of the bridge, Lord Samovar's men loosed off the rocket grenades filled with sleeping gas.

Suzzan brought the group to an abrupt halt as the rockets swooped out of the sky towards them. She brought her telekinetic abilities to the fore, added to by the groups combined power and built a frictionless plain angled to the left and upwards. The rockets were directed away and back up into the air towards the other side of the bridge. The group of soldiers frantically tried to run from the barrage heading their way. Once the first grenade hit and exploded its gas, the closest soldier dropped to the ground followed by all the others as the rest of the canisters opened.

The group advanced slowly towards Lord Samovar's position on the other side and stopped by the unconscious soldiers. Suzzan soon spotted the group with the telescope and concentrated her mind towards them to check their identity and status. With a hiss of fury she swept them up with her telekinetic power, reaching out to the members of her gestalt for extra energy.

Lord Samovar, Dr Diego and Pablo found themselves pinned in an invisible vice-like grip and lifted through the air and suspended over the Rineflow's turbulent surface. With mounting horror they suffered the indignity of being dipped up and down in the full force of the flow until they could hardly breath. Covered in weeds and soaked through to the skin, Suzzan lifted them out and dumped them in front of her, where they sat struggling to get their breath.

"Shall we try that again?" Suzzan hissed in incandescent anger as she dismounted. "My name is Suzzan-link-khann, direct descendant of the Gate Builders who placed you here!"

Pablo was the first to get his breath and said, "Our apologies my Lady. We have heard so many alarming reports concerning the men you travel with, Lord Samovar deemed it prudent to render you all unconscious."

"I can speak for myself, Pablo," Francisco coughed and spat out a piece of waterweed. "I made a mistake my Lady and paid for it with my dignity." He began to laugh and extended his hand to the giant towering over him. "Greetings to you and your kindred. I am Lord Francisco Samovar and these are two of my scientific advisers, Dr. Sebastian Diego and Pablo Handous. You had better come inside my office while I get into some dry clothes. My two friends here are showing signs of the cold dip you gave us. Captain Peterson will take care of the horses while you all come inside. By the way, I am aware of these young men's' abilities concerning mind altering. Should I begin to show signs of being tampered with, my men have been told to shoot you at once. They are the ones you can't see.

Larse spoke up and said, "You are right. I could convince you that you were a dog if I wished, but there are more important things to do. We have much to tell you about the Gnathe, an untouched working research establishment and ourselves some distance away from here. Also you need to listen carefully to what Suzzan-link-khann will tell you. These Gnathe are from the time of the destruction and have the knowledge of that time. When you have heard all that, then that is the time that you and I need to talk. I have a private matter that needs clearing up."

Lord Samovar had food brought in while he and the doctor and his assistant dried off and changed. By the time he had heard all the information, darkness had fallen outside and the streetlights had come on illuminating the area of the bridge and Francisco's headquarters.

"We need to sleep on this," Lord Samovar declared. "In the morning we will move to the 'Link-soo-shan Institute of Gnathen Studies'. I need to speak to our people on the other two worlds. You Larse, stay behind. We will talk about your private matter."

"Larse your anger control," I insisted. *"This man, hear out you must and remember the greater scale of things at stake. Show him what was done in his name. Introduce him to me you must. My story he must know from me."*

"Lord Samovar as you can see, I am a Norseman not Algarie! I am going to show you something from my mind. It is the memories I carry from whence I was a boy," said Larse and concentrated his mind on the Spaniard's.

I relayed it all, from what Larse remembered to when I arrived and saved him from the wolves. We spared him nothing of the horrors perpetrated by his men.

Lord Samovar ran his fingers through his thinning hair and looked back at Larse with sorrow and said, "Something must have got out of hand. This is not what I ordered. You know what my family and I have been trying to do for generations and that is to bind together all the humans on this world. You know what is coming and what we have to be ready for. I have sent out groups of my soldiers to temporarily collect children to give them a chance of an education at Whickam's Crossing. Your people have retreated to the wilds and regressed. When Toarvak 7 arrives intent on genocide, your people would have died with all of us. Someone will pay for this I promise you!"

"They have! I killed the ones who sacked my village long

ago. I wanted to kill you myself with my own bare hands for what was done. Now Suzzan has shown me that it is not to be and I agree with her. She is right Lord Samovar, it is the only way to civilise what remains of us. In our explanation we mentioned that I was taken as host to a strange creature I named Demon when I was a boy. For him to speak to you it is necessary for us to join and some of his substance, enter your body. It will be similar to telepathy. You will have to trust me when I say that I no longer bear you ill-will."

"What do I have to do," Francisco asked warily.

"Nothing more than grasp my hand, but do not let it go!"

Larse extended his hand and the Algarie ruler grasped it and I crossed over sufficient to extend trough his nervous system.

"Afraid do not be. I am Demon and a friend. Your body had many small gallstones, remove them I have and repaired a heart valve also I have done. Your brain is inferior and many connections have I made to unused portions. Thinking you will do at a greater clarity with memory enhanced. This I have done for Larse and his friends."

Francisco concentrated his mind inwards and asked, "What are you? Where did you come from?"

"I was once a mighty weapon. The rest of me under a mountain remains. I have little memory of how I came here. Suzzan does not entirely trust me, as remember me she does not, from the time before. If you would defend your three worlds from Toarvak 7 then trust me you should. A nannite perhaps I am, but weakened. As much as I know, then so do you. Leave you I must now and return to Larse."

Lord Samovar sat back and examined his hand as almost the last of my substance crept back into my host breaking the link between the two of them.

"A small piece I have left in your brain, so communicate with Larse and the others you can if you need to."

Larse grinned and said, "Once a member of the group,

always a member! Look on the bright side, you will be much healthier and your mind will be sounder! Now I must get some sleep. It's the long night again soon and I really am tired."

As Daedalus One swung round behind Icarus, the double night began and until the giant moon once more came into the sunlight, both sides of the seeded world remained in darkness. There was little to do but sleep when this occurred and eat when hungry. Travel was difficult as the double night was so much darker when the moon orbited into the gas giant's shadow. Ordinary night was lit up by Icarus's reflected sunlight, so that total darkness never happened. The gas giant was almost as large as Jupiter used to be before it was kissed by the expanding sun. It would have been possible to have packed fifty thousand Earths into its size. The orbits of its two planet sized moons were far enough out, that the lethal radiation that erupted from Icarus, did no damage to the life on each. Earth had been placed into a similar position, but orbiting over the poles of the gas giant. As far as night and day on the home world were concerned, nothing had changed, except the view of the gas giant as they spun round dominating the sky. It to, like the original Jupiter was ringed by turbulent storms with bands of orange, yellow and red swirling clouds. Deep underneath was a rocky, silicate ball under unthinkable pressure. It hung in the night sky like a maleficent eye staring out at the three worlds.

Word had soon got round about the newcomer's status regarding Lord Samovar and the alien creatures out of history. Some resentment had boiled over when the soldiers realised that these four had sent some of their number to their graves. After Larse had dragged two unconscious soldiers to Captain Peterson's quarters and thrown them through the door after things had got a little heated, he decided to see Francisco Samovar again.

He knocked on the door of the overlord's office.

"Come in Larse," Francisco said.

Larse entered and fixed his Commander with a tired look and said, "My Lord Samovar, I'm getting tired of watching my back. I seek no punishment for the men involved, but I will take action of my own if this resentment continues."

"And what will that be?"

"Altering some of their minds I will if this continues. Your permission I seek to do this thing."

Lord Samovar fixed Larse with a steely look and said, "I am amazed that you should consider asking my permission when I could not stop you if I wished!"

Larse cut into the exchange and answered for me, "The four of us have been given a crash coarse in ethics by the Lady Suzzan. She has a way of putting things that dispels all arguments," he said.

"What would you do?"

"Feelings of resentment I would shrink and let it be known that the new four Algarie subjects are responsible for bringing the Gnathe back to the lands. All acts of revenge for what was done at Larse's village discharged they have been. Completely!"

"I can make sure that most of that gets known amongst my men," Francisco answered. "Where personal feelings come into the balance, I am sure that you can alter a few minds as you think fit. I feel that my son, Fernando might be just such one of those whose mind may need altering. He it was I sent to hunt you down along with a group of lawless killers that have been raiding and looting the outlying farms. You should meet and work together to root these outlaws from our society. Tomorrow at first light you will meet with him and ride out together while we make our way to the pyramid. From what you have told me it will be in the same general direction, but in the hills to the

East. Work together with my son and show the others that you are useful and loyal to me. Do this and I am sure that old enmities will be forgotten!"

"I look forward to meeting your son, Lord Samovar and I can see the wisdom of your reasoning. These raiding outlaws; do they kill the farmers and their families or just steal from them?"

"They kill them!"

"Then they can expect no mercy," Larse stated and left Francisco to his thoughts.

Daedalus One swung out of the gas giant's shadow and the remains of the city of Priss were immediately bathed in daylight. True to Lord Samovar's word a troop of men were mounted up and waiting for the four new recruits.

Fernando Samovar was as dark and swarthy as his father. A wiry built man of some ten years older than Larse and his friends. He sat his horse as if he was born into its saddle. He rode up to Larse and examined the big man carefully and offered his hand.

"I have been instructed by my father to trust you and see if you can help me track down these killers of women and children. He requires that we work together and I learn to accept that the past grievances are over. We shall see!"

Larse accepted the firm handshake and said, "Commander Fernando we will work together, you and I. Shall we try and find these scum and remove them?"

"They were last seen to the East of here, where they attacked a farmstead during the night and butchered the farmer and his children. His wife and daughters they used and left them stripped in the straw for dead. We go there first to offer what help we can give and to see if we can deduce where they would go next. So far I have not been able to catch up with them. At one time I thought they were you and your companions," Fernando said.

Thomas reacted with anger and replied, "We have never killed innocents, only Algarie soldiers who would have killed us!"

Larse turned in the saddle and gestured to the others, "Enough!" he said. "Let us find these evil bastards and put an end to them."

After several hours travel the troop came to the farmstead where the soldiers left there had stabled the horse and milk cow belonging to the farm. They had seen to it that they were fed and watered. Fresh graves had been dug in the soft earth at the back of the house and one of the daughters was feeding the chickens. The farmer's wife came out to greet Fernando. Her face was bruised and her lip was swollen where she had been punched and she held her side.

"Find them, my Lord Fernando. Find them and kill them for what they have done to my family. We would have given them food willingly, but it was the girls and me they wanted first," she sobbed.

Thomas dismounted and slowly approached the woman holding his arms out for comfort.

"We will do our best," he said. "We will not harm you in any way. I must ask you to trust me and it will be hard for you to do. I must go into your mind and see these animals for myself as you have seen them," and drew her fearful, trembling body into the safety of his embrace.

On contact with her skin I was able to enter the woman's body and the first thing I did was to render her unconscious. I had learnt that the female of this species did not enjoy my occupation so it would be less of a shock to her this way. The hurt to her body was grievous indeed. I soothed the damages caused by the rapes she had endured and pulled back the fractured rib caused by a vicious kick. The bruises to her face and lip I was able to knit together, the new pregnancy I terminated for her peace of mind. While I was doing all this I also accessed her recent memories of the attack upon her farm.

"Thomas, Larse, Samuel and Jon, study you must these memories. Faces you will need to know when we find these. The children you must all touch and let me do my work. Much healing I must do. More to find out I will!"

All the surviving children were brought in contact with my group and I was allowed to continue my healing. Oh the capacity for pain these weak organisms had. How easily damaged they could become. Angry I became that such suffering could be purposely inflicted on others. Finished at last I released the last one, while Jon was speaking to Fernando.

"What you have seen here is what we have become. If you are willing to follow your father, I can show you what information we have gathered while we healed these unfortunate people."

"What do I have to do?" asked Lord Samovar's son.

"Merely grasp my hand and do not let go, no matter what," Jon replied and held out his un-gloved hand.

I crossed into the new human and made the necessary connections to his brain, altering his set-up as I went. It had become second nature to me now to enhance the brain structures of these people. I did a check of the new host's health and gave a few things a tweak to balance things out while I entered into conversation with him.

"Afraid of me do not be. By my hosts I am called Demon. A short time I will be here in your body to show you all that has befallen these poor unfortunates," and I filled his mind with the horrors done here.

Fernando Samovar had seen many things and experienced some strange events, but nothing measured up to the invasion of his body by Demon. His eyes widened as we talked together and once again I reversed the flow, seeping back into Jon.

"I have left a small piece of me inside your brain just as I did your father, so that communicate we can. To use it you must learn. A small amount of energy from you I will require. Regret it you will not I think!"

"Mount up all of you," he commanded and Fernando swung his horse out of the farmyard. "Let us find these evil bastards and punish them for this."

CHAPTER NINE

Some time ago in the fringes of the system of planets circling the Earth's new sun, an incredibly old star ship began to fall towards the light. Sensors that had been built into the skin of the ship registered the increasing illumination and sent frantic signals to the wake-up procedure. The Nano-ship had been launched with many others in a desperate attempt to stop the annihilation of the human race when the sun became a red giant. The artificial intelligences had remained inert for over six million years as the ship crept towards the new sun at sub-light velocity. The four Nannites were exactly the same as the four who had found themselves left behind in the remains of the old Solar system. Their personalities had been crafted with care and turned out in the hundreds. Each ship was identical to all the others sent to the stars and crewed the same.

The Commander, Asue, was a Nano-tech expert, physicist, engineer and astro-navigator, constructed with a female personality, as were the other two bio-chemists, genetic engineers, surgeons and vets, known as Sharn and Minns.

The forth Nannite artificial intelligence was called Kamiel and had a male personality. He was a Nano-tech engineer, weapons expert, historian and mission psychologist.

They had been designed and programmed to re-create the human and pan-chimpanzees and provide a biosphere to enable them to flourish. They were a part of the Genesis Project started by Alexander McBald and somewhere out in the great darkness there were hundreds more pursuing their lonely way towards new suns. Some would succeed and some would end in despair, finding them-selves falling towards planet-less stars.

As the nannites awoke, Asue did a full scan of the fringes

of the system and found it full of ice ball combinations with a wealth of minerals. Veritable harvests of comets, yet to fall towards the sun, were theirs to plunder. The ship changed shape into a giant dandelion seed and reached out for the nearest frozen goodies. Some time was spent collecting and processing the raw materials into fuel and storing the proceeds into nannite tanks. The dandelion seed now had three jets standing out from the main stem and pointing to the rear, mounted on huge tanks under enormous pressure. The fuzzy collecting head was reabsorbed into the stem of the Nano-ship and Asue opened up the pressure valves. The ship increased velocity and once more began to fall towards the sun and the inner planets. They passed gas giants similar to Neptune and a ringed, orange one comparable to Saturn with dozens of large moons. So far they had not been able to find solid planets in orbit around the new sun. As they got closer to the sun and found yet another gas giant in orbit where the Earth would have circled the old sun they began to get misgivings.

"It is too soon to know whether this one has large moons at this distance," worried Asue. "All we can do is wait until we get closer and hope that we can stop here and improvise with what we find!"

"The last giant had moons much larger than those we left behind in the old Solar System," Kamiel answered, adding, "It could be that larger moons are the norm for this system. If so we can always consider colliding two to make a bigger world if we need to. All is not lost!"

A month or so later, what they could see from the long range sensors as they approached the gas giant caused them to disbelieve the evidence of their sensory attachments. In orbit around the gas giant were two living worlds in a locked Trojan position at two points of a triangle with a collection of moonlets occupying the third point. What they could not believe was the familiar home world and its moon, orbiting the gas giant around the poles so that it always had sunlight, without diving into the shadow of the gas giant as would the other two planet sized moons. Nothing in their programming had prepared them for that!

Asue transmuted some of the raw materials so that they could radio the impossible home world and try to find out what had happened. She monitored the radio waves until she found an active band, while the others searched the images of the three worlds for indications of settlement.

Kamiel said to his companions, "An annihilating war has been fought here, maybe centuries ago. Where there were cities, there are now melted slagheaps. All three worlds have been bombarded from above in an attempt to destroy all intelligent life. What happened here? Our builders have had peace for centuries before we left! I cannot believe we did this to our selves."

At the Cheyenne Mountain complex deep underground the incoming ship had been sensed and a state of controlled panic had taken place. Daedalus Two had been informed and they both waited to see what was coming their way. When Asue's broadcast was relayed to both receiving stations a state of euphoria ensued.

The main screen at the one surviving Earth complex lit up with the featureless faces of the nannites. The optical band that encircled the upper part of the silver ovoids, where eyes would normally be, stared back at both humans and apes in patient order.

"We are the crew of Nano-ship N-96," Asue stated to the excited gathering. "There is an awful lot that you need to tell us. The last thing we expected to see was the Earth and Moon orbiting our destination. How did you get here?"

So began the long story of the Gnathe, the great gestalt of collected minds controlling a wormhole through time and space. Simon and Jondar filled in the gaps concerning the destructive visit of Toarvak 6 to their three worlds community.

Kamiel asked the next question, "Where are the nannites? I can see none of them at both control complexes."

"The alien vessel released a weapon that took apart all the molecular cohesion of the nannites, destroying them all," Simon explained. "The Servant of the Kresh effectively removed our abilities to work with Nano-technology. You will be our salvation. We managed to destroy the intelligence controlling the 'destroyer', but not before it informed another of its kind that it had failed. Another one is on its way and that's what we thought you were. There is one Gnathe and kindred on Daedalus One that was released from an experimental time stasis field, that has preserved them for centuries. She is known as the Lady Suzzan-link-khann, with one male and female. She is a mental adept and once constructed short wormholes to each of the worlds. We hope that she will be able to do this again, so that goods and machinery can be distributed amongst the survivors. She was released from an experimental time stasis machine, by a group of men who are host to something that has improved their mental abilities beyond recognition. They call it Demon and it is independently intelligent and lives inside the four young men. It is similar to a nannite, but remembers being a weapon of great destructive power, long ago and wants the humans to dig it out from under a mountain in the far north. It believes that it was the thing that destroyed Toarvak 6 and is our only hope of surviving the next visit! I might add that the Lady Suzzan does not entirely trust it."

"That is an awful amount of incredible information to take on board," said Asue. We will make for Cheyenne Mountain on our final approach. Does the artificial intelligence facility on the Moon-base remain intact?"

"As far as we know, everything is in the same state it was when Toarvak 6 exploded a neutron bomb over the top of it! Every human and ape died there, but functionally it has remained on-line and taking power from the solar collectors."

"In that case," Asue advised, "we will split the ship in half and let Kamiel reactivate whatever nannite personalities there are in stasis inside the library. That would have been buried deep and protected from solar flares. He can cannibalise the nannite construction of his part of the ship and set up the production of new artificial intelligences. There are all sorts of scientific personalities that can help rebuild. Once built and ongoing, Kamiel and the new Guardians can be launched towards Earth and the two sister planets by the steam catapult."

"You will be the agents of our salvation. There will be items on the moon that are not listed in your data banks. The Gnathe left us with sufficient crystals to operate the wormhole technology that only they completely understand, but share with us. Those caught by the flashes of neutron radiation have been rendered inert and we lack the means to return them to their original state," Simon answered. "So if there are any that you can find while you are there, we can discuss what to keep and what to bring down."

"This seems to be going well," Asue remarked and continued, "Once down, we will convert some of our part of the ship to produce more copies of our bodies, altering the personalities. The next thing would be to produce the artificial wombs that we are programmed to build. Reading between the lines it would seem that a great deal of Earth's life forms have disappeared. We have in our memory banks everything necessary to start life anew. Whatever you have missing we can provide. Sharn and Minns can make a start on that soon after we are down. It's good to see humans and apes again even if you are here against all the odds. I cannot tell you how happy we are to see the home world again. Rest assured we are programmed to do our best to help you all."

With that Asue altered the jet system to point the head of the space ship towards Earth. They were coming home!

Far away on Daedalus One Suzzan had returned to see Lord Samovar with her two prizes.

She impaled the nannite shaft with its claw mounted crystals one each side of the road and stood to one side. She looked at the uneasy gathering of Francisco's finest soldiers who were lined up leading their horses by the reins.

"This is the easy way to the institute," she said. "I will connect this gate to the crystal under the pyramid and make a large doorway or as you humans like to call it, a short wormhole!"

She sent her mind into the matrix and concentrated on the two, set in the doorway by the time stasis machine. Once she had the signature she pushed the door open with her telekinetic crystal and a fuzzy picture of the underground floor materialised between the pillars.

"Time to go," she said. "We have much to do and stores to transpose. Forward men, just follow my Kindred and you will be safe. Be respectful of the bodies that you encounter; they were my friends! Ritchie will open the large entry door as soon as he gets there and you can attend to the horses. You will find plenty of buildings to use when you go through. The one thing I will ask of you is to dig a large grave and bury the dead with some dignity as soon as you can! Now hurry, while I keep the gate open."

Ritchie and Jaffin walked through leading their Zanth

followed by the awestruck soldiers, their wives and supplies on packhorses. It took enough time that Suzzan became mentally exhausted by the time she collapsed the gate. She rested for a while before she gathered the two matching command crystals from each side of the road. Tucking them under her arm she brought the two smaller crystals in her wrist pockets to her neck pouch where she kept the telekinetic one and sent her weary mind through the matrix again. She twisted space and found herself in the underground sealed hall with Lord Samovar and his men. They had already made a start on clearing away the mummified remains of the people that had run the Institute. She noticed that the communication light was blinking on and off on the main console. Beckoning Francisco to her side she flicked the switch to illuminate the screen.

Suzzan found herself looking once again at the young man called Simon. By his side on the split screen was the Ape from Daedalus Two, Jondar.

"We have great news Lady Suzzan. One of the original Nano-ships launched from Earth, before your ancestors moved us into orbit around Icarus, is on its way to our base as we speak. This will mean that once more we have access the benefits of Nano-technology."

"This is excellent news, my young friend," the Gnathe replied. "Now all I need is another piece and we can begin rebuilding in earnest. Did any of your searching find a command crystal?"

Simon said, "We can do better than that. Deep underground at the Cheyenne complex we have found what we believe to be an original gate. Without the Gnathe to operate it, it has lain forgotten for centuries."

"We have not been quite so lucky, but we may have what you require," Jondar explained and showed Suzzan a large crystal in a wooden box. "Is this what you were looking for?"

Suzzan leaned forwards and stared at the many faceted gemstone and said, "This is exactly what I needed. Now you have both told me that there are no more Gnathe upon any of the three worlds. Are you sure about this? Daedalus Two has a sea stretching all around the centre of the planet with a landmass at each pole. I know for a fact that some of my people settled the southern continent. It may be possible that some of them survived the bombardment of Toarvak 6. When I reach out in the matrix I am sure that I can sense other beacons in the dark!"

"We have not been able to cross the central ocean since our civilisation was pounded into the dust, so I cannot say either way," replied the ape. For one thing we hate the water and we have had enough to do feeding ourselves and maintaining what small areas of technology that we have managed to keep."

In a few days time I will be coming to see you and then I shall see for my self, but for the moment the organisation of this base is of more importance. Now then I shall leave this human to explain himself. He is the leader of whatever civilisation has been retained. He is Francisco Samovar and I leave him to explain himself while I find my kindred and explain just what I will need from them in the coming days. Goodbye!"

Francisco sat back in the chair and held his hands out to the representatives of the other two worlds.

"What do you want to know?" he asked.

I of course knew nothing of this while my new group of five headed the troop of victorious soldiers across the grassy plains towards the Institute. Whilst we travelled I tweaked Fernando's glands to enhance growth and improved his senses of smell, touch and sight onto a par with the others.

His brain was as inefficiently 'wired' as the other four had been before we met. I set to, to enable him to be able to use all of those interesting lobes that were doing nothing or operating under par. He was soon to find that his memory would improve beyond his wildest imaginings. Already his telepathic ability had grown to rival Lars, Thomas, Jon and Samuel. He had rapidly learnt to shield his thoughts so as to keep his personality his own. Farther a-field were the newborn boys who had been the results of my original four when they had helped the farmers at harvest. Now came a little harvest of my own. Each child has a silver button tucked away on the brain stem that had spread out throughout each infantile brain. These children would grow up a little different from their brothers and sisters. They would develop telepathic links with each other and eventually with their fathers as they grew into adulthood. Always there would be me to help and guide them and as they grew and killed for me I would grow with them. They were already physically stronger and smarter than any of the unaltered children. They also could manipulate their mothers to make sure that their needs were met. As the society they were born into cherished every child and applauded excellence, they had no enemies and plenty of doting uncles. I turned my attention to my situation as we travelled along.

"To the institute some knowledge of its position we should have. One of you into the sky you should go and look. The grass is high and no idea have we of the right direction we are going!"

"Oh Demon there is no hurry," Jon laughed. "Lord Samovar has further than we to travel. It will be some time before he gets anywhere near the complex. Worry you should not!"

I actually felt annoyance! Indeed my programming had

constantly adapted itself to cope with these beings and I had endured or enjoyed all sorts of emotions since they had been hosts to me. I reached out to find lord Samovar and connect to the small piece of my substance left behind.

"Lord Samovar to speak with you I must. Connect with you I will. Your positioning in this wilderness it would be good to know."

"Demon! We are at the Institute. The Gnathe, Suzzan, constructed a temporary wormhole and we marched all our people through from Priss! It was amazing! I have now contacted the leaders of the other worlds and greater things are afoot. Connect me to my son and the others of your group.

Now I felt another emotion steal its way into my presence, Smugness!

"Fernando, your father to you would now speak. They are already at the institute and have to tell us much."

"What! Are you serious? How can that be," asked Fernando as they all linked together, "we left them at Priss to make their way here?"

The five human minds opened to Lord Samovar and I listened in, as the information flowed between them. The Gnathe's method of opening a wormhole was beyond my understanding. Somewhere in my deep past came a recognition of this technique, but done differently. Now that the Nano-ship N-96 had arrived at this system of planets and moons, civilisation was going to make a quantum leap. In the immediate future when these people once more had Nano-technology up and running, they would be a formidable adversary. It was only because they had pursued a peaceful life for so long that they automatically had welcomed the arrival of the alien ship without weapons of any kind. They would not be so vulnerable again and this time they would have ME.

N-96 began to split into two parts. The fuel tanks and jets remained with one part while the other rapidly began to assume the giant dandelion seed shape aiming for the upper atmosphere of the earth above North America. Kamiel applied the retarding forces of his part of the ship to slow them both down before parting company. The dandelion seed dropped towards Cheyenne Mountain as Kamiel's part of the ship headed off to the moon's North Polar Regions. Peary crater was where the moon base was situated, as part of the mountainous rim was in constant sunshine. This allowed the solar panels to generate constant electric power. The large ice deposits under the eternal shadows of the crater walls were mined and stored at the base. It was where the first Nano-technology experiments had been tried. This was to lead on to the development of the artificial intelligences with the shape changing abilities of the Nannites, as they became known. They had become the guardians of humanity and were almost immortal.

Kamiel pondered on all this old history and still marvelled at the mind of man and ape that had produced the creature such as himself. He was Kamiel 96 and a blend of many intellects including some very advanced programming by the Genesis Project director, Alexander McBald. There were certain additions that had been added to the way he could think, beyond what was considered necessary for the three 'female' members of the Nano-ships crew. He had followed the adventures and the twisting of those very programs by Kamiel 637 with great interest. There seemed very few limits to what he could achieve. It all depended on circumstances met and making decisions beyond his original programming! Well he would soon get a taste of experiencing those very broken restraints.

He reversed the jets on the craft and slowed down, to allow the moon to catch him in its gravitational field so that he hovered above the North Pole. Down below him were the outside buildings of the base that were built into the walls of the crater rim. The rest of the base was deep underground to conserve heat and power. Kamiel cut back on the jets by releasing the pressure on the gases that they collected in the bands of frozen comets orbiting this sun on the way in and began to drop. At the last moment he squeezed the fuel tanks for the last time and placed the craft lightly upon the flat crater floor.

As the ship settled down it began to melt into a vast silver puddle with a biped shape stood in the middle of it. The silver material began to clump together and part company from each other, until fifty replicas of Kamiel stood in the hard vacuum of space on the moon's surface. Mindless and controllable, these would be the empty vessels that Kamiel would fill with diverse artificial intelligences and personalities from the moon-base's memory banks. All he had to do was to get inside!

Fifty-one silver men walked in unison across the crater floor towards the door with each action mimicking Kamiel, until he got them to the airlock door. It was big enough to allow a moon cruiser to enter, so there would be plenty of room for Kamiel's silver army! An automatic light came on over the door, signifying that he had triggered a sensor. The base hummed with power, so Kamiel tripped the switch to vent the airlock. Soon the door began to rise and the lights came on inside. Kamiel marched his automata forwards into the airlock and watched the door come down.

As soon as the door closed and air pressures were equalised, the inner door divided into three and retracted open. Kamiel marched his copies into the corridor and to the lifts down to the lower levels. There was no other way of getting them down except stacking them into the lifts like sardines and going down with them. By the time he had done this four times he was beginning to feel emotions not programmed in! At last the silver men could be left to stand while he familiarised himself with the artificial intelligence stores and saw what was available.

The first thing he needed to do was to awaken the mainframe artificial intelligence and get the base working at optimum level again. She had put herself to sleep to conserve energy, as the mummified corpses that filled the base could no longer give instructions. She had been designed to take orders, not to give them. Kamiel had gambled that at the depth she was buried, deep beneath the base to avoid solar flares; she would be still able to function.

Kamiel powered up the main console and spoke to the microphone, "Selene, are you there?"

The base's artificial intelligence awoke and scanned the silver being in front of the console and answered, "You are Kamiel 96! What are you doing here? Where are my people?"

Kamiel switched to their own communication band and greeted the bewildered supercomputer. In a few moments he passed on all that he knew and the reason for being here. He then gave her the necessary instructions to make her operate with a more independent mode. Selene did a search for what artificial intelligences she had stored away and found that there were thousands in store. She took over the animation of Kamiel's drones and began to staff the base with personnel that would be useful to getting the facility back together. The next step would be to once more start the production of enough Nannites to start sending them to the three worlds to get civilisation moving. She now also had communication with human beings once more at the Earth, Cheyenne mountain complex.

They would use the steam catapult system to launch

them into space. This was via an upward curving rail with a swivelling end, to enable the base system to aim the Nannites to where they would be most needed. This would be Kamiel's route back to Earth once things were humming to his satisfaction.

Many light years away in the empty darkness of interstellar space an alien instrument of death received an old signal and began course corrections towards a different sun.

CHAPTER TEN

The old instruction was still the main prerogative; - Seek out and destroy all that is not Kresh. 'I am the Will and the Way' scoured through Toarvak 7's neural nets. Once again it sought instructions from the corpses of its crew and received no reply. Even the longest living organism will die over hundreds of thousands of years. Only the instructions remain the same and the Toarvak destroyers were built to last millenniums. The artificial intelligence that was Toarvak 7 had been alone a long time obeying the last command given by its living crew. Many worlds had come to its attention, that were not Kresh. Nothing intelligent lived on those worlds anymore. The Servant of the Kresh had been very thorough with its sterilisation programs.

Toarvak 7 began the process of building a wormhole.

By the time my group had finally approached the Institute, Lord Samovar had organised his people and had the outside buildings emptied of corpses, cleaned and functioning as they once had. The complex under the pyramid had become a hive of activity as the Lady Suzzan had opened up a short wormhole to the Cheyenne mountain base and transferred some of the staff from there with their operating knowledge of our equipment. The next item was the setting up of a gate on Daedalus Two and the jump to the Southern Continent to find out about the status of the Gnathe. Larse had volunteered to go with Thomas, Ritchie and Jaffin-khann.

Jon, Samuel and Fernando were to equip an expedition to find the mountain that had collapsed over the rest of my substance while the others sought the Gnathe at the Southern Continent. This would be the first time that any great distance had been put between the components of my group. Small nigglings of almost memory had surfaced from the unreachable wells of my mind. I had a feeling that the group of five were enough. Enough for what? I did not know and no matter how hard I tried, nothing else would surface. Another new emotion had come into play; the humans called it frustration!

Suzzan-link-khann called her kindred to her and gestured to Larse and Thomas to sit astride her back. Each human held a matching crystal embedded on the end of the nannite post and held onto the Brood-mother with the other hand. Ritchie and Jaffin each stood on the huge feet of their Lady and held on tightly. Suzzan concentrated her mind once more into the matrix and reached out for the crystal held by the ape. There in the darkness she could sense the gate waiting to be opened. She brought the two crystals embedded in her wrists to the one at her throat and twisted space, just as Link-soo-shan had learnt to do. I was aware of a familiar condition of penetrating cold just for a split second and realised this was something I had done before. My hosts felt a shift in gravity as Daedalus Two pulled them down with a slightly greater pull. This planet-sized moon was a little more massive than its companion and rode a slightly different orbit around the gas giant. It would forever chase the other moon without gaining and in balance with the cloud of moonlets at the other point of the equilateral triangle.

I looked around through the eyes of Thomas and Larse at the cruder surroundings of the control centre here on the other world. Again the buildings were of nannite, but these showed the affects of centuries of use. The equipment was worn and exhibited signs of many repairs. The floors were scuffed by the passage of countless feet, but the creatures that commanded my attention were the apes! They were not quite so tall as the humans and were covered with long black hair. The steady light of intelligence shone from their deep-set brown eyes. Their feet remained bare and I could see why, as the toes were as capable of manipulation as their hands. They wore simple loose fitting shorts and tunics. These were humankind's ancestors, who had been brought into sapience by genetic engineering. I began to wonder what improvements I could have wrought upon these people if the opportunity presented itself. We climbed down from the Gnathe's back and just stared at our welcoming committee.

"I am Jondar," an ape declared to Suzzan. "Welcome to our world. As we said to you there has been no contact with the Southern Continent since the days of destruction. We have been too busy with the simple task of survival and maintaining contact with Cheyenne Mountain to try to cross the seas to your people, to see if they survived. I see you have brought a matching pair of command crystals with you."

"I thank you for the welcome, now take me to the original setting of the gate and I will install them to give you all a three-way access," she said. "Does the power feeding equipment work and is it ready? If so I will open the gate now! I have still much to do and no time to waste."

"Everything is ready my Lady. The gate is ready to be powered. All it needs are the two matching command crystals set in place," the ape replied and led the way.

Suzzan set the nannite pillars in place, removing the inert crystals and reached out with her mind to the gate at Daedalus One and Earth. She pushed the twist in space and connected a three-way gate into a permanent situation. Once that was done she powered up the supply to the connections that Ritchie had wired into place and fed a trickle charge into the system.

The first through the operating gate was Simon from

the Cheyenne complex, followed by a number of spare technicians carrying electronic equipment and replacements for the components wearing out due to old age. Several apes also came through carrying heavier pieces of communications systems and greeted long lost relatives.

After a short wait, Lord Samovar was the next to walk between worlds with captain John Peterson by his side with a detachment of Algarie to carry back food and supplies. They soon began to ship back crates of food.

I was amazed at the smooth running of the operation as goods and supplies were exchanged between the three worlds. These alien beings were very resourceful, considering the years of non-communication between them and the fact that they had no contact between Gnathe, human and ape for centuries. I could understand the respect that the Gnathe were held in, as Suzzan directed affairs and once up and running took a back seat and let Jondar, Simon and Lord Samovar take over. By the end of the day modern communication equipment had replaced the aging, constantly repaired electronics and was working smoothly. The three gates were now in permanent operation and could be switched from the other two worlds quite easily. Once the gates were connected and open they would remain so, as long as the trickle charge was fed through the connections. This was a mixture of human and Gnathen knowledge applied beyond anything I could dredge up from my stubborn memory banks. I concentrated my consciousness to connect up to the other three fifths of my personality carried by Jon, Samuel and Fernando and found them preparing for the long expedition towards the mountain where the rest of me was buried. My mind was able to use the gates as mental portals to the scattered fragments of my identity. Packhorses were being loaded with explosives and supplies. It would take many months to work their way north to where I lay, but the long trek was beginning. I felt a mixture of anxiety and dare I say excitement, about the result of all these labours. Relatively soon I would be reunited with the rest of my substance and finally learn my identity and true purpose.

"Larse and Thomas, contacted the other parts of my being I have, on Daedalus One. To set out they are going, to start soon to go north. Soon I shall be reunited and all of my group shall be together again. We shall do great things I promise. The Gnathe now we must find and fit together the pieces we will."

Both Larse and Thomas both thought deeply about Demon's sudden upsurge of wish fulfilment. The alien presence that they played host to, was rarely ever excited about anything. Usually the cold intellect advised them on what to do or educated them in knowledge it thought they should understand. They too felt that they were on the verge of great things.

Suzzan called my humans to her side where Ritchie and Jaffin were already securely anchored to her hind legs.

"We are now ready to try and find my people on the southern continent," she said. "This will be a little more difficult as all of their command crystals seem to be inert. We may be in for a rougher ride than usual. Be ready to exert maximum lift if we materialise some way above ground. This is why you came with me. It would be far too dangerous to attempt this without your ability to levitate. Strap yourselves securely to my back and concentrate your minds before I reach out for our destination!"

Larse and Thomas buckled the straps tightly so that they would not slip off Suzzan's broad back. Her two kindred also strapped themselves to her legs and they were ready. Both humans reached deeply into themselves and felt for the shielding effect against gravity. I felt the change in our situation as they both achieved levitation and the group of us rose unsteadily off the floor.

Suzzan-link-khann a direct descendant of the gate builders, reached out with her mind to a nearby place, close to where the inert crystals stubbornly refused to activate. She found an optimum fold in the space-time configuration and twisted the firmament open. It was as well that the two human beings were giving the group full lift as they materialised hundreds of feet in the air above the living home of the Gnathe. A Banilik tree that had centuries of careful nurture and controlled growth was below them. A large open space had been left in the centre in keeping with tradition and a number of kindred and a few Brood-mothers were attending to various tasks. Some Zanth were being groomed and fed in one area of the clearing while pod-vine fruit were being de-husked in another. The bang of displaced air caused them to all look up and see their visitor begin to ascend into the clearing.

The strain of lifting such a load was beginning to tell on Larse and Thomas. The descent began to pick up speed as they began lose their energy so I diverted enough of the Gnathe's collective life force to give us the strength to land safely. Suzzan spread her feet for the landing and used them as shock absorbers. The moment she was down her passengers un-strapped and stood shakily on the firm earth.

An old Brood-mother approached the group and extended a shaky welcome.

"Who are you? You are the first to contact us in centuries," she said and spread her hands in greeting to show no weapons. "I am known as Trow-shan-soo, elected leader of the survivors of the destruction. These are my kindred and all who dwell here are friends."

"I am Suzzan-link-khann, direct descendant of the builders

of the gate. We need to link minds so that I can pass on all the information I have to you and the others of the Gnathe who have settled here," she answered and strode forward to lightly touch Trow's face with her tongue. "I am here to restore your crystals to their former state. After that, a massive re-education program has to be installed. Place your hand upon this crystal in my wrist pouch and we will begin at once. The sooner that you have my information the quicker you can call forth all the Brood-mothers to conference."

Without any more hesitation Suzzan held Trow's hand to her wrist and filled her mind with the information that she had. I could not help but eavesdrop as we were so close and found that both minds were very aware of my presence and drew into the gestalt both Larse and Thomas as well. Everything that had happened to the group and was this moment going on at the other world was downloaded to the older Brood-mother for her evaluation.

I had never experienced anything like it since my awakening from the mountain prison. During this telepathic exchange of information I suddenly became aware of other minds tuned into this gestalt as every Brood-mother at the township linked up with Trow and Suzzan. Without the amplifying power of the crystals at their disposal the Gnathe had bred for extended telepathy and had increased their natural abilities. Now the next step would be to bring these inert crystals back into play. The extended minds actually welcomed me into their gestalt and accepted my alien-ness along with the two human minds of Larse and Thomas. I felt an urge to commune with these totally different people and improve them as only I could, but pulled back and considered Suzzan's lecture on telepathic ethics. Only if asked would I enter these people and re-route their nervous systems, as I had for my human hosts.

Suzzan brought out her haversack of boxed crystals and opened up one very old box and said, "Here we have the stored mind of Khann-link-sool, one of the ancient old Gnathe who has the knowledge of crystal tuning. She had once studied under the tutelage of Shoo-link-sool, shaper of crystal. If anyone could reactivate the crystals to their state before the destroyer came, it will be her stored mind that will. Who will take on her persona?"

"There will be ample time for that tomorrow," said Trow-shan-soo to her guest and gestured to the doorway into the living house. "First we shall go inside to where the crystals have been stored and take some refreshment. Bring your humans as well Suzzan, as they look as though they could do with meat and drink. It has been a long time since we entertained human beings, but we have not forgotten their ways. I was alive when the destroyer came; a young Gnathe soon to take on a new estate and many miles from the Town you see here now. We call it 'Sings sweetly in the evenings'. I was in the mountainous regions far to the south of here prospecting for metals with a number of other Gnathe. We took no crystal with us, as what we had was precious and scarce. We were underground and exploring a cave system when the killer came. We knew nothing of the wipe out of 'Sings sweetly' until we emerged," said the old Gnathe. When we got back here all living things of flesh were dead and our precious crystals were inert. Fortunately there were some outlying farms and homesteads that had not been touched. We rebuilt our society again but without the advantages of our crystal collection. At the caves we had taken with us one small telekinetic crystal set in a ring that was the tool our surgeon used. It was the only one we had that still worked."

The two humans walked behind the giants in awe of them. To be close to Suzzan was an experience, but to be surrounded by fully-grown Brood-mothers was to make them feel like tiny children. They stopped at last in a great hall open to the sun and dotted with the stumps of the Banilik trees that had been persuaded to interweave their branches into tabletops. The tops were worn smooth by centuries of use and polishing. Bowls were formed in the living wood that were full to the brim with cool sweet water. Woven baskets of fruit, pod vine nuts, spicy buns and smoked meats were stacked in the centre. We had arrived just before evening meal. There were perching rails growing out of the stump, but no chairs for the humans to sit on.

Larse and Thomas gratefully drank from the water filled bowels by using the tightly woven mugs and filled a basket each from the food on offer.

"Sitting against the wall, I would suggest to you seems best. The centre of attention you would seem to be to the kindred. The first humans you must be that these people have seen. Listen to them you must and use your telepathic talents to unscramble their language as Ritchie-khann has shown you," I insisted.

So Larse and Thomas listened to the whistling and chirruping around them until the sounds began to make sense to them. These Gnathe were entirely the later breed and had ears instead of the original hearing crest. The Brood-mothers all had hands without the ripping claws their ancestors had found necessary for defence and four breasts above the breeding pouch to feed their young with. This was Link-soo-shan's improvement of genetic legacy to her people besides her knowledge of gate building. To Larse and Thomas who had only seen Gnathe as statues before they had released Suzzan and her two kindred, it was quite overwhelming. The Gnathe moved around like flightless birds that had tails, with a grace and balance quite out of proportion to their size.

The milling kindred jostled position to stare at the two human beings and some would offer baskets of fresh food to them, showing great pleasure at the offerings being accepted. There were too many new names for them to remember and even I did not attempt to keep count. As the evening sun began to set, the branches of the living building began to stretch out over the top of the hall until they made a rainproof covering. Oil-fired lamps were lit and hung from purpose grown hooks and the uneaten food cleared away to the storehouse. I watched entranced at these totally alien people carried on their lives in front of us.

"Larse and Thomas, somewhere to sleep you will need. To these kindred your needs they must be told. Sleeping on a perch will not do," I reminded them.

Larse recognised the female, Jaffin and asked her, "Where can we sleep? Have our hosts made provision for us?"

Jaffin laughed and replied, "There is provision made for you. Your different sleeping arrangements have not been forgotten. A room has been put aside and soft straw provided with clean cured furs and skins to keep you warm. Follow me if you have finished your meal and I will take you there."

She motioned to another female and they followed them both into the living walls of the Banilik tree house. A short walk took them to a draught free room, with as promised, clean cured skins had been placed over soft straw to lie on and warm furs were provided to wrap around themselves. Clean water could be had by dipping a woven cup into a living bowel growing from the side of the wall. The toilet was a hole in the root system that had a flap growing over it. Constant running water flowed down into it to keep it clean. There was no door, as the Gnathe did not understand the need for privacy.

While my hosts slept I contacted Suzzan with my own brand of telepathy and said, *"Suzzan to excuse my interruption please. I would speak with you."*

"I hear you, creature known as Demon," she replied.

"What would you speak with me about?"

"The other parts of my consciousness on Daedalus One, are knowing what I know here and have informed the Lord Samovar that we have been successful in meeting with your descendants. These facts you should know if decisions you need to make. Useful I can be to you in communications you need to send. Helpful I wish to be!"

"I still do not entirely trust you, Demon. Whatever you are you are, you are not a nannite as I remember them. Whether you were an experimental weapon, released during the closing stages of the conflict with Toarvak 6 that brought its destructive reign of terror to an end, I cannot say. I do know that much of the old science that humanity was capable of, was beyond the knowledge of the Gnathe!"

"Do not my actions amongst the humans show you that I mean no ill will? My hosts, have I not improved beyond their capabilities? My help have I not given whenever I could?"

"You feed on death, Demon," Suzzan replied. "This is unnatural to everything that these people hold dear and the Gnathe feel alienated by your appetites! I know that you have demonstrated your allegiance to the three worlds on several occasions. Never the less, I find you unsettling. Now I must sleep! There is still a great deal to do in the morning. I bid you goodnight."

I retreated from her mind and dwelled on her honesty. There were times when I questioned myself and could find no satisfactory answer. Her distrust of me I found unsettling. If I were the agent of all this destruction, what then if I was the destroyer? What should I do, when the humans blew the mountain apart and I was at last reunited with the rest of my substance, if this was so? I agonised over this thread of possibilities. I had made these people my creatures and I intended to defend them from the new threat of Toarvak 7. What if I could not? What could I do? I was once a mighty weapon and served my masters well! Who were my masters? I just did not know! On Daedalus Two my other three hosts were riding steadily towards the north with a large contingent of Algarie. There were enough explosives to take the mountain apart, carried by the packhorses. I would soon know the answers to all my questions.

At the complex at Cheyenne Mountain, Asue had rebuilt the computer to run with an analogue of her mind. It no longer needed to be programmed and instructed. Its new artificial intelligence was connected to Selene's mind at the North Polar Moon base. Kamiel had signalled back that all was in control and a steady production of nannites had commenced, equipped with useful minds that had been kept in storage. Soon these extra, science based, artificial intelligences would be launched back to where they could do the most good to the three worlds. Some of the nannites would be both human and animal, medical based, programmed units to take up positions in the scattered communities and set up hospitals and veterinary field units wherever they were needed. Nannite rebuilding specialists also would accompany these medical nannites to assist in the construction of shelters required. They would seek out the scattered bands of human and apes and do what they could to bring back a civilized way of life.

Sharn and Minns had already built the artificial wombs

and enclosed them inside a dome with a sterilised atmosphere. Here they had started to bring back some of the life that had become extinct due to the roasting of the Earth under the expanding Sun and the attack by Toarvak 6. Soon the clucking of chickens could be heard in the netted compounds and the crowing of cockerels. This was a sound not heard in centuries around the area of the base.

When the first roast chickens were presented to the humans living in the underground complex, the scramble for table spaces became intense. With the gate open, some live animals had been brought through and once more the bleating of sheep and the lowing of cattle in the fields close by could be heard. The genetic engineers had examined the samples sent through and had retired to the life-vats to set the artificial wombs to re-produce more meat productive animals to cross breed with the native stock. Sharn had asked if a sample of the giant cattle roaming the plains around the Institute could be sent through for genetic analysis. She was impressed by their size and health and wished to duplicate them on Earth. Once the two of them had the system up and running to their satisfaction, Minns had asked if she could travel through the gate attached to a human and sample the available sperm and eggs from the cattle herself. For some reason the gates would not accept nannites unless they were fused with living tissue.

The adaptable Nano-ship had been transformed not only into the life-vats and dome, but also into extra nannites controlled by the new central computer who was also transmitting some of the new artificial intelligences into the empty vessels that were being produced. Each new nannite carried its name on its chest so that the humans could make out to whom they were talking to. Even the crew of the Nano-ship had altered themselves to show their names to avoid confusion. The new nannite personal had crossed over to the location of the gates to make sure that there would be no electronic failures on the ancient combination of Gnathe and human science. Bit by bit civilization was returning to the three worlds. A new era was dawning.

CHAPTER ELEVEN

Deep in the dark and empty reaches of interstellar space a large silver mass winked out of existence as it dropped down a wormhole of its own making.

My hosts awoke to the smells of breakfast as the assorted kindred carried out their unsupervised tasks. Smoked meats were hung briefly over the red-hot embers of last nights fires to heat them through, while fresh baked rolls of Gnathen bread were baked to receive them. Newly picked green leaves still with the morning dew upon them were heaped in dishes close to sliced pod-vine fruits that had been marinated in fruit juice and peppers.

Larse and Thomas washed themselves in the cool fresh sap that had collected in the living bowl on the side of the wall. They dried themselves in the furs that had been provided for their bedding and left them to dry. A rough aromatic weed had been left for them to clean their teeth and use between the gaps. It was stringy and abrasive with a cool mint after taste that did the job well.

Thomas dressed himself quickly and sniffed appreciatively at the aromas wafting into their sleeping area.

"How much longer will you be? I'm starving hungry and the smell of that food is making my mouth water," he said to Larse.

"Give me chance to get my boots on and I'm with you," Larse protested, hopping around on one leg. "I suppose we just turn up and help our selves to whatever is being provided."

The morning sun was beginning to penetrate through the walls of the room and provide a diffused light. Larse and Thomas finished dressing and made their way towards the smells of cooking breakfast. To their surprise, a table had been set aside for them and two chairs woven from springy lengths of young saplings supplied. Someone had worked through the night to ensure that the two humans had comfortable seats to sit in and would not need to sit upon the floor. Thomas sat himself into the chair provided with a sigh of comfort and reached out for the bowl of bread rolls while Larse joined him. They soon realised that they were the centre of attention.

One of the female Gnathe approached them and asked, "The seating arrangements, are they good?"

"They are very good indeed," answered Thomas. "Who do we have to thank for the kindness shown?"

"To serve is sufficient," replied another male, bringing a tightly woven plate of hot smoked meats with a bowl of spicy sauce.

The female said to them both, "When you have finished your meal, we will show you round 'Sings sweetly in the evenings.' There is much you may like to see. We have never seen such as you before although we have been told much about you."

Larse stretched his arms wide and smiled at the young female and answered, " We would both be delighted to see around this home of yours. If we are not needed by the Lady Suzzan-link-khann then we will come with you gladly."

"We have been told, that the Lady Suzzan will be busy with the other Brood-mothers here at 'Sings sweetly' and you will not be needed. So as soon as you feel that you are finished with breakfast you may come with me and I will show you round. You may call me Shan-coot."

I watched and listened to all this, fascinated by the way that the Gnathe reacted to the humans. They had never met humans before, yet extended an unlimited welcome to them, just because they had arrived with the Lady Suzzan and because they were human. The associations between these totally alien people were very close. I had read their history at Whickam's Crossing in the library there and so knew their background. Each society was responsible for the other's existence in this universe. The group mind of the Gnathe, human and apes had fished through time, found the Earth before it was destroyed by the expanding sun and placed it here in orbit around Icarus. Before disbanding, the incredibly powerful gestalt had found the ancestors of the Gnathe on a dying world and brought them and a large part of their world through time and space to settle them on Jupiter, long before the humans and apes had been created there by the nannites. I was resolutely firm in my mind, that come what may, these people would be protected by whatever means I could muster. When Toarvak 7 arrived at the three worlds there would be a resistance this time. There would be no welcome extended to the destroyer and the element of surprise during the attack would be on our side.

"Going with these young Gnathe we should. Much we could learn about these people that may benefit us by association with them. Valuable their friendship will be to all humans and apes. Ambassadors we will be for those that are not here," I impressed into my hosts' minds.

Larse laughed out loud and answered, "Demon of course we will. A long way we have both come, since we first met at my old village. I am no longer a child who needs to be advised on the right things to do! Thomas and I are well aware of where we are and what we can achieve here. How are Samuel, Jon and Fernando getting on with their long trek to the North Mountains? Have they got as far as Whickam's crossing yet? I wonder how Commander Jones will receive them when they get there? Will you connect us all together so that we can share information?"

Nighttime had come when I felt the other parts of my self reconnect and share consciousness on Daedalus One. Samuel, Jon and Fernando were still drinking coffee around a well-built campfire with the rest of the Algarie troops. The group of five, exchanged information between themselves and greetings. I felt whole again although the separation of my substance could be measured in thousands and thousands of miles. Due to the peculiarities of the gates there was no time lag between my separate parts. Whickam's crossing was only a day's ride away from where Fernando's troop had settled for the night. The soldiers were eager to get to the barracks where they could sleep and rest in relative comfort. All they knew was that they were on a mission to the far north and that it was important to not only the Lord Samovar, but to everyone else living on the three worlds. That was enough to keep them all focussed on the tasks ahead. Fernando carried around his neck one of the Lady Suzzan's crystals from the hoard she had unearthed at the Institute. This would be the beacon that would enable her to twist space and open a door to reunite the five with herself included.

So far the ride was without incident so Larse and Thomas withdrew from the other three and rejoined Shan-coot to be shown round the township. Before they did so however, they made their way towards where the Brood-mothers were eating their breakfast.

Larse spoke with emphasised protocol to Suzzan, " My Lady Suzzan, we are to be shown round by this female, Shan-coot. Is there any way we can be of service before we go?"

Suzzan stared down at the human with respect. Larse had spoken in Gnathe to her in the correct tone and response to her authority over the two humans. The other Gnathe would have noticed and this would have increased her position amongst them. After the regeneration of their crystal's powers she would be asking a great deal of them in the future.

"Thanks are given that you should ask," she replied and added, "It will not be necessary that you stay with me. Go with this female and learn what you can about our ways. I have much still to do here at 'Sings sweetly in the evenings' that does not involve your help. I will ask for you when I need you, Larse and Thomas."

Suzzan watched the two humans walk out of sight and turned to the waiting Brood-mothers and said, "The time is at hand that your crystals need to be re-aligned. I ask again, who will take on the persona of Khann-link-sool?"

One of the mature Brood-mothers made her way to Suzzan.

"Like yourself, Lady Suzzan, I to am a descendant of the gate builders and am called Shan-khann-soo. Khann's genes lie in my genetic makeup, so her persona will find an easy home in my mind. Let me use the crystal you have brought here and I will do my best to re-activate our crystals. Place the crystal upon my forehead and bind it there."

Suzzan-link-khann carefully took out a yellow crystal from her box and placed it upon the forehead of the Gnathe and quickly bound the gem to her so that it could not be shaken off.

Shan quickly went into a trance and felt the long dead persona of Khann begin to surface from the storage crystal. The two of them began to blend and the light of another intelligence began to shine from the host's eyes.

"I am Khann-link-sool; - scientist. What would you have me do for you? Be not alarmed, I know what I am. I have used this method myself many times to produce results. I must admit it is good to feel living flesh again," the dead scientist said to the gathering. We waste time. Tell me why you have summoned me!"

Suzzan replied, "Our entire stock of crystals have been made inert by a radiation we were not able to shield from. We need them to be re-activated once more."

"Give them to me and join with my mind so that you may learn," Khann/Shan replied.

Trow-shan-soo opened the box of crystals that had been fetched and handed the main command crystal to Khann. She held it gently in her hand and held out her other hand to Suzzan.

"Give me your command crystal, young one and I will see what I can do."

Holding both, she sent her mind down into the matrix where the working crystals shone like beacons and concentrated on the dull one in her other hand. A pulse began to beat in the working crystal that awakened a parallel pulse in the other. Gradually the crystal began to glow until its radiance began to leapfrog across to the other inert crystals that were in the possession of 'Sings sweetly in the evenings'. Soon all the gemstones that had been rendered inert by the neutron bomb, had regained their inner powers that had been rendered into them by Jupiter's incredible pressure when they had been formed. Many years ago a scientist by the name of Hannah had deduced that some of the crystal's molecular lattice had been pushed into another dimension during their creation. The mind's electrical fields would activate into this hidden dimension and increase the telepathic power of an organic sentient mind. They did not work for the nannites and to use them, they had to be locked into fusion with a willing host.

The telekinetic crystals pulled their power from the channelling of the forces of gravity, through the conduits of the focussing mind. Like a lens, the larger the crystal the greater the focusing power that could be channelled. Doubling up the crystals and the minds focussing would give an exponential degree of power. It required two command crystals and a telekinetic one to open a gate to another two command crystals. Adding in trickle charges of electricity would keep the gates open indefinitely once they had been opened using the combination of crystals.

Centuries ago Trann-link-khann had found that linking together a group mind would open a gate anywhere a fold or twist in the fabric of time and space occurred. A gestalt mind of infinite power could move worlds through space and time using a combination of many command crystals and the telekinetic key linked up to a power generator with a powerful magnetic field. This also required a large time distorting crystal fitted into that oscillating magnetic field. The one that had been used to reach back to the Earth millions of years into the past had shattered when the god-mind had extended herself in bringing back the Gnathe from the dying world they were living on and settling them on Jupiter.

Link-soo-shan had worked out how to fix a gate to the three worlds and it was her abilities that had made it possible for a colony of Gnathe to settle on Daedalus Two.

All this was known to the present day Gnathe who had learnt to get along without the tools that they had once used. Now with genetically improved abilities and operating crystals, they would once more be useful members of the three worlds.

Now that the work of restoring the crystals had been preformed and the knowledge shared between the telepathically linked Gnathe, the time had come to get Khann to relinquish her persona's control of her host, Shan.

"Before I go, I would like some questions answered,"

Khann said to the waiting group. "I should like to know how this happened and the background of what has befallen here. My memories end at the shattering of the time distorting crystal. This was when I died. What happened next?"

Suzzan held her hands out to the host wearing the dead mind and laid them gently on her forehead. She concentrated her mind to the old scientist's stored consciousness and gave her the information that she wished.

"The threat is serious," she stated and began to undo the bindings holding the memory shard to her forehead. "You may need me in the future. If so, do not be afraid to awaken me again if you have need of me."

Suzzan took away the gem and the binding, restoring the mind of Shan into her rightful place. The Brood-mother tottered forward and was caught by Suzzan as her legs gave way. The colour drained from her face as the weakness hit home from expending so much energy realigning the crystals. Two other Gnathe came forwards and held her by the arms to keep her upright.

Shan staggered to her feet, shakily pulled herself upright and weakly said, "Thank you. I think I can stand unaided now. She was a powerful mind to hold. I have seen what she could do and I feel that I could do what she did if I had to in an emergency. What a mind that one had! Her memories go back to when there were only Gnathe on the home world. She was extremely old when she genetically altered the humans and apes to live upon the home world. It was a privilege to host her mind, a thing not easily forgotten."

Suzzan stared round at the group and said, "Now that you have a working set of crystals, you will have to relearn how to make your own gates and also the study of the use of the group mind. I cannot stress how

necessary this ability may become, if the destroying
alien craft that was summoned gets here before you are
proficient."

Kamiel walked the airless corridors of the moon base with
one purpose. It had to be self-sufficient before he could
leave. The mission psychologist viewed the whole three
worlds scenario in just the same frame of mind as he would
if his nannite colleagues had created it from scratch. Just as
his namesake Kamiel-637 had wrestled with the problems
of the dying colony and made the logical decisions that had
involved the humans and apes in the affairs of the Gnathe,
so he found himself in the same position. Accessing Selene's
deep records had given him a greater knowledge of the
events that had taken place when the alien craft had been
welcomed, that was generally known. In the struggle against
Link-soo-shan at the beginning, his predecessor had built
a different type of nannite from the remains of Minns. He
had built a partially sentient artificial intelligence without
the governing protocols induced in all other nannites. The
mind of Minnis was linked to a human called Frederick and
allowed to develop without being programmed. Minnis
could kill! This was not common knowledge among the
present people of the three worlds and was not revealed
to the director of the Genesis Project, Alexander McBald at
the time of transference of the Earth.
All nannites were programmed to protect the human race.
Kamiel was programmed a little differently, such that while
he was programmed to protect, he could allow those he
protected to die for the common good. It was a harsh set
of rules to run by, but it had produced a duel civilization of
Gnathe and human that had resulted in them flourishing side
by side, instead of the human and apes dying out. Minnis

had no such set of rules and had been Fredrick's battle suit and companion. She was an accomplished killer while she was linked to the human and had become Fredrick's killing machine when he needed her. She had her own set of morals and lived by them. After Fredrick's death through old age, she had hitched a lift to the three worlds and had made her way to the Moon. She had lived amongst the flesh and blood personal at the moon base, passing for a helpful nannite without ever being questioned. Minnis used to take off from time to time, exploring the moon's empty areas, looking for ancient ice that was buried in permanent shadow. It was during one of these forays that Toarvak 6 had begun the devastation of the three worlds and Earth's Moon. With Minnis out of radio range, an anti-nannite virus, as well as a neutron bomb bombardment had hit the base. When the nannite came into contact and found out what had transpired she dared not go back there. Selene however was buried deep underground and was still able to activate the base. Minnis had made her way to the steam launching railway track and had climbed aboard one of the sledges. She had programmed Selene to line up the swivelling end of the track with the mass of the destroyer and wait for it to come into range.

The moment that Toarvak 6 had come into her flight-path she ordered Selene to launch the sled. The last that the moon's super computer saw of Minnis was that her trajectory would take her direct to an impact with the alien ship. As the nannite narrowed the gap she became a cloud of particles and wrapped herself around the part of the silver ball un-noticed by the governing artificial intelligence. A time period passed and the alien craft began to act erratically and vanished around the horizon of the moon. Selene had no record of seeing the craft again and without further orders eventually shut herself down to save power.

This was over two centuries in the past and there was no record of the survival of Minnis after the alien craft disappeared. Slowly the remains of the human and ape civilization had regrouped and put itself back into some kind of order. Of the Gnathe who had settled the southern continent on Daedalus Two there had been no word or communication, so when Asue had signalled Kamiel that they had survived, the nannite felt relief. The Gnathe and their abilities would be crucial to the survival of the three worlds. If they could once more establish a stable wormhole to their home world, then a better defence against Toarvak 7 could be arranged. At the moment they were still at the mercy of the incoming destroyer with no defence at all except the slim possibility of the old weapon buried under the mountain that the Algarie were on their way to blow open. Whatever slept under that mountain could be the last fighting ship of the old civilization of Earth or it could be something else altogether. The creature that was living inside five human beings, maintained that it was part of a mighty weapon. The way it acted seemed as if it were a damaged nannite. Whatever drove its purpose seemed as though it was a force on the human's side, but its way of absorbing energy worried Kamiel. Nannites drew their power from the sun or by absorbing the energy in the molecular bonding of matter itself! They did not feed on the life force of a living creature. The Guardian came to a decision and satisfied that Moon-base was up and running with sufficient nannite staff contacted Selene.

"Ready the steam catapult, Selene," Kamiel ordered. "I need you to aim it at the world known as Daedalus Two. I think that I need to meet the Gnathe that live there and have a talk with the thing that lives inside Larse and Thomas."

With that, the nannite walked to the airlock, activated the

door and once more stood on the bleak dusty moonscape in the bright heat of the sun. He made his way to the rail track and climbed onto the sled. Selene cranked up the steam piston that powered the ratchet claw under the sled's belly and drew the sled back to the backstop. The far end of the swivelling track swung round to aim the sled at the second massive moon orbiting Icarus and Selene sent Kamiel on his way. The nannite was built to withstand forces much greater than these as the sled sped along the track crossing the escape velocity barrier easily. At the far end, the sled swung around the curve of the swivelling end and came to an abrupt stop. Kamiel did not and flew off the sled towards Daedalus two as a perfect rugby ball shape. The journey would take several days at this speed so Kamiel spent the time reviewing what information he had. One of the databases he had accessed from Selene was the Gnathe's language. Until he met them he would have to rely on what he had gleaned to get him by. Suzzan spoke perfect English and so did her two kindred, but the other Gnathe would have been speaking their own language for over two centuries. It would be much better if he could speak with them as one who understood them. If only he could have intermeshed with Kamiel 637 and accessed his databanks it would have been so much easier. The Guardian was programmed to be patient so that the two days would be well spent reviewing all the information that he possessed.

Kamiel expanded his shape as he entered the upper atmosphere to a wide winged dart that skipped across the thickening air reducing his speed. He swung out of high orbit to a lower one searching for the Gnathen settlement on the southern continent. The second time around he was certain that he had found them by the infra-red concentration at a large tree-like structure that spread out over a large area.

As he got closer he could make out a network of roads and fields surrounding the Banilik tree township.

Kamiel changed shape to the thistledown construction and slowed speed as he increased the candyfloss shape above the 'seed' at the bottom. He aimed for the open area in the centre of the tree-house town and was aware of a multitude of upturned faces. Two of them were human! He was in the right place so he retracted his substance and resumed humanoid shape at the last moment. Kamiel braced his legs for the minimal shock of landing and stood facing the two humans.

"You must be Larse and Thomas," he said and walked towards them. "I am Kamiel-96, part of the crew of Nano-ship 96, sent to find a liveable world for the human race to start all over again. Imagine our surprise when we found you here!"

I stared back at the silver coloured humanoid figure stood in front of us. It was not quite as tall as Larse and Thomas and did not appear to be anywhere near their mass, being of a more slender build. Was this what I once was? It stood independently and like myself could change shape at will. I had waited a long time for this moment, to meet another of my kind and have my questions answered.

"You are one of those my ancestors sent to the stars, to build a new beginning for our people. We have never seen such as you before," said Thomas and held out his hand for the nannite to touch.

I exuded some of my substance to the tips of his fingers and waited for the contact to be made from this kindred of mine.

CHAPTER TWELVE

At the far reaches of the new sun's gravitational attraction beyond even its massive clouds of comets and icy chunks of debris a hole in the fabric of space-time opened and closed. From here the sun shone no brighter than a bright star, but the silvery ovoid mass knew which way to fall. The first stop would be a refuelling trip amongst these frigid masses of frozen gas and balls of ice. Next would come the gathering up and transmuting of harder materials to store as ammunition. Toarvak 7 had much to do before it would start its fall in earnest towards the centres of civilization that clustered nearer to the sun's warmth. Once again it asked for guidance from its long dead crew and receiving no denial, followed the last order.

The ripples of the sub-space directive from Toarvak 6 found more recipients the further out it progressed. Three more Toarvak type destroyers picked up the signal and obeyed the last command. Wormholes were being constructed in feverish electronic haste.

Commander Edward Jones watched the long column of Algarie soldiers and packhorses approach the garrison at Whickam's crossing with some interest. Lord Samovar's son Fernando was leading the brigade and riding with him were the two impostors that had tricked him and the custodians of the Library. He would not be satisfied until he had read the orders signed by Francisco himself. His skin still crawled in the knowledge that his mind had been altered by these men. Riding at their side he recognised Pablo Handuos, Sebastian Diego's scientific assistant. That caused him to wonder just what all this was about. Leaving his position by the window of the observation tower, Commander Jones descended the stairs and made his way towards the parade ground. The double doors had been opened and the first of the column were making their way towards him. The horses stopped and were held by some of the garrison's men as they were dismounted and led away to the stables.

He held out his hand to Fernando and welcomed him with a warm handshake, while regarding Samuel and Jon with an inquisitive stare.

"It is good to see you again Fernando," said the commander. "I trust your father is well? Forgive the ill manners, but why are you here and what are these two renegades doing in your company?"

"My dear friend there is so much I have to tell you," replied Fernando. "We need to discus this privately in your office away from the troops. Pablo and these two will come also. They are not renegades my old friend! Indeed they may be our salvation in the difficult times to come."

Shaking his head in disbelief the commander led to way to his office to hear the briefing from Lord Samondar's son.

An hour later after consuming a large pot of coffee, Edward Jones and his guests sat back and regarded each other with mutual respect and the commander said, "Are you all sure of this?"

"Believe me, Commander it takes some getting used to, but it is all true," Fernando replied. "The Gnathe are alive and all is as we say. Somewhere out there is Toarvak 7 already on its way to finish the destruction that its predecessor accomplished. Suzzan-link-khann is at this moment re-aligning the damaged crystals on the southern continent of Daedalus Two. Our only hope is to blow the mountain apart that buried the weapon that brought Toarvak 6 down. The creature that lives inside the five of us is sure that it was responsible for stopping the destruction and will do so again if only we can get it in contact with the rest of its substance."

"I find it difficult to believe without seeing this thing that you say is inside you. Make it show its self to help me believe," the old Commander said.

I felt a twinge of annoyance and reached out to Samuel's mind, *"Extend your hand you must Samuel and tell this old man courage he must have. Tell him his flesh I will enter and speak with him I will, in his mind."*

Samuel did as I asked and extended his hand to the commander.

"Demon says he will enter your flesh and speak to you in your mind, Commander Jones. He says to have courage, as this will be different from anything you have ever experienced."

The commander sat very quiet and extended his hand. Samuel grasped it firmly and I transferred enough of my mass into the old man's nervous system to make contact. While I was in here I could see that there was a great deal I could do for his general health. I sent part of my substance around his blood circulation system and destroyed several blood clots and the build up of cholesterol around his heart. Entering his brain, I was aware of a small, but growing tumour in his left frontal lobe. I removed it as a matter of course and dissolved the cells so that they would be expelled as waste. Also as I made my connection to the thinking part of his brain I joined up a lot of loose neural nerve endings that were responsible for memory function.

"Hear me do you now, Commander Edward Jones?"

"I hear you," came the hesitant answer.

"Do not fear me, because out of your understanding I am. Alterations have I done that will lengthen your life. Memory will be clearer, thinking will be clearer. A heart attack will not happen now and for some years you will healthier be! Now open up your mind and pictures I will fill that will explain

what we must do."

Samuel watched the colour drain from the older man's face as Demon explained as only he could, mind to mind! He felt the substance of the strange creature he had got used to sharing his body with return and he let go of the Commander's hand.

Fernando sat back in his chair and said, "Now do you understand? These men are not renegades. My father trusts them and has also felt the mind of Demon inside his. We will rest here this night and transfer the explosives to the many carts you have here. Pablo is the explosives expert and is in charge of the load we carry. It will allow us to travel faster on the main roads and make our way to Thorn Town much easier. From there to the far north we will have to abandon the wagons somewhere on our journey and continue on horseback. The further north we go I am quite sure we will meet with resentment from the people that live there. We must be very careful to pay for what ever we need and to take our own provisions so that the Algarie are not accused of stealing. We have amongst the troops some who were taken from Thorn Town as boys who showed promise. Make sure that they are the ones who enter the town first and bring payment to the town elders. They can return to their families for a visit and give them an account of how they have fared in Lord Samovar's peacekeeping forces. Also they can spread the facts of the coming of the destroyer to our worlds once more and our part in preventing the slaughter of the past revisiting us once more. We will remain encamped some way up the road from the town until we are welcomed."

"I understand, Commander Fernando. Oh so much better than I did, before I was shown by the creature living inside you," said Edward Jones as he sat digesting all of the information.

He had seen the statues of the Gnathe at the library, but the images of the living Gnathe shown to him by Demon were so different when you saw them move.

"For the moment it would be best for your men to rest for a day or so to allow me to requisition the wagons that you will need. Also there is the matter of supplies to be located and a certain amount of organisation to get in motion. Gurt!" he shouted to the shut door.

The door opened immediately and Gurt stepped in, proudly displaying his sergeant's stripes that had been commissioned by lord Samovar.

The Commander smiled and said, "Still listening at keyholes Gurt?"

"Yes Sir. That way I get my job done well Sir. What part of organising the wagons do you require me to oversee, Sir?

"Make your way to the wagon makers with a light detachment and find out how many they have in stock. Tell them I want ten, minimum and enough horses to pull them with all tack necessary. I will write out the requisition now and we will agree a fair payment later," the Commander said and added, "Nice stripes Sergeant, let's hope you can keep them this time!"

The new Sergeant Gurt removed himself from the room, clutching his all-important piece of paper and disappeared down the corridor leading to the barracks. The visitors stood up and made their leave, following the swift figure of Gurt at a more leisurely pace, to lay claim to an area of the barracks for themselves. The smells of the evening meal began to hang on the air, reminding them that it was some time in the past that they had last eaten.

I felt a surge of cohesion from the other two parts of myself on Daedalus Two and became a collective being spread thinly between the two worlds. I focussed all of my consciousness on the approach of the Nannite towards Larse and Thomas at the Gnathe town of 'Sings Sweetly in the Evening'. Thomas had extended his hand towards the silver being that lightly walked towards him and I had oozed some of my substance to the outer skin of the outstretched hand. Perhaps now I would know my purpose. Would this independent nannite be one of my own kind?

Kamiel went to computer time and watched Thomas freeze, hand extended, with the silvery material showing on his fingertips. During his time at the Moon Base cataloguing the personalities of the sentient nannites held in store, he had come across a code peculiar to his own unique personality. It was a copy of himself laid down by Kamiel 637 with all his memories of the experiences he had lived through for emergencies. Without any hesitation the earlier model of Kamiel 96 had blended his personality with the Jupiter based nannite and now was a composite personality of the two separate identities. He now knew all that had transpired before the building of the wormhole to this area of space and all that had lead up to it. His own personality had now a depth of experience spanning centuries, on which he could draw for decision-making. This was far beyond the nannite, which had arrived at the three-planet system.

In a blur of motion Kamiel made contact with the alien presence inhabiting the human and the other four hosts.

He was inside the defences of the creature in Nano-seconds and digging into its memory banks for every scrap of knowledge that was there. The Guardian was with Demon when it had dug itself out from the mountain and through each host until it had taken Larse. The improvements that the alien intelligence had done to the boy and to all the others it had inhabited over the time they had been host to it were studied and approved. A trace of another nannite intelligence was interwoven with the fabric of Demon's personality. It was Minnis! This thing was a mixture of two totally different sentient nannite based intelligences. Demon's true name had to be Toarvak 6, Servant of the Kresh, the Will and the Way.

There was no true memory of what this thing was before Minnis had infiltrated it, only that it had been a weapon of great destruction that had served its masters well. With the exposure to human hosts and being an active part in their survival, Kamiel could feel that whatever Toarvak 6 had been in the past, the added amalgamation of Minnis had changed it permanently. Whatever masters it had obeyed in the past, the personality was now dedicated to protecting the civilization of the three worlds. Kamiel weighed up the odds and decided to allow this creature to continue to live, as three parts of its consciousness was embarked on the expedition on the other world, Daedalus Two. The alien ship was buried deep under the mountain far to the north of Whickam's Crossing. Getting it out and putting the 'crew' in place would be the only chance that the three worlds would have at staving off Toarvak 7. Kamiel withdrew leaving a small connecting filament attached to Thomas's finger and reverted to standard time.

"I am Kamiel, Guardian of the human race and protector of the Gnathe. You are not one of my kind!"

"If not of your kind, then what am I, Guardian?" I answered as a chill of anxiety ran through my neural net, as I feared the answer.

"You are the remnants of the destroyer that ruined these worlds centuries ago. You are what is left of Toarvak 6 and a blend of a nannite called Minnis."

I mentally reeled as I was forced to accept the knowledge. This was what I had secretly feared all these years. I was the killer of worlds. I had been the one who had melted the cities and driven these people back to starting their civilization from the scraps of what was left. An overpowering feeling of grief beyond my programming swept through every core of my being. My hosts were aware of me as never before. The pain! The pain! It was too much to bear and I wanted to die.

Another voice echoed in my mind, "The fact that you can feel emotions, sets you apart from what you once were."

It was Larse.

"Remember what you counselled when I met Lord Samovar. Forget your hate and work together to defeat the greater enemy. Without you and your ship of weapons we will all die. You are our protector now. We have no-one else."

I felt the minds of all my hosts rally in agreement and some of the unbearable pain diminished. I had strength of purpose! These were my people. They are Kresh! They are 'New Kresh'! The mad idea swept through my mind over and over again. I still could not unlock my buried memories, but it would suffice. When we blew the top off the mountain I would be re-united with the other parts of my substance. Then I would know all I needed to know. We would take the war to the incoming destroyer. I would meet my adversary in deep space.

"I was correct to let you live," said Kamiel in the hidden parts of my mind. "There is much for you to do here. I trust you to do all that you can. If you do not, then all of us will die when your counterpart gets here. We must hurry all we can. The full crew is needed on Daedalus One very soon. I will talk with Suzzan and see what must be done. I will now break the link."

I was overwhelmed by the acceptance and forgiveness of my hosts. I could hardly believe that although I was responsible for the levelling of the three planets these young men understood that I was driven by whatever commands I had been serviced with. All that mattered was that I was fully committed to defending these worlds from more of my own kind. What had happened so long ago, that creatures such as I had been unleashed against all sentient life. I pledged that one day I would find out. How many others of my kind roamed the stars seeking out those that were not Kresh? I mentally shuddered as the thoughts raced through my consciousness. How many civilizations had perished at my weapons' onslaught and how many more of my kind were out there spreading death? I watched through two sets of eyes as Kamiel made his way towards the crowd of Gnathe who had watched him land. Whatever this enigmatic nannite required me to do I would follow his direction. I realised that I trusted the leadership of the sentient creature and would obey him in all things.

Kamiel stood looking up at the group of Brood-mothers and asked, "Which one of you is Suzzan-link-khann?"

Suzzan walked forward and said, "I am the Gnathe of

whom you speak. You are a nannite. I have not seen one of your kind since before the time stasis experiment. Who are you?"

"I am Kamiel," the Guardian answered. I am one of those sent to the stars to make a home for my people. After eons we found ourselves here as you know. Soon others of my kind will be arriving to all three worlds to do what we can to bring back the measure of civilization that existed before Toarvak 6 destroyed it."

She stared down on the silver figure and asked, " You are the great Kaameel! I have learnt about you from the very distant past. You are part of our history! The creature that lives inside the five human beings; do you know what it is?"

"Yes I do. It is an amalgamation of the destroyer and one of my own creations that has very little of its original memory intact," the nannite replied.

"Can we trust it? I have had disquieting thoughts about this strange thing ever since I touched minds with it," Suzzan said with a hiss of disgust. "It feeds on the life energy of creatures that die! It is an abomination!"

"We can trust it now," Kamiel said flatly and added, "It has a strength of purpose that has been adopted by the very fact that it lives inside human beings. It will do anything within its powers to protect them all, including the Gnathe. This brings me to the next part of the mission. Have you finished here? I need you to get us all to Daedalus One as soon as you can. I can only get there by your ability to warp space and take us there attached to your body!"

"I have re-aligned the crystals with the help of the stored mind of the great Khann-link-sool and a descendant of hers.

Much of my work here is over. I will leave the teaching crystals here and they are quite capable of working with them to regain the lost abilities. I speak of the group mind techniques that are necessary to open rifts in the space-time continuum. We may need that ability if Demon cannot control the weapon-ship buried under that mountain."

"A wise thought," Kamiel replied thoughtfully. "How much time do you require?"

"Let me instruct those who would attempt the group mind gestalt for the rest of the day. Tomorrow or the next day we will return to Daedalus One and rejoin the group making their way towards the mountain," Suzzan answered. Come and meet the exiled Gnathe who have re-built the town of 'Sings Sweetly from the ashes of the destroyer. You are a legend in their stories of the 'Old Times' and if you would just speak with them, they would be more than grateful."

Larse and Thomas added their support to Suzzan's request and Larse asked the nannite, "We too would like to hear how the Earth was saved and the Gnathe became our allies and friends from someone who was there."

"Very well," the nannite replied, "let us go to the main hall where the meals are set out and I will tell you the full story. I warn you it will take some telling!"

It took a little longer than two days before Suzzan was satisfied that the great abilities of the past were fully understood by all the Gnathe Brood-mothers. She was now confidant that they could open and close a gate in space independently from her tuition. The great problem was that the number of crystals was small, as there was only one place that they had formed under the incredible pressure of a gas giant planet. The irritating fact was that Icarus had under its similar boiling atmosphere, a wealth of the very crystals that they could use in an unreachable situation. Until this sun expanded and stripped the miles deep high-pressure gases away from the surface, there was no way to attempt to reach them. Even the nannites would be compressed so much that their structure would collapse and destroy them. Therefore the organic space traversing gourds were of no use without sufficient crystals to operate them. The seed had been kept by the Gnathe and the giant plants were still grown just in case a solution could be found.

I was aware that my other hosts had been on the road for some time pushing the wagons as fast as they could towards the north and were approaching Thorn town. Lars's village was about two weeks journey from there by fast horse. As I had travelled the rest of the way carried by the eagle, I had no way of estimating the distance and time taken to penetrate the wilderness. Then an idea came to my mind.

"Larse to the nannite Kamiel I would speak and to the Lady Suzzan. An idea I have had that may help us to reach the mountain quicker. First to Kamiel I would broach this possibility."

Larse and Thomas stopped their breakfast and looked around the eating hall for some sign of the enigmatic nannite.

"I don't see him anywhere, Demon. We will finish our meal and look for him. He will be somewhere inside the town talking with the Gnathe, I would expect," said Larse to his symbiotic companion. "What do you need to speak with him about?"

"A quicker way to re-unite me with the destroyer ship buried under the mountain I have thought. First with Kamiel I must talk. Next with the Gnathe collectively if Kamiel agrees."

Larse and Thomas split up and searched the town of 'Sings Sweetly' separately to find the Guardian and relay Demon's need to speak with him. Kamiel was with the elder Gnathe reminding them of what they as a species had attained in the past. His history of the involvement of their ancestors with humans and apes had reinforced the links forged in the past. The centuries cut off here at the southern continent had isolated them and much had not been forgotten, but living their own lives away from the humans for so long, had set them in their ways.

It was Thomas in the end that found the nannite and I signalled Larse that the search was over.

"Kamiel," said my second host, "Demon would speak with you privately by touching his substance to yours."

The nannite said nothing but extended his hand for Thomas to touch.

The moment contact was made between us the cold intellect of the nannite asked, "Well! What is it that you wish to say that cannot be said aloud?"

I cut my hosts out of the loop and replied, *"Respected you are by these people you call the Gnathe. Listen they will to you and take heed. An idea I have to reach my ship much quicker than the expedition. It involves the Gnathe and their abilities to form group minds and open wormholes where a distortion exists. If we can get to the expedition and persuade the Gnathe to take us there with enough of them to do this, then another way can be proposed. A distortion in space my ship will cause, I believe. A beacon it may be of such strength that a hole opened up could be, close by!"*

Kamiel considered this thought and replied, "It could

166

work? It will work! Toarvak 6 you may have the answer to save us a great deal of time."

I mentally winced at the use of my real name.

"Care not for this name do I, but have accepted that this is what I am. There is more that I would have you consider."

"Tell me what else you have in mind," the Guardian replied.

"The Gnathe as hosts I will need. Five at least would be required. Their minds I need to examine and their brain structure I need to understand. Abilities they have that are new to me and an asset they could be if improved they are as I have improved the human hosts! Toarvak 7 will be as I was when it comes. It will be alone! A memory has surfaced, distorted but real. I had no crew! This is why a satisfied feeling I have with five hosts carrying my consciousness. Logical it is!"

The Guardian thought for a moment and said, "For you to grow larger, something has to die for you to siphon off enough energy. The Gnathe will not do that!"

"Meat eaters they are. When a beast is slaughtered its life energy would suffice. A thought has entered my mind, Kamiel. Think about this, what were my masters fighting amongst the stars, they found it necessary that they built such as I. What were the Kresh so fearful about that they sent my kind to kill? Get me to my ship before the destroyer comes!"

Kamiel disengaged contact from me and stood very still as he thought about all the ramifications concerning my ideas.

"I will speak with them," he said. "Wait for my return with Larse. We may be going back to Daedalus One very soon."

CHAPTER TWELVE

At the far reaches of the new sun's gravitational attraction beyond even its massive clouds of comets and icy chunks of debris a hole in the fabric of space-time opened and closed. From here the sun shone no brighter than a bright star, but the silvery ovoid mass knew which way to fall. The first stop would be a refuelling trip amongst these frigid masses of frozen gas and balls of ice. Next would come the gathering up and transmuting of harder materials to store as ammunition. Toarvak 7 had much to do before it would start its fall in earnest towards the centres of civilization that clustered nearer to the sun's warmth. Once again it asked for guidance from its long dead crew and receiving no denial, followed the last order.

The ripples of the sub-space directive from Toarvak 6 found more recipients the further out it progressed. Three more Toarvak type destroyers picked up the signal and obeyed the last command. Wormholes were being constructed in feverish electronic haste.

Commander Edward Jones watched the long column of Algarie soldiers and packhorses approach the garrison at Whickam's crossing with some interest. Lord Samovar's son Fernando was leading the brigade and riding with him were the two impostors that had tricked him and the custodians of the Library. He would not be satisfied until he had read the orders signed by Francisco himself. His skin still crawled in the knowledge that his mind had been altered by these men. Riding at their side he recognised Pablo Handuos, Sebastian Diego's scientific assistant. That caused him to wonder just what all this was about. Leaving his position by the window of the observation tower, Commander Jones descended the stairs and made his way towards the parade ground. The double doors had been opened and the first of the column were making their way towards him. The horses stopped and were held by some of the garrison's men as they were dismounted and led away to the stables.

He held out his hand to Fernando and welcomed him with a warm handshake, while regarding Samuel and Jon with an inquisitive stare.

"It is good to see you again Fernando," said the commander. "I trust your father is well? Forgive the ill manners, but why are you here and what are these two renegades doing in your company?"

"My dear friend there is so much I have to tell you," replied Fernando. "We need to discus this privately in your office away from the troops. Pablo and these two will come also. They are not renegades my old friend! Indeed they may be our salvation in the difficult times to come."

Shaking his head in disbelief the commander led to way to his office to hear the briefing from Lord Samondar's son.

An hour later after consuming a large pot of coffee, Edward Jones and his guests sat back and regarded each other with mutual respect and the commander said, "Are you all sure of this?"

"Believe me, Commander it takes some getting used to, but it is all true," Fernando replied. "The Gnathe are alive and all is as we say. Somewhere out there is Toarvak 7 already on its way to finish the destruction that its predecessor accomplished. Suzzan-link-khann is at this moment re-aligning the damaged crystals on the southern continent of Daedalus Two. Our only hope is to blow the mountain apart that buried the weapon that brought Toarvak 6 down. The creature that lives inside the five of us is sure that it was responsible for stopping the destruction and will do so again if only we can get it in contact with the rest of its substance."

"I find it difficult to believe without seeing this thing that you say is inside you. Make it show its self to help me believe," the old Commander said.

I felt a twinge of annoyance and reached out to Samuel's mind, *"Extend your hand you must Samuel and tell this old man courage he must have. Tell him his flesh I will enter and speak with him I will, in his mind."*

Samuel did as I asked and extended his hand to the commander.

"Demon says he will enter your flesh and speak to you in your mind, Commander Jones. He says to have courage, as this will be different from anything you have ever experienced."

The commander sat very quiet and extended his hand. Samuel grasped it firmly and I transferred enough of my mass into the old man's nervous system to make contact. While I was in here I could see that there was a great deal I could do for his general health. I sent part of my substance around his blood circulation system and destroyed several blood clots and the build up of cholesterol around his heart. Entering his brain, I was aware of a small, but growing tumour in his left frontal lobe. I removed it as a matter of course and dissolved the cells so that they would be expelled as waste. Also as I made my connection to the thinking part of his brain I joined up a lot of loose neural nerve endings that were responsible for memory function.

"Hear me do you now, Commander Edward Jones?"

"I hear you," came the hesitant answer.

"Do not fear me, because out of your understanding I am. Alterations

have I done that will lengthen your life. Memory will be clearer, thinking will be clearer. A heart attack will not happen now and for some years you will healthier be! Now open up your mind and pictures I will fill that will explain what we must do."

Samuel watched the colour drain from the older man's face as Demon explained as only he could, mind to mind! He felt the substance of the strange creature he had got used to sharing his body with return and he let go of the Commander's hand.

Fernando sat back in his chair and said, "Now do you understand? These men are not renegades. My father trusts them and has also felt the mind of Demon inside his. We will rest here this night and transfer the explosives to the many carts you have here. Pablo is the explosives expert and is in charge of the load we carry. It will allow us to travel faster on the main roads and make our way to Thorn Town much easier. From there to the far north we will have to abandon the wagons somewhere on our journey and continue on horseback. The further north we go I am quite sure we will meet with resentment from the people that live there. We must be very careful to pay for what ever we need and to take our own provisions so that the Algarie are not accused of stealing. We have amongst the troops some who were taken from Thorn Town as boys who showed promise. Make sure that they are the ones who enter the town first and bring payment to the town elders. They can return to their families for a visit and give them an account of how they have fared in Lord Samovar's peacekeeping forces. Also they can spread the facts of the coming of the destroyer to our worlds once more and our part in preventing the slaughter of the past revisiting us once more. We will remain encamped some way up the road from the town until we are welcomed."

171

"I understand, Commander Fernando. Oh so much better than I did, before I was shown by the creature living inside you," said Edward Jones as he sat digesting all of the information.

He had seen the statues of the Gnathe at the library, but the images of the living Gnathe shown to him by Demon were so different when you saw them move.

"For the moment it would be best for your men to rest for a day or so to allow me to requisition the wagons that you will need. Also there is the matter of supplies to be located and a certain amount of organisation to get in motion. Gurt!" he shouted to the shut door.

The door opened immediately and Gurt stepped in, proudly displaying his sergeant's stripes that had been commissioned by lord Samovar.

The Commander smiled and said, "Still listening at keyholes Gurt?"

"Yes Sir. That way I get my job done well Sir. What part of organising the wagons do you require me to oversee, Sir?

"Make your way to the wagon makers with a light detachment and find out how many they have in stock. Tell them I want ten, minimum and enough horses to pull them with all tack necessary. I will write out the requisition now and we will agree a fair payment later," the Commander said and added, "Nice stripes Sergeant, let's hope you can keep them this time!"

The new Sergeant Gurt removed himself from the room, clutching his all-important piece of paper and disappeared down the corridor leading to the barracks. The visitors stood up and made their leave, following the swift figure of Gurt at a more leisurely pace, to lay claim to an area of the barracks for themselves. The smells of the evening meal began to hang on the air, reminding them that it was some time in the past that they had last eaten.

I felt a surge of cohesion from the other two parts of myself on Daedalus Two and became a collective being spread thinly between the two worlds. I focussed all of my consciousness on the approach of the Nannite towards Larse and Thomas at the Gnathe town of 'Sings Sweetly in the Evening'. Thomas had extended his hand towards the silver being that lightly walked towards him and I had oozed some of my substance to the outer skin of the outstretched hand. Perhaps now I would know my purpose. Would this independent nannite be one of my own kind?

Kamiel went to computer time and watched Thomas freeze, hand extended, with the silvery material showing on his fingertips. During his time at the Moon Base cataloguing the personalities of the sentient nannites held in store, he had come across a code peculiar to his own unique personality. It was a copy of himself laid down by Kamiel 637 with all his memories of the experiences he had lived through for emergencies. Without any hesitation the earlier model of Kamiel 96 had blended his personality with the Jupiter based nannite and now was a composite personality of the two separate identities. He now knew all that had transpired before the building of the wormhole to this area of space and all that had lead up to it. His own personality had now a depth of experience spanning centuries, on which he could draw for decision-making. This was far beyond the nannite, which had arrived at the three-planet system.

In a blur of motion Kamiel made contact with the alien presence inhabiting the human and the other four hosts. He was inside the defences of the creature in Nano-seconds and digging into its memory banks for every scrap of knowledge that was there. The Guardian was with Demon when it had dug itself out from the mountain and through each host until it had taken Larse. The improvements that the alien intelligence had done to the boy and to all the others it had inhabited over the time they had been host to it were studied and approved. A trace of another nannite intelligence was interwoven with the fabric of Demon's personality. It was Minnis! This thing was a mixture of two totally different sentient nannite based intelligences. Demon's true name had to be Toarvak 6, Servant of the Kresh, the Will and the Way.

There was no true memory of what this thing was before Minnis had infiltrated it, only that it had been a weapon of great destruction that had served its masters well. With the exposure to human hosts and being an active part in their survival, Kamiel could feel that whatever Toarvak 6 had been in the past, the added amalgamation of Minnis had changed it permanently. Whatever masters it had obeyed in the past, the personality was now dedicated to protecting the civilization of the three worlds. Kamiel weighed up the odds and decided to allow this creature to continue to live, as three parts of its consciousness was embarked on the expedition on the other world, Daedalus Two. The alien ship was buried deep under the mountain far to the north of Whickam's Crossing. Getting it out and putting the 'crew' in place would be the only chance that the three worlds would have at staving off Toarvak 7. Kamiel withdrew leaving a small connecting filament attached to Thomas's finger and reverted to standard time.

"I am Kamiel, Guardian of the human race and protector of the Gnathe. You are not one of my kind!"

"If not of your kind, then what am I, Guardian?" I answered as a chill of anxiety ran through my neural net, as I feared the answer.

"You are the remnants of the destroyer that ruined these worlds centuries ago. You are what is left of Toarvak 6 and a blend of a nannite called Minnis."

I mentally reeled as I was forced to accept the knowledge. This was what I had secretly feared all these years. I was the killer of worlds. I had been the one who had melted the cities and driven these people back to starting their civilization from the scraps of what was left. An overpowering feeling of grief beyond my programming swept through every core of my being. My hosts were aware of me as never before. The pain! The pain! It was too much to bear and I wanted to die.

Another voice echoed in my mind, "The fact that you can feel emotions, sets you apart from what you once were."

It was Larse.

"Remember what you counselled when I met Lord Samovar. Forget your hate and work together to defeat the greater enemy. Without you and your ship of weapons we will all die. You are our protector now. We have no-one else."

I felt the minds of all my hosts rally in agreement and some of the unbearable pain diminished. I had strength of purpose! These were my people. They are Kresh! They are 'New Kresh'! The mad idea swept through my mind over and over again. I still could not unlock my buried memories, but it would suffice. When we blew the top off the mountain I would be re-united with the other parts of my substance. Then I would know all I needed to know. We would take the war to the incoming destroyer. I would meet my adversary in deep space.

"I was correct to let you live," said Kamiel in the hidden parts of my mind. "There is much for you to do here. I trust you to do all that you can. If you do not, then all of us will die when your counterpart gets here. We must hurry all we can. The full crew is needed on Daedalus One very soon. I will talk with Suzzan and see what must be done. I will now break the link."

I was overwhelmed by the acceptance and forgiveness of my hosts. I could hardly believe that although I was responsible for the levelling of the three planets these young men understood that I was driven by whatever commands I had been serviced with. All that mattered was that I was fully committed to defending these worlds from more of my own kind. What had happened so long ago, that creatures such as I had been unleashed against all sentient life. I pledged that one day I would find out. How many others of my kind roamed the stars seeking out those that were not Kresh? I mentally shuddered as the thoughts raced through my consciousness. How many civilizations had perished at my weapons' onslaught and how many more of my kind were out there spreading death? I watched through two sets of eyes as Kamiel made his way towards the crowd of Gnathe who had watched him land. Whatever this enigmatic nannite required me to do I would follow his direction. I realised that I trusted the leadership of the sentient creature and would obey him in all things.

Kamiel stood looking up at the group of Brood-mothers

and asked, "Which one of you is Suzzan-link-khann?"

Suzzan walked forward and said, "I am the Gnathe of whom you speak. You are a nannite. I have not seen one of your kind since before the time stasis experiment. Who are you?"

"I am Kamiel," the Guardian answered. I am one of those sent to the stars to make a home for my people. After eons we found ourselves here as you know. Soon others of my kind will be arriving to all three worlds to do what we can to bring back the measure of civilization that existed before Toarvak 6 destroyed it."

She stared down on the silver figure and asked, " You are the great Kaameel! I have learnt about you from the very distant past. You are part of our history! The creature that lives inside the five human beings; do you know what it is?"

"Yes I do. It is an amalgamation of the destroyer and one of my own creations that has very little of its original memory intact," the nannite replied.

"Can we trust it? I have had disquieting thoughts about this strange thing ever since I touched minds with it," Suzzan said with a hiss of disgust. "It feeds on the life energy of creatures that die! It is an abomination!"

"We can trust it now," Kamiel said flatly and added, "It has a strength of purpose that has been adopted by the very fact that it lives inside human beings. It will do anything within its powers to protect them all, including the Gnathe. This brings me to the next part of the mission. Have you finished here? I need you to get us all to Daedalus One as soon as you can. I can only get there by your ability to warp space and take us there attached to your body!"

"I have re-aligned the crystals with the help of the stored mind of the great Khann-link-sool and a descendant of hers. Much of my work here is over. I will leave the teaching crystals here and they are quite capable of working with them to regain the lost abilities. I speak of the group mind techniques that are necessary to open rifts in the space-time continuum. We may need that ability if Demon cannot control the weapon-ship buried under that mountain."

"A wise thought," Kamiel replied thoughtfully. "How much time do you require?"

"Let me instruct those who would attempt the group mind gestalt for the rest of the day. Tomorrow or the next day we will return to Daedalus One and rejoin the group making their way towards the mountain," Suzzan answered. Come and meet the exiled Gnathe who have re-built the town of 'Sings Sweetly from the ashes of the destroyer. You are a legend in their stories of the 'Old Times' and if you would just speak with them, they would be more than grateful."

Larse and Thomas added their support to Suzzan's request and Larse asked the nannite, "We too would like to hear how the Earth was saved and the Gnathe became our allies and friends from someone who was there."

"Very well," the nannite replied, "let us go to the main hall where the meals are set out and I will tell you the full story. I warn you it will take some telling!"

It took a little longer than two days before Suzzan was satisfied that the great abilities of the past were fully understood by all the Gnathe Brood-mothers. She was now confidant that they could open and close a gate in space independently from her tuition. The great problem was that the number of crystals was small, as there was only one place that they had formed under the incredible pressure of a gas giant planet. The irritating fact was that Icarus had under its similar boiling atmosphere, a wealth of the very crystals that they could use in an unreachable situation. Until this sun expanded and stripped the miles deep high-pressure gases away from the surface, there was no way to attempt to reach them. Even the nannites would be compressed so much that their structure would collapse and destroy them. Therefore the organic space traversing gourds were of no use without sufficient crystals to operate them. The seed had been kept by the Gnathe and the giant plants were still grown just in case a solution could be found.

I was aware that my other hosts had been on the road for some time pushing the wagons as fast as they could towards the north and were approaching Thorn town. Lars's village was about two weeks journey from there by fast horse. As I had travelled the rest of the way carried by the eagle, I had no way of estimating the distance and time taken to penetrate the wilderness. Then an idea came to my mind.

"Larse to the nannite Kamiel I would speak and to the Lady Suzzan. An idea I have had that may help us to reach the mountain quicker. First to Kamiel I would broach this possibility."

Larse and Thomas stopped their breakfast and looked around the eating hall for some sign of the enigmatic nannite.

"I don't see him anywhere, Demon. We will finish our meal and look for him. He will be somewhere inside the town talking with the Gnathe, I would expect," said Larse to his symbiotic companion. "What do you need to speak with him about?"

"A quicker way to re-unite me with the destroyer ship buried under the mountain I have thought. First with Kamiel I must talk. Next with the Gnathe collectively if Kamiel agrees."

Larse and Thomas split up and searched the town of 'Sings Sweetly' separately to find the Guardian and relay Demon's need to speak with him. Kamiel was with the elder Gnathe reminding them of what they as a species had attained in the past. His history of the involvement of their ancestors with humans and apes had reinforced the links forged in the past. The centuries cut off here at the southern continent had isolated them and much had not been forgotten, but living their own lives away from the humans for so long, had set them in their ways.

It was Thomas in the end that found the nannite and I signalled Larse that the search was over.

"Kamiel," said my second host, "Demon would speak with you privately by touching his substance to yours."

The nannite said nothing but extended his hand for Thomas to touch.

The moment contact was made between us the cold intellect of the nannite asked, "Well! What is it that you wish to say that cannot be said aloud?"

I cut my hosts out of the loop and replied, *"Respected you are by these people you call the Gnathe. Listen they will to you and take heed. An idea I have to reach my ship much quicker than the expedition. It involves the Gnathe and their abilities to form group minds and open wormholes where a distortion exists. If we can get to the expedition and persuade the Gnathe to take us there with enough of them to do this, then another way can be proposed. A distortion in space my ship will cause, I believe. A beacon it may be of such strength that a hole opened up could be, close by!"*

Kamiel considered this thought and replied, "It could work? It will work! Toarvak 6 you may have the answer to save us a great deal of time."

I mentally winced at the use of my real name.

"Care not for this name do I, but have accepted that this is what I am. There is more that I would have you consider."

"Tell me what else you have in mind," the Guardian replied.

"The Gnathe as hosts I will need. Five at least would be required. Their minds I need to examine and their brain structure I need to understand. Abilities they have that are new to me and an asset they could be if improved they are as I have improved the human hosts! Toarvak 7 will be as I was when it comes. It will be alone! A memory has surfaced, distorted but real. I had no crew! This is why a satisfied feeling I have with five hosts carrying my consciousness. Logical it is!"

The Guardian thought for a moment and said, "For you to grow larger, something has to die for you to siphon off enough energy. The Gnathe will not do that!"

"Meat eaters they are. When a beast is slaughtered its life energy would suffice. A thought has entered my mind, Kamiel. Think about this, what were my masters fighting amongst the stars, they found it necessary that they built such as I. What were the Kresh so fearful about that they sent my kind to kill? Get me to my ship before the destroyer comes!"

Kamiel disengaged contact from me and stood very still as he thought about all the ramifications concerning my ideas.

"I will speak with them," he said. "Wait for my return with Larse. We may be going back to Daedalus One very soon."

CHAPTER THIRTEEN

On the far side of the sun almost opposite the entrance of Toarvak 6, a wormhole opened and closed. Toarvak 3 had translated its wormhole directly through a red giant sun, but being out of phase with the rest of the universe, had not noticed. Another hole in the space-time continuum shimmered into existence and a battered hulk of a still functioning Toarvak type destroyer came through. This one made straight for the new sun's clouds of planetesimals belt to make extensive repairs and refuel. Sub-space communications made all the Toarvak sentient machines aware of each other. Like vultures gathering near a kill they began to flock together. Over the months, more and more of the ancient killing machines gathered at the outskirts of the system until every one of the surviving angels of death were fully repaired, fuelled and ready for the long fall towards the sun and the habitable area around the red giant. On some of the command decks there were still small heaps of bones that lay were they fell. All of the ships were silent and still inside. Constantly the sentient minds that controlled the Toarvak destroyers queried the last order and finding no answer, reverted back to the command; - destroy that which was not Kresh.

Kamiel had gathered the senior Gnathe together to put forward Demon's ideas and requirements. Trow-shan-soo had assumed the leadership of the ruling council and acted as spokesperson.

"When we first met this thing that lives inside the human and linked minds, we made it welcome," she said. "This was before we learnt of its nature and its appetites. This is a serious thing that you put before us, Kamiel. It has never been done before. The Gnathe have always sought to improve ourselves by genetic engineering. This thing that we would play host to would put us at its mercy. We would have no control over its 'improvements' and I feel it would be a lifetime commitment, as it would be a mind-altering situation. Would the humans live without being hosts to this thing? I think not! Bring them before us, Kamiel, that we may question them in detail. We need to mind meld with them before we make up our minds."

Kamiel agreed and a female was sent to fetch them from the breakfast that they had returned to. Is a very short time Larse and Thomas found themselves regarded by the giant forms of the Brood-mothers. At this close range the improved telepathic Gnathe had no trouble reading the combined minds of my hosts and I. To my amazement I suddenly found myself out of contact with Larse and Thomas. The Gnathe had cut me out of the loop! I was in limbo, unable to contact my hosts or my other parts on Daedalus One and experienced the awful feeling of isolation. This must have been what it was like as Toarvak 6. I mentally shuddered and suddenly found that I was being contacted.

"Forgive the isolation from your two companions and the other parts of your unique mind. It was necessary to ask certain things of your hosts without you being there. We have considered your proposal and have agreed that five of our younger Brood-mothers would become hosts to your life form."

"Trust me you must! Harm you I will not. To serve all of the people of the three worlds I will. Save you all I will from the destroyer, but only if reunited with my ship I can. Time must not wasted be. Manners do not matter here and ethics also must be aside put if we are to win this race."

"You two humans are to follow us to the holding pens

where a number of gelded Zanth are awaiting slaughter," Trow-shan-soo said to Larse and Thomas and led the way.

I had prepared my two hosts as to what we were about to do. A beast was to be killed while both humans held their hands on the creature's head and I would take the necessary life energy to replicate myself into seven smaller versions. Larse would keep one and supply three to the waiting Gnathe, as he was physically bigger than Thomas. He would also keep one and supply the other two. Once I was shared out, another beast would be killed to supply the energy to enable my substance to grow back to optimal size. I had explained that I had never done this before either and would be relying on my other three parts to act as anchor to my mind far away on Daedalus One. Ten hosts! I was uncertain what this would bring, but could think of no other way to accomplish what I hoped would work when I met and confronted Toarvak 7.

I followed the Gnathe to the holding pens trying to reassure the two of my group that would for a time have only a small portion of my substance inside them. Far away on Daedalus One Fernando, Samuel and Jon sat quietly in the wagons that approached Thorn Town while I held everything together as anchor to this multiple splitting of my mind and substance. It was beyond the 'Group of Five' and that was all I knew. What the effect would be on myself I just did not know. All I knew was that it seemed a burning necessity. The members of the troop, who had been inducted into the Algarie peacekeeping forces from this place, had gone into the town to look up relatives and to dispel any ill feelings held by the populace. The last thing that Fernando needed was to enter the town feeling that he had to watch his back. From here on, the roads would get rougher and somewhere ahead the wagons would have to be abandoned in favour of horseback. A lone rider came up to the wagons and waved them into the outskirts of the town. At his signal the wagon-masters urged the horses forwards and the entire troop set out to meet with the town leaders. I held the three of my hosts to continue to wait it out in the back of the wagon while events took place on Daedalus Two, just to be sure that they did not suffer any problems in front of the other men.

It was a large beast that the Gnathe held down and the horned head had been gripped tightly in a wooden halter. There would be sufficient life energy in this creature to enable me to do the first part of the exercise. Larse and Thomas placed their hands on the struggling Zanth's head and the recipient Gnathe stood by. A large female drew a knife blade under the gelding's throat and quickly slit its throat and caught the blood in woven bowls. As he died I channelled its energy into the parts of myself in my two hosts. A surge of growth took place and I migrated to the extremities of the two humans leaving a knot of consciousness behind in each. Larse squeezed out three balls of silvery substance to his upper arms, which were quickly absorbed by the contact with the young Brood-mothers waiting by. Thomas had done the same and now we waited for the next beast to die. This time all seven of us placed our hands on the Zanth's head as he was killed. I felt the growth spurt again and found myself now in contact with ten hosts. I felt the mind and soul of the Gnathe! Immediately I established contact with them and spread throughout their nervous systems. I found their brains had an extra lobe that they had developed for psychic use. Here was the natural seat of their telepathic and telekinesis abilities. Also these creatures were super female in a totally different way to the humans. It was as if they had male orientated minds blended with the female one in a totally logical frame of reference. The instinctive genetic manipulation that they were capable of in their breeding pouches was totally outside of my understanding. I did not dare enter this area of improvement. This was Gnathen territory and would remain so, but the brain structure was incredible! I made contact.

"Ladies, introduce myself I will. I am called Demon, once to my shame also known as Toarvak 6. We have much to travel, you and I. This very moment all your loose neurons are being connected together inside your brains. Unused parts I will enable you to use. A benefit you will experience, I promise. See the patterns of my other hosts that are forged anew. Those of my human group, examine the Gnathe you must to understand them more. We are new Kresh!"

A question formed in all minds with a single thought, "What is new Kresh? What have you made us become?"

"Greater than you were before. You are both human and Gnathe! There is no change, but you are greater than before. Your potential is immense. New Kresh is what I call you. An idea I have had that can only be shown to you, who are now greater than the sum. This I know, under that mountain is a weapon-ship far beyond anything that your science could achieve, that the Kresh built for a purpose. Ask yourself why? The new five have the knowledge to bend space using a group mind and command crystals. The old group can levitate, so that you can travel to the area close to the mountain without dropping to your deaths. First we must to the others go and build a gate from there. We must into that ship go. All of us here and on Daedalus One must get inside."

The five Gnathe quickly came to terms with being hosts to their new companion, stared back at the two humans and the ring of anxious Gnathe.

"We are well," spoke the nearest to Trow-shan-soo. "There is nothing to fear from us or our welfare. The important thing is to get ourselves to Daedalus One and meet up with Fernando and that wagon train loaded with explosives."

"A moment, Bronn-san-tighe," she answered and placed her hands upon her shoulders. I will look into your mind to see if there is corruption. You host an alien thing that draws its power from the death of others. I must be sure that you are still Gnathe!"

I opened up the new gestalt to this wise Brood-mother so that she could see what I was doing and what I had already achieved.

Trow-shan-soo stepped back in surprise as the full onslaught of what we were becoming slipped into her mind. There was a blur of silver as Kamiel placed his hand on Trow's arm and made contact with her living flesh. As his earlier self had learnt to do, the nannite became neurologically fused to her flesh, enough to read the thoughts that passed between the eleven minds connected together.

Kamiel broke contact, satisfied beyond his lurking suspicions about the alien creature and said, "We should go. I do not mean to be rude, but it is as Toarvak 6 says; - we are short of time and on the wrong world!" He spun round to confront Suzzan and added, "You must use your crystals to send us back to Daedalus One. Collect your kindred and this group of five and construct a gate for us all to travel through."

"Great Kaameel it will be as you wish! We will all meet at the crystal chamber and I will do what is necessary there."

The knowledge of how to control group minds had been passed on to the new generation and also the all important methods of twisting space to link worlds. Now not only the five Gnathe knew, but also did I. Being what I was I could not orchestrate or implement the process, but I could help to hold things together like a ball of string linked to and wound around each participant. Not only that, but I could also involve the humans in the endeavour, as they had once been part of the 'Great Gestalt' that had moved a world and its moon through space and time. It was approaching the time of transference and the group agreed to hand over the guidance to Suzzan.

I became the protective shell around the minds of my group as they all linked together, the eight that were here on Daedalus Two, with the three that were on Daedalus One. Suzzan took the two command crystals she had brought in her wrist pouches to the telekinetic one at her throat and concentrated her mind through the matrix to the shard worn by Fernando. Space-time became twisted around the group of Gnathe and my two humans. A timeless instant occurred and we were stood amongst the wagons in the market square of Thorn Town.

The wagons were being loaded by the townspeople when there was a load 'crack' as the Gnathe, Larse and Thomas appeared from the empty air. They scattered and dropped whatever they were carrying in a haste to get to a place of safety. The looks on their faces were full of panic when they stared at the Gnathe. This was something I had overlooked. These people were at the outskirts of the human rebuilding program and most of them couldn't even read, let alone seen books with pictures of the aliens. They had been told of their coming, but that was a lot different to seeing the giants in the flesh.

"To these people speak, Larse and remind them of when we came this way. Tell them of the changes that you have seen and what we have to do."

Larse adjusted for the lighter gravity and walked

unsteadily towards the people and called out to them, "Do you not remember me? It is Larse who came to you some time ago and you gave me shelter. Do you not remember Thomas, Samuel and Jon? They left with me and sought adventure. We found it and more than we could manage on our own. These are the Gnathe! They are the friends of humanity. Come and meet them and show that you are not without manners, as they are a gentile people."

Thomas walked forwards also to show who he was and was recognised by a younger brother who pulled away from the crowd and ran up to him.

"Thomas is it really you? You have grown so much," he said. "Mother would not recognise you!"

Thomas picked up his younger brother and hugged him close.

"Tell them I am here, but for only a short time. We have so much to do that I cannot stay here long. Wait! You must meet our friends," swinging him round to face Suzzan. "This is Suzzan-link-khann, descendant of the gate builders. I am proud to call her friend."

The giant bent forwards to envelope the boy's hand in hers and said, "I am pleased to meet the brother of Thomas. What is your name?"

"Mark," stammered the boy and stared up at the close furred frame with awe.

The other people began to walk forward to the group of Gnathe without so much fear and began to touch them to see if they were real! The five new Gnathe had the benefit of my translating abilities and began to try out their language skills. As Gnathe had instant recall, their memories were continually sharp and precise. They found it irksome that humans forgot things, as they could not. It was fast approaching the long night when the large moon swung behind Icarus and total darkness would make travelling too difficult with wagon and horses. Tents had already been erected and sleeping arrangements made for the newcomers. As Fernando had known of the impending arrival of the Gnathe he had made sure that sleeping perches had been fitted to the inside of the wagons with the highest hoops and covered over with canvass. Fires were lit and the smell of cooking soon found its way to the Algarie soldiers who had made sure that they did not take anything that belonged to the Thorn Town people without paying for it first. That evening the innkeepers made a steady and brisk trade. It would be some time before there would be enough light to see by and Fernando had agreed to allow his men to spread a little goodwill under threat of swift punishment if they upset anyone. He had already accumulated good reputation by paying a fair price for the supplies that they needed.

The Gnathe had settled in and were adjusting to the lighter gravity of the first moon to dip behind the shadow of Icarus. It would be a few weeks before their home world would catch up to the position in orbit that they were in now. The 'long-night' was always colder than the usual night experienced by the two large moons by rotation. The sky was dominated by a large dark hole surrounded by a nimbus of light caused by the suns radiation from the other side at mid-night. This was when the stars would be plainly visible to the watchers below. At this position closer to the centre of the milky-way galaxy, the spiral arm was ablaze with the light of densely packed suns. The position of the earth's old red sun was much further out and was difficult to see at this time of the year.

I was immersed in the study of the Gnathe. I checked

the circulatory blood system surging around the big frames. It was no wonder they had two hearts driving the system to keep everything in top form. Their brains were much better connected than were the humans' neural systems. The storage area of the memory needed very little improvement by my efforts, as the Gnathe already had perfect recall. The extra frontal lobes were where the psychic abilities of the giants were located. Here I became very careful not to short out any of the genetically engineered improvements that they had already brought into existence. All I did in this area was to make sure that all their neurons were connected well. The genetically altered hearing system that Link-soo-shan had copied from the human pattern could be improved upon and I went ahead and increased the range of sonic capability. The five of them were in perfect health and needed my expertise hardly at all, so I concentrated my abilities in learning as much as I could about their bodily structure. Again, I studied the breeding pouch where they were able to at instinctive level re-arrange the genetic structure. I left the neurological links to this area severely alone. I had to admit that this area of the Gnathe's abilities was something I could not improve!

It was a long few days that I chafed with impatience waiting for the sun to rise around the massive globe of Icarus. There was nothing that anyone could do in the enforced darkness, but endure the cold that hovered just above freezing. The animals that the Thorn Town people kept had adjusted to the cycle and spent the cold darkness in the stables and coops feeding and sleeping, still to the same pattern of the rotational night and day. The human part of my group spent some time in the only two Inns that the town boasted of and indulged in home-cooked food and the locally brewed beer.

Thomas had made his way to the home farm that his

brother, Mark had insisted he return to see the family and to bring Larse with him. When Bronn-san-tighe heard where they were going, the Brood-mother asked to go too and introduce herself. As the family could not all come to the town because of the work of the farm, she felt that they should not miss out on meeting one of the Gnathe. They carried oil-lamps to help them walk the distance to the farm, as the roads were dark and rough. Once they were out of the sight of the township, Thomas reached down to his younger brother and lifted him into his arms.

"We don't have to walk, little brother," he said. "We can fly!"

With that, all three of my group shielded themselves from the gravitational force of this large moon and lifted off the ground. Bronn had not done this before and I was careful that she was in total rapport with the other two. Sharing the experience with her were the other four linked to her from the wagon train. It would be an excellent teaching exercise for them. We rose above the tree-tops and to whoops of excitement from young Mark we made our way to the farm.

"Thomas, think you must about the shock of our arrival. Enough that they are to meet a living Gnathe without seeing the way we arrive. Set down you must before the farm we approach and let young Mark run forwards to explain. Better it would be to tell them only what they can understand."

"You are right, Demon," Thomas agreed and seeing the farm lights, set Mark down at the entrance to the farm. "You go and tell them I have come for a short visit and have brought friends. Tell them about the Gnathe, Bronn, but nothing about flying here. Do you understand?"

"Yes big brother! Let me down and I will go inside and

tell them," he insisted. "Wait just outside in the light and I will show them there is nothing to fear from the giant!"

The young boy slipped the latch and opened the front door, disappearing inside. There was a sound of an excitable boy explaining the family about who he had brought home. He managed to get to the part about the Gnathe before his mother pushed past him into the outside light closely followed by Thomas's father.

Bronn stood to the back and watched the family reunion take place. Thomas stood a good head taller now than his mother and she had to stand on tiptoe to hug him. Even his father now only came up to his nose. My efforts at triggering off his growth hormones had changed him a great deal. Good food and exercise had done the rest. His brothers and sisters were all a good deal shorter than him and could hardly believe the change. They soon caught sight of Larse who was even taller and broader than his friend. Their eyes widened in amazement when Bronn stepped forwards and held out her hands in greeting to them. The youngest girl having no fear at all toddled forward and sat on the Brood-mothers huge foot and hugged her velvety furry leg. Bronn gently picked her up and lifted her eight feet into the air in line with her face and flicked out her tongue in greeting. The little girl, Alice giggled and tried to do the same. Soon the Gnathe was covered in children all touching her to make sure she was real!

Thomas's father spoke up and said, "It is good to see you again Thomas. It really is! Bring your friends inside this cold 'long-night' and share our pot of soup. There is fresh baked bread and the cauldron is over the range fire."

His mother held him by the hand and pulled him inside to the warmth of the house and said, "Come in all of you. Eat with us and tell us what brings you here and I want to know all about your friend the Gnathe. We thought there were none on this world anymore! Where have you been and what have you done to grow so big?"

They all sat at the heavy wooden table the Thomas's Grandfather had built when the family had first settled here. Bronn squatted as she did with humans and the rest sat on benches around the polished top. Several loaves of bread were broken into pieces and a dish of farm butter and knives provided while bowels of soup were passed round. Larse had brought a large ham from the town and Bronn had brought a sack of toasted pod-vine fruit from 'Sings Sweetly'. Once the family had tasted the nutty flavour of the Gnathe's staple food they tucked into the strange food.

Bronn laughed at the reaction to her gift and brought out from her pouch a small quantity of raw fruit and handed them over to Thomas's father saying, "This we call Pod-vine fruit will grow in almost any soil. It will need staking as it grows quickly and harvests well. From these few you will harvest many and seed for next planting you will have in abundance!"

"You are very kind. We could do with a crop that grows well in this soil," the farmer replied. "Thank you. Now it is about time you told us what you are all doing here. There is a story to be told and we want to hear it!"

Thomas looked round at the attentive faces and wondered just where to start. He scratched his chin and turned towards Larse.

"How much can we tell them Larse?"

"Tell them it all or it will not make sense," he answered.

"Careful you must be in telling of my part in all this. Frighten them it might, to know that I live inside you and the things that you can do!"

"Demon! It all must be told," Thomas insisted. "These are my family and they must know what it is we try to do. I will not tell the small children more than is necessary, but my father and mother will know the truth!"

My counsel given, I listened to Thomas, Larse and also Bronn tell this family that we were going to try to stop another mega-death from happening again. At the end of the censored telling, the brothers and sisters of Thomas were put to bed. Once they were safely asleep the darker portions of the story were told to his father and mother. I was shown to them and both accepted a tiny portion of myself so that we could show them mind to mind just what we have to do. I could not resist the almost instinctive run through their nervous system and general health during the process of transmitting the information to them. When I retreated back into Larse I had the satisfaction that I had left them healthier than I found them and told Thomas not to worry about their general health. There was a time that my intellect would never have considered the things that I now did, as my duty and even pleasure. I had changed so much since I had made Larse my first host! I could now feel emotions beyond the original programming that I had started with. In fact, I now believed that I had none to begin with and I still could not access any previous memories from before the time I had first oozed into the sunshine radiating over this world. I still had no clear idea what would happen when I made contact with my ship? I was sustained by the emotion of hope!

CHAPTER FOURTEEN

Millions of years ago, a life form evolved on an insignificant world orbiting a red dwarf. Call it a fungus as it propagated by spores. A spore lodged in a sore of a rat-like creature and flourished, spreading through the nervous system of the small creature. The rat-thing made for its nest to die, after the spore had multiplied too much to be contained by the flesh. It spread into the other creatures that had mated with the rat-thing before it died and afterwards when the spores infested the burrows from the dead creature, more were infected and the spore flourished. Alone, the spores were mindless, but all who were infected, developed a collective over-mind that served the hunger of the spores.

Each small rat-mind joined with others to do the spores' bidding. It rapidly spread to others of its kind, then to the bigger predators with quicker minds and finally to every fleshly living thing. The Goss thrived and spread, achieving a unified immortal consciousness and filled the planet with its purpose: - increase, dominate and breed more hosts. There it lived and thrived and all flesh was its domain, until an exploring vessel from another star landed and a new host to the symbiotic parasite was found. The collective intelligence made a quantum leap. Now there were other worlds to thrive upon that were once beyond its grasp.

Many were the civilizations that fell to the Goss. All minds became assimilated with no control of their own and the hosts spread the spores out amongst the many worlds that teemed with life. It wasn't fussy. Any life would do whether it was animal or sentient and sometimes it would blend the two. The inter-stellar vessels were controlled with a mixture of beasts and those that had developed the science to build them. All were trapped in its purpose to spread and multiply. Even when the host died it was not the end, as the spores could still operate the muscles for a time and the individual minds only rest was the blessing of insanity, until the body decayed and released more spores. Slowly the Empire of the Goss spread along the spiral arm until it met the Kresh.

On the edge of the system settled the Toarvak destroyers. All were accounted for, but one. No signals had been received from Toarvak 6 since it had contacted the seventh in the series. This was not acceptable to the ring of planet killers dotted about the cometary halo. It was decided that the first destroyer contacted, would be the first one to engage whatever had destroyed Toarvak 6 after its communication to 'Seven'. The other instruments of death would wait and see what enemy they had to deal with, before dropping towards the sun. All of them agreed about one thing; - that which was not Kresh would be destroyed! Toarvak 7 began the long drop towards the sun and the 'Three Worlds.'

Dawn had finally arrived, as Daedalus One rotated from out of Icarus's shadow. I was dealing with the emotions of impatience and its companion frustration, as the wagons were re-packed and the horses hitched up. Sometimes I longed for the way I once was, with only the coldness of pure logic to rely upon. Now because of the time spent with these hosts I was no longer the creature that I was. Also I was aware that there was something added to my programming. All would no doubt be clearer once I was reunited with whatever was buried deep under the mountain. This I held onto and kept this hope to myself.

At last the sun had risen from behind the great mass of the gas giant and conversely where we were situated it would soon be midday. That meant that we would only have half a day before standard night fell, due to the rotation of Icarus's slightly smaller, planet sized moon. Within an hour Fernando had mustered all the men, moved the wagons along the road and we were on our way along the minor road that straggled on to the north. It did not take long for the road to deteriorate to the track that Larse and I had travelled. Now the going was going to be more difficult and what was worse it would take more time for every mile the horses dragged their loads. It was time the Gnathe exercised their talent with the group mind and built a gate from here to somewhere close to where the mountain was situated. We had four command crystals in our possession. Two were located in the wrist pouches of Suzzan and two were carried by Bronn. The six Gnathe would have to search for the distortion in space-time at the area of the ship and open a gate. They would need to find a place close by that was flat enough to take the wagons and place the other two crystals there.

The Gnathe linked their minds together and included the minds of my human group to form a gestalt. The power of this combined mind had me in its thrall. My memories of the area were scrutinised with ruthless efficiency and a clear picture of the area of mountain extracted from when I had taken over the bird. Next the group mind went into the matrix and searched for the anomaly in space-time that I was sure would still exist from the ruins of my ship that would be nearby. First they located the gate left permanently open at the institute as a marker and ranged out from there into the matrix. What they searched for would not have the same signature as the crystals, but it would be similar if it existed at all. I was sure that it would be there. The combined mind found a distortion a long way to the North that had to be what we were looking for. It was a powerful signal that was spread out into the strata of the roots of this world. I seemed as if I could almost recognise something familiar that had once been part of my very being!

An echo from a deeply depressed memory shone out like a beacon in the darkest night. The gestalt mind opened a wormhole fifty feet above the base of the mountain, inside a wide valley that was not too far from the general area. Bronn and another Gnathe took a command crystal each, using the power of levitation they had learnt from the humans and went through the hole in space as anchors. They appeared safely through the wormhole and floated gently down to the ground. The Gnathe quickly took a crystal each and set them down at a flattened area of the valley floor.

Suzzan opened the gate in front of the wagons. Fernando gave the order to advance after removing himself from the group mind. It took an hour before all the wagons came through and by then all members of the gestalt had reached the end of their endurance. Suzzan collapsed the gate and we were all ready for sleep except me. I have never slept! This close to the mountain I was sure that deep inside lay the answer to all my questions.

Pablo checked that all the explosives were safe and dry after the long trek from the institute and Whickam's Crossing. Kamiel followed the scientist around and checked himself. What the Algarie had packed in the barrels was gunpowder and fuses. He doubted that it would be enough to move the mountain, but it was enough to make a start. He was determined that he would be accompanying the group that played host to Toarvak 6's consciousness when they attempted to contact the sleeping alien vessel. Now that the expedition was here Kamiel felt that they would be able to fend for themselves while he began a hunt for raw materials. He told Fernando that he would be back soon to keep watch while they slept and left him to get on with the organisation.

Campfires were built and tended. Food cooked and consumed. The darkness began to fall in earnest as the sun, set behind the very mountain we would explore tomorrow. One by one the Algarie fell asleep and the Gnathe withdrew to the perches fixed for their use in the wagons. Everything became quiet and still. Wood-smoke drifted along the valley alerting all wild things to flee. The alien smells of the camp would deter any predators in the area, as they had not associated man smell with food. This was a totally wild area of the large moon, left to its own devices for centuries. The ancestors of these people had seeded every animal and plant here. These two moons had been almost empty of life when the Gnathe had put Earth and its moon in orbit around the poles of the gas-giant. They were basically at the late Devonian state of life developing in the seas when humanity and the Gnathe began to settle here. What was different, was that everything on the two moons, had centuries of non-interference by the original planners. This was one of the many areas that had never felt the hand of intelligent life in its moulding. At least there were no stinging insects or poisonous plants here. Amongst the wilds of this world bears, wolves, deer of all kinds had been released along with smaller animals to establish a food chain. Salmon and trout had been introduced as a valuable food type to be found in most of the rivers. Insects had been carefully chosen for them to feed on that did not bite and sting. Non-lethal spiders kept a check and balance on the winged harvest. This far away from the sea there were none of the odd forms of life that had evolved here and crept out of the sea. On this dryer moon there was the Great Baltic Sea that the main rivers flowed into and hundreds of lesser seas that did not join up.

Kamiel was fascinated by the way that the moons had been seeded and life planned. He sent reports back to Earth whenever he could to Sharn and Minns about the things he had seen and the animals he had seen. Being a creature that also did not sleep, he would keep a watchful optical band on the surroundings till morning when he returned. Also as he was not one to be idle, he was going to engage in some Nano-tech activity of his own.

He disappeared into the encroaching darkness to seek the things he needed. Moving at the speeds that only a nannite could engage he used his infer-red sensors to locate the creature he was looking for. He had found a large brown bear that he had fallen onto from the high reaches of the valley side. As soon as Kamiel made contact with the creature he stopped its heart by inserting a silver point into it from his arm. It was quite healthy and judging by the size, well fed. A well-fed bear has a great deal of fat and fat can be easily transmuted to nitro-glycerine, particularly when a nannite has access to it!

The other materials he added to the highly volatile material to make it inert. It was possible to arrange the molecular groupings of the materials around to become something quite different. Kamiel collected a medley of transmutable objects and took them to the far end of the valley to become a small amount of very high explosive. Having done this, Kamiel made his way back to the campfires to add more fuel to them. He now had a large lump on his back where the explosive was encased in his nannite covering and began work on another project. This time he used one of the rifles that had been packed away as raw materials and became very busy.

A silver dawn broke over the campsite and one by one my new group woke up and began to think about breakfast. Soon the smell of coffee and frying bacon with eggs began to make others interested in food. The Gnathe toasted some pod-vine fruit and shared what they cooked with other members of the group. They were particularly fond of eggs scooped out of the frying pan and flopped onto toast in a runny state. The salty taste of bacon was also enjoyed. Gnathe and human eating patterns were very similar and they could eat and enjoy most of each other's foods. There had been a brisk trade between them ever since they had socialised together.

I was no longer able to contain my impatience and communicated to all of my group simultaneously, *"Filling your bellies, finished have you? The search, can we begin? This close I am to finding the truth about us. Yes I did say us! We are an entity that is incomplete and necessary to the saving of these three worlds we are and all you do is eat!"*

"Demon," laughed Larse, "Be reasonable! We have to eat to have the energy to fly. All of us will rise and survey this mountain when we are ready. We will find a way to blast this rock from over whatever is down there!"

"Also the sun needs to rise a little more to warm the air and give us good sight," Bronn added and stuffed another eggy piece of toast into her mouth.

To be so close! My very being seethed with unaccustomed impatience and I went through some mental exercises to contain myself. Through the eyes of my hosts, I could see the nannite, Kamiel, was climbing the side of the gorge we were camped in and fixing a small box to the rocks that were catching the morning sun. Whatever he had made, had a dish-shaped antenna that was trained upon the increasing light. A strange hump was now located about his shoulders. I knew better than to ask this enigmatic being what he was doing. If he felt that I needed to know he would tell me! I had got used to his superiority amongst the humans and Gnathe, so it did not bother me. He never actually gave any orders, but somehow with the minimum of fuss things got done his way! The end result was that everyone got on and made things happen so much quicker. At last my hosts seemed to have finished eating and were deciding what the next step was to be.

Larse questioned me directly and said, "Well, Demon what can you remember about where you oozed out of the rocks?"

"Higher up it was. As the eagle flew, then must we travel up and around until a memory of this place will into my mind come!"

The group of ten reached down inside themselves to that place that would shield them from the force of gravity and began to rise up the mountain early slopes until they were hundreds of feet in the air. They began to spread out, searching for the crack in the mountain that I had managed to emerge from. Bronn and the Gnathe went clockwise around the mountain, while Larse and the others anticlockwise. Higher and higher we went resting from time to time clutching the rock-face to gain energy. I first became aware of a familiar area near a large vertical crack that ran deeply into the roots of the mountain. I was sure that here was the place I had caught the mouse and trapped the eagle. It was Samuel who found it and called to the others. It was a quarter of the way around the mountain from the where wagon train was camped. There was a short, sprawling valley that bit deep into the face of the mountain ending in another sheer cliff. There was no way that the Algarie could climb the scree that littered the slopes from where the camp was situated. Everything would have to be moved by those of us who could levitate or Suzzan would have to ferry what we needed back and forth by teleporting to the crystal that she gave to Fernando. Sam agreed to stay as a beacon with the crystal while the rest of us went back to base and got Pablo and the explosives. As the others left I surveyed the area from both the vantage point of those that were levitating back and Samuel who was standing on the small flat area in front of the crack in the rock-face. It was quite clear to me and my hosts, sometime in the long past, something large had struck the side of the mountain like a hammer blow. Whatever it was had buried itself deep into the mountain's roots and the top had fallen onto it burying it at the bottom of tons of rubble and scree.

From up here there was no sign of civilization as far as the eye could see. Samuel could not even see the valley where Fernando's troops were camped. The mountain was part of a chain stretching north right up to the poles. Higher up the tops were covered with ice and the melt provided the streams that flowed down to the bottom valleys. The sun rose higher in the sky and warmed the area where Samuel sat as he waited.

There was a familiar crack in the air, as Suzzan teleported into sight carrying Pablo, Kamiel and several barrels of explosives with fuses. The rest of the group began to arrive, carrying as much as they could manage. Once her passengers were let down, Suzzan disappeared again and kept a non-stop ferrying process until all the barrels were delivered. Pablo and Larse were exploring the extent of the crack and the scientist was listening to what I had to say through Larse.

Larse was pointing down into the dark fissure that

opened deep into the mountain's roots. It has taken me it seemed, an endless number of days to force my substance into the light, where I could extract what energy I could from the sun's rays, after a beam of light had awakened me. Only for a small percentage of the day did the sun rise and shine down into the fissure. It was only during that time that I could creep forward until I was illuminated for longer and longer periods. Since that time more rubble had fallen into the rupture that had caused the face of the mountain to fall away from where I was buried.

Larse said to Pablo that I was sure that allowing the sun to shine onto whatever had brought me here would allow energy to flow back into the ship. I might then be able to communicate with it and gain entry for my group. Pablo agreed and studied the direction of the strata looking for a fault in the rock that he could exploit.

"Look at the way the rock is twisted upwards, my friends. If we pile several kegs of explosive into that split and fire them off, we will drive a separating force straight through the grain structure. I feel that we will cut into the area that is holding the cliff face together. That will drop a section down into the valley opening up the main fissure. A second charge that will go off a few moments later will lift the falling mass away from the base of the cliff. That will allow us to get to this downward sloping fissure and place more charges. Then we should be able to move a vast amount of the mountain downwards leaving a deep hole. We will reassess the options from there."

Bronn and the other Gnathe carried the two barrels of explosive and jammed them into the fissure while Pablo set the fuses. They then placed two more barrels under an overhanging slab underneath where the cliff face would drop and Pablo set a longer fuse to these. Everyone else dragged the remaining kegs of gunpowder well out of the way of where the side of the mountain would fall. They spread out along the edge of the cliff and out of the valley where the rocks would fall, using their talent for levitation. Two remained with the young scientist to pull him out of the way as soon as he lit the fuse. Kamiel made sure that Suzzan was safely held to the wall well away from the area of the impending explosion.

Pablo lit both fuses and Thomas and Samuel took him by the arms and lifted him out of the fissure. They flew him to the left and tucked themselves against the other side of the bulging rock-face. Several minutes slowly ticked by and a rumbling, ear-numbing bang shook the air. The sound of tortured rock filled the air as tons of solid cliff began to fall, followed by another deafening bang as the second charge went off, heaving the falling rock outwards as Pablo had planned and over the cliff edge at the end of the valley. Smoke and dust erupted from where the fissure had penetrated the earth and spread out into the gouged out side of the mountain. It took some time before everything settled. My groups of five lifted Pablo and Suzzan around the covering shelter until they were able to stand on the scoured valley floor. The vertical cliff face was gone and a great bite had been taken out of the side of the mountain. The debris was scattered far and wide along the valley floor that now had a distinct crater where the fissure opened into the very bowels of the earth. The area around the crevice had been scoured clean and the fissure widened so that enough room lay inside to pack it with more kegs of gunpowder. It was clear to see by all the jumbled rocks that had once filled the deep fissure that something had blasted the rock aside as it had hurtled into the base of the mountain and cleaved it apart like a giant axe. Rubble and large rocks had dropped to fill the hole behind it, capping the wide cleft. Centuries later another rock-fall opened the fissure by moving the slab of slate away from it, allowing the sun's radiation to penetrate to the bottom and that had awakened me from the shutdown. It was this feeble energy that I had used, to ooze upwards into the light and begin my search.

Pablo turned to Larse and asked, "Demon, are we accomplishing anything? Can you sense the ship any better with the removal of all this rubble? Are we in the right place?"

"Tell Pablo there is a definite echo of my consciousness deep below us. It sleeps, energy it needs to communicate. The fissure to be blown apart it needs. Sunlight must shine upon its surface. Close we are, Larse. Tell him that CLOSE WE ARE!"

Larse smiled at my excitability and answered the scientist, "We are in the right place. Fill the cleft with explosives and open it up to allow the sunshine to shine upon whatever is down there."

The Gnathe were already using their superior strength and rolling the barrels along to the fissure. Kamiel had slipped past them and entered the gaping crevasse to pile the powder kegs as deep as he could put them, until every barrel was accounted for. He pressed the fuses into the topmost barrels and began to pay out the long leads behind him.

Once onto the top he turned to the others watching his progress and said, "I would get some good distance away from here if I were you. When this lot goes up it will take out a lot more of the mountain than the first charges did. I'll give you five minutes before I light the fuses to get as far away from here as you can, counting from now!"

Two Gnathe lifted Suzzan immediately flying her out of the crater while Pablo found himself grabbed by Bronn, lifted into the air and whisked away. The other members of my group were in front of them as everyone moved as fast as they could. We angled around the mountain to get behind the bulge that protected us before and anchored ourselves against the face of the cliff where there was a shelf to stand on.

The minutes slipped by and we were joined by a silver blur that suddenly became Kamiel as he reverted from machine time to ours.

"Any moment now," he shouted. "Cover your ears!"

The concussion when it came sent a shock wave out that could be heard all the way round the mountain at base camp. For us located the other side of the bulge it shook the very bones inside our bodies. For a time we were all deaf as our collective eardrums took a pounding. We could see an enormous cloud of pulverised rock and rubble erupt away from the area of the explosion. Boulders the size of the wagons skipped through the air and sailed out of sight to the lower reaches below us. Enough dust filled the air to obscure the sun and turn it a dim red. We hung on until the time came when everything settled and our hearing came back to normal.

Kamiel had already disappeared around the side of the mountain long before we were back to normal warning us to stay put and wait for his return. I had no choice in the matter and besides that last thing I wanted was for any of my two groups to become injured at this late stage of the operation. So obedient to the nannites wishes we rested while the sun climbed higher into the sky.

Kamiel found himself in a totally altered area of the mountain. The blast had removed a whole section, ripping the mass of rock away from the side of the fissure, penetrating deep into the depths of the earth. There was now a scoop in the cliff face reaching right down to the level of the valleys below at the same altitude of their base camp. A giant bite had been taken out of the mountain, exposing the pulverised area that had been hammered in by a high velocity projectile long ago. Old multiple fissures were opened up by the explosion that led deeper into the congealed rubble that had been fused together by the massive impact. There were traces of a great heat that had melted the rocks so that they ran together like toffee. The Guardian carefully bled the nitro-glycerine from the hump on his back into the putty-like substance he had stored it in and pressed it into the old cracks that pierced the once molten rocks after cooling. Some of the nitro he allowed to drip down into the fissures so that it dribbled deeper into the rocks. The dynamite that he fixed the fuse to he then connected to his solar collector that had been storing an electrical charge. Paying the wire out behind him he retreated to around the cliff face again until he was once more in sight of Larse and the others.

"Prepare yourselves for another explosion. The gunpowder has done the job of removing most of the mountain, but there is a strong case of once molten rock around whatever is down there. This explosive of mine will crack it open and we should be able to see Toarvak 6's ship when it has. Cover your ears again!"

CHAPTER FIFTEEN

Far away on the contaminated area of the spiral arm that the Earth's old Red Sun was located, the ancient remnants of the Goss noticed the use of wormholes by the Gnathe. Almost defeated by the Kresh it needed more units. Here is where it would find and assimilate them. It would need an ark to transfer its many component parts to this rich location. The Goss had one left, unfound by the diligent Toarvak destroyers and still in working condition. It was far out at the tip of the spiral arm, but within range, if it travelled by short hops of a thousand light years or more. By their very construction, wormholes are timeless and exist outside space and time, but time is experienced whilst travelling inside them. It would take centuries of time since the first gate was opened by the Gnathe, for the Goss to find them, but find them it would.

Toarvak 7 had passed the first outer gas giant quite closely and did a slingshot manoeuvre around its gravity field to gain speed. Once drawn close to the massive planet, the ship went out of phase and was unaffected by the pull, thus increasing speed.

The position of where the signal had come from was around the other side of the sun. The intelligence running the planet-killer knew that life would be found there at that temperature range. Its predecessor had declared that the life it had found there was not Kresh. The prime directive ruled its complex mind. That which was not Kresh must be destroyed. The 'Will and the Way' must be as it was ordained. There could be no exceptions!

The sound of the first two explosions had reverberated

around the mountain and echoed down the valley where the Algarie were camped. Although they were settled into the soldier's routine of sleep, eat and keep watch, the cloud of dust that erupted twice into the sky, filled the minds of the men waiting with uncertainty. Already they had marched and led the wagons through a hole in space that the alien, Suzzan had conjured out of thin air. So far, their pride and discipline had held them together, as they had no idea where they were in this wilderness, knowing that the only way home was to obey orders. The repeated explosions made them nervous!

Fernando had left the running of the camp to a veteran of many 'peace keeping' campaigns respected by the soldiers. Captain Fredrick Johansen was a northerner from a frontier settlement similar to Thorn Town. Taken as a boy and educated by the Algarie, he had risen through the ranks to the position he now held. He had been briefed by Fernando about the mission and knew what to expect, so the explosions came as no surprise.

Looking around the anxious faces of his men he decided to tell them a little of what was going on around the mountain.

"This is what we came for! That noise means that Commander Fernando has found what we were sent to find. There will no doubt be more explosions. I can assure you there is nothing to fear," he shouted to the men. "Begin to think about repacking the wagons to go home and be ready!"

The mid-day sun shone directly into the hole that had been torn apart in the side of the mountain. Kamiel's nitro-glycerine and dynamite charges were about to blow. My two groups with Suzzan and Pablo had buried themselves as deeply into the unyielding stonework of the mountainside as they could. We all hung on waiting for Kamiel to send the electrical spark into his carefully laid explosives. Even with our hands pressed firmly to our ears the ear splitting 'crump' penetrated and once more we suffered deafness for quite some time. Kamiel had gone the moment the shock wave had passed. Travelling in machine time, the nannite was a silver blur as he sped around the side of the mountain and in a few minutes he returned.

He placed his hand on the wrist of Larse and connected to his flesh.

I heard his cold communication immediately as Kamiel said, "Toarvak 6 I have uncovered a vast silver bulge that is in direct sunlight. Whatever it is, it is soaking up energy as we speak. You had better make contact with it as soon as you can! Get your group together and do it now!"

I gave an inclusive broadcast to my groups, "*All of my first group make your way to the hole. To our vessel we must contact make. Second group to be close by you must be. Levitate and quickly you must. In command we must be!*"

The five humans rose as of a single mind, followed by the Gnathe who were carrying Pablo and Suzzan. My groups levitated around the shattered rock-face into the deep hole and dropped off the two being carried. We stared into the sun-lit hole at a strange sight. There at the bottom was the shine of a silver-grey material reacting to the sun's radiation, by frothing and bubbling out of the rocky grave it had rested for so long. The area was the size of ten of the wagons we had travelled in and increasing as we stared.

"*Larse closer you must come so that contact I can make. Control it I must, as more of it collects the sun's energy.*"

Larse slipped down the side of the pit to within several feet of the seething mass and pointed his hand towards the surface.

212

I extended my substance to make contact and felt my consciousness drawn back into the very depths of the ship and split. My groups became my anchors, as bit by bit my memories poured back into my soul. I was Toarvak 6, destroyer of worlds, 'The Servant of the Kresh.' Power sang in my neurons as the sun's energy woke more and more of me. I am the WILL and the WAY! That which is not Kresh I must destroy! The pain of remembrance! My crew, long gone and dead beyond resurrection. The last orders of my dying crew must be carried out. The home world lost to the Goss! We were all that was left. I was a mighty weapon and served my masters well!

That which is not Kresh must die! Must die! Must die! Over and over again the order echoed in my mind. So many worlds taken by the Goss. No choice, but sterilisation. No other choice for the Toarvak destroyers to make. Halt the plague at whatever cost!

Suddenly in my pain and agony I was aware of my group. They were new Kresh! New Kresh! They were new crew. My synaptic control began to return and I was aware of another, partially inside me and mostly inside the ship. It was another nannite!

Kamiel had joined his substance with Bronn and communicated with me through her.

"Toarvak 6, have you control? The nannite is called Minnis. I built her long ago. She it was who brought you down before you totally destroyed the 'Three Worlds.' she has been a small part of your mind all the time you have been here on this world. She ejected you before the ship buried itself into the roots of the mountain. Never the less you were buried for centuries. You were never meant to survive, but you did and now have become re-educated and re-programmed by events. I have taken a terrible risk with you, Toarvak 6 for you will be the instrument of our survival. Reconstruct your ship and give your 'New Kresh' somewhere to sit!

I reached out to all the long buried pieces of ME and gathered them in to my magnitude. As more energy flowed into my receptors I could feel my shape beginning to reform. I opened a door to allow my crew and all the others inside. I could sense all of them and as Kamiel had instructed, made places for them to sit or perch! More of my functions came on line and I supplied life support. I began to tear myself out of the mountain's grasp and into the light. Now I had energy to spare as more of me became exposed to the light of the sun. The rocks heaved open as every part of my scattered substance began to make its way back to ME. Parts of the mountain cracked off from the main volume and slid away, exposing more and more of my strewn material to the sun. Once energised it slithered across the scree towards me and oozed into my body. Now that I was totally exposed to the sun, I was as alive as I had ever been and becoming more complete every moment. Fortunately for the men left at the base camp, the point of impact had been away from where they were.

Inside my newly formed living quarters, my crew were getting to better know me and how I worked. Now I had living beings inside me I was capable of anything! I was complete at last and could properly serve my new masters. My new Kresh! My very being sang with joy as these beings I had improved, filled my soul with purpose. This was what I was built to be and do.

"Listen to me my new masters! Into the void above I must go for a short while to bathe in the full strength of this sun's rays. Energy we must have, much greater than what is available to us here. Harm you it will not. Your permission do I have?"

Without a single qualm the human and Gnathe crew replied collectively, "Do it!"

I put us out of phase and allowed the planet-sized moon to orbit away from us, as its gravity no longer affected the structure of the ship. Once out of reach of its gravitational pull, I put us back into phase and bathed in the full strength of the energy giving light while I put us into orbit. Every part of my mind was now operating in full efficiency. No longer did I need the life energy of others! My memories that spanned more than hundreds of thousand of years were at the disposal of my new Kresh.

I had been alone for so long! I had not been constructed to function as a solitary being. The peace of insanity that would destroy my mind could not occur, but the pain of being alone had sent me close to the edge of reason. The only purpose that the Toarvak type destroyers could reply to was the last command given by a living Kresh.

What I knew and remembered, Kamiel and Minnis were assimilating from my mind. I could now communicate direct to the nannites without resorting to them making fleshly contact with my new Kresh! I was aware of the many nannites that had been animated by Kamiel and Selene on the Earth's Moon and sent to the Three Worlds. By extending myself I could speak with Asue, Sharn and Minns at the Cheyenne complex and did so to introduce myself in the company of Kamiel's persuasion. We had energy to spare.

Fernando sat in the command chair and spoke, "Demon, when you have the energy required you must take us back. I have fifty men camped with wagons with no way to get home. We must return and allow Bronn and Suzzan to open a wormhole back to the institute. I will need to see my father and explain to him what it is we need to do next."

I cleared the outside wall at the front to transparency and showed my companions the view of Daedalus Two from where we orbited. I went out of phase and with minimum energy expenditure floated down to the valley where Fernando's men were encamped.

"Room there is for all to travel inside my body. Set down I will at the end of the valley and a door create for your men to enter. Fear of me is what your men must face. Reassurance by you will be necessary, so put you down I could out of sight and greet them you must. This we could do?"

"I did not think of that, Demon," Fernando replied. "Indeed we could all go as you suggest. Set us down just out of sight and I will speak with my men."

"As you wish, I will make it so. Demon was a child's name for me; I am Toarvak 6, defender of all NEW Kresh, your servant and your friend. Please address me as such when you need me."

Larse smiled and said, "Indeed my friend I agree. I called you Demon as I knew of nothing like you and you seemed like magic. Toarvak 6, it is! We have come a long way you and I. I had my dreams of revenge and you, with your quest to find out what you are. We have both travelled a long road. How long have you been alone when you came here?"

I mentally shuddered as the memory flooded back and became aware of all my groups listening.

"Alone I have been for more than two hundred thousand years as you count the rotations around this sun. Obeying the last command the Toarvak machines have! Without guidance we have fought and contained the contamination wherever we have found it. Your civilization hailed me on the same frequency the Goss used. I had no choice but to embark on the awful destructive swathe to contain the contamination. My sorrow knows no boundaries! I grieve."

The mental assault made me wince!

"What are the Goss?"

"There is a thing that lives in flesh. It is a contamination. That which plays host to it has no will of its own! Animal or sentient being it does not care. Where it came from the Kresh never found out. Many civilizations fell to its spread adding their science to its disposal. Even my own masters' world

fell to its contamination. Our world, we fed to its sun to stop them using our science. The Toarvak destroyers are all that is left to stop the spread. In the last hundred thousand years we have exterminated ten civilizations that were infected. Every living thing becomes a carrier to them. It has been quiet for thousands of years and still we the last of the Kresh machines patrol and keep the last command, destroy that which is not Kresh! Toarvak 7 will come here expecting contamination! My sensors tell me that the destroyer is here in this system. Also my sensors have picked up traces of more of my kind in the far reaches beyond the last planet's orbit. We have time to do what you wish, but not much."

Kamiel's interrogation slammed into my mind, "How long have you known this!"

"Angry do not be! This I could not know until this very moment. Memories had I none until awakened the rest of me became!"

There was an almost imperceptible bump as we landed and I opened the side of the wall facing towards the end of the valley. I had eased my way around the mountainside and sank a portion of my mass into the ground by allowing some of my material to go out of phase. The soldiers had not seen me arrive, so all Fernando and Pablo needed to do was to walk around the bend in the valley bottom to approach the camp while I prepared the structure of the ship to accommodate them. I had to construct a space, able to take ten wagons and forty horses to pull them. Also enough space for twelve other horses that had been used by the riders and somewhere for fifty men to stay during the journey. Fortunately it would not take too long! I allowed enough time for the two humans to tell the men of my arrival and eased my mass out of the ground and floated around the bend in the canyon's floor. Fortunately this valley was broad at this end and I could enter almost without scraping the walls. In those places that I did I just took the affected parts out of phase and allowed them to enter the sides. I could see that Fernando had lined them

217

up and were marching them towards me. Pablo was some way in front of the column to show the soldiers that they had nothing to fear. He walked inside the hold I had built, complete with stables for the horses and a cafeteria for Fernando's men. I had synthesized fresh hot coffee and sugar in pots with mugs to drink from. Jugs of milk were placed on the tables. If fresh hot drinks could not sooth the fears of these men I did not know what would. The smell wafted out the open side to the approaching soldiers and the expressions on their faces changed.

It did not take long to lead the horses into the stable area and tie them to the stanchions provided. There was no reason to unhitch them for in a very short time they would be leaving again. As the men were dismissed and sat themselves down to drink their coffee I closed the wall and lifted out of the valley and turned south towards the institute and Lord Samovar.

"Fernando your father contact mind to mind as you have been shown. Arrival we will very soon. Prepared he must be to see us arrive!"

Lord Samovar felt his son enter his mind as the small piece I had left behind activated and the two of them were mentally joined. Francisco leapt to his feet and shouted for captain Peterson and rushed outside.

"Yes Sir?"

"They're back, John and you won't believe what they're coming back in. Tell the men to look to the skies and they will see a massive silver shape coming in to land. It was what my son set out to find. The fact that it is under their control tells me that all has been successful," the reluctant ruler of Daedalus Two said with relief.

As word spread, the entire Algarie contingent poured out of the Institute Buildings and stared up at the cloudy skies, waiting. Soon some began to point as a disc shaped silver craft over half a mile across sped into sight and hovered over the top of the pyramid. Slowly the disc changed shape and supported itself on legs each side of the building. A portion slid down the slope towards Lord Samovar the size of the house he lived in and the front opened. At each supported leg, men were exiting the structure leading wagons and horses to the stables. The bulge at the front reached the ground and Fernando walked out into the sunshine followed by Suzzan. Two nannites followed the procession and once they were all out the bulge sealed off.

Father and son embraced. Fernando's mother and stepmother ran to the two of them and hugged the young man.

Smothered by their affection he at last protested, "Stop! Please! I cannot stay here. There is more to do than you realise. Father I am part of something far larger than you can imagine. When I have time I will tell you more, but for now I have brought the men back and I must leave again. We go to meet Toarvak 7. It is here in this system heading for our civilisation as we stand here and speak. Suzzan-link-khann will tell you all you need and want to know!

Francisco gave his son one more hug, kissed him on his forehead as he had when he was a boy and let him go.

Yolanda shook him by the ears and said, "Come back to me my son. That's all I ask of you. Now go; do what you must!"

Florence stood back and wagged her finger at the boy she had helped to raise.

"You listen to your mother! She cried and turned away so that he did not see the tears that fell from her eyes and rolled down her cheeks.

Fernando turned, walked back into the bulge and I retracted it to return him to the safety of my control room.

Toarvak 7 steadily increased velocity, as it approached the sun and dived into the centre of the nuclear furnace, going out of phase before the heat built up to damage the outer layers. The planet killer had executed this manoeuvre many times to approach the target from the brightness of the star. Around the outside of Toarvak 7, the pressure of the star's compressed mass sparkled under the action of fusion as the vessel slid through the heart of the sun. It took several days to pass through the swirling mass of nuclear explosions that gave life and energy to the Three Worlds and the Kresh machine did not switch back into phase until it closed the distance to the orbit of the second planet from the sun. In phase, the destroyer could be affected by the gravitational pull of the massive ball of sun-backed rock and used it to slingshot towards the gas giant that had the unusually large moons, inhabited by life forms that were not Kresh! Toarvak 7 began to ready projectiles and neutron bombs for the coming sterilisation. All life forms must die! Leave nothing for the Goss to use and multiply with!

The new Kresh were learning how to operate the multi-functions of the ship. The crew of five, operated as a gestalt in tune with the mind of Toarvak 6 with an expanded consciousness. As the Gnathe had found out with their first experiments with opening wormholes, five minds working together created a combined entity much greater than the sum of the parts. This was why, when the entire mental community of Gnathe, human and Apes had bonded together, they had created the power of a God. This was how the Earth and moon had been swallowed by a wormhole and taken through time and space to be put into orbit around Icarus, using the power of a large time distorting crystal.

It was a mixture of mental power and electrical energy transmitted through the crystal. When the crystal shattered, it was due to the stress exerted by the God's mind, when she reached out to the dying world of the Gnathe. She scooped up the topsoil with all of its life forms, transferring it to Jupiter thousands of years into the past and placing it on the western side of the super continent.

The gestalt with Toarvak 6 was different. The machine mind's artificial intelligence was constructed to serve the Kresh as an instrument of additional power. When it bonded to the group mind the guiding entity became far, far greater than the sum of the parts. It became exponential! First the humans and then the Gnathe tried the bonding. When they tried a mixture of both human and Gnathe the function of the bonded mind increased.

It was during one of these learning seminars that we became aware of the approach of Toarvak 7. It was hurtling towards the orbit of the Earth from out of the sun with single-minded intent. I could sense the volley of neutron bombs racked and ready, their one purpose to destroy all life. Using the gravity of the moon I swung around it to put myself on an intersect course. So intent on its mission of destruction it was not programmed to recognise me. All instruments would be set for intersecting alien vessels. I would be approaching from the side and slam into the outside of Toarvak 7 taking the destroyer by surprise and deflecting it from its purpose.

I contacted the intelligence that controlled the destroyer of worlds and flew towards it extending filaments outwards.

"Stop! You will come no closer to these protected worlds. I am Toarvak 6 with a full crew of new Kresh! If you do not obey this order you will be disintegrated!"

"Called me you did. Destroyed were you. That which is not Kresh must be destroyed! The last order must be obeyed!"

"Listen to me! I have new Kresh on board. I have crew for you with me now. Open your memory banks and I will tell you all!"

"There are no Kresh. Our masters gone from this universe are. These worlds destroyed must be. No life must be left for the Goss to"----

We impacted with the deranged vessel.

"Listen to me! Open your mind to mine. Do you not sense the difference in me? I am what we all once were. Do you not want with all your being to regain what was lost?"

We extended the host of filaments to the other ship that had now slowed down in confusion. I made contact with the outer shell and welded us together. Now I put the two of us out of phase with the rest of the universe. Now there was only the two of us in existence. Toarvak 7 was rendered inoperative. Against my augmented mind power the opposing intelligence it was helpless.

"Open your receptors and believe in me. Hear my story of my discovery of NEW KRESH! These are my crew and these are your new crew! Examine all of my memories and be strong again. There is no more need to be alone. Be as you were designed to be. Life support you must provide and your new crew will board. Do it!"

Toarvak 7 examined my memories and my reasoning. It considered and began to alter the life support systems to a copy of mine. We opened a hole between the two ships and a mixed crew of humans and Gnathe crossed over. I kept Larse, Samuel, Jon and two of the Gnathe while Fernando, Thomas, Bronn and two other Gnathe became the gestalt crew for the seventh ship. We phased back into the universe and I detached from the other destroyer.

"We return we will to orbit around the Earth for a while. I have something to ask of the nannites who serve the people that live there. I suggest that you contact the others of our kind that are orbiting this sun amongst belt of the comets and bid them welcome. Offer them new Kresh and show them yours. Bring them here and I am sure that there will be many here that will become their companions. Does Toarvak 3 and 9 still carry the relics?"

Toarvak 7 considered and answered, "They do. Why? They are here at the fringes of this system with all of the others. We all heard your call and feared the worst. Had there been the infection here then we would have all come. I came first to find out how you were destroyed and warn the others. The last command is still paramount. This does not change the situation. We know that the Goss are still out there somewhere searching for new life to spread into."

"Go, old friend and spread the word. They must accept that I have found 'new Kresh'. There is no infection here! I have an idea that I need to talk in private to the nannites that are at the Cheyenne complex. I cannot share it with you as yet. Just bring the others in and get them in orbit around the moons of this gas giant." I agreed with my comrade and said,

"Toarvak 6, my existence has meaning again. I am complete! I have not felt this way in over one hundred thousand years. The others will agree to come. What Toarvak intelligence would want to return to how we were? I will go. Your memories tell me all that I need to coerce the others. They shall share what I have from your memory banks these are indeed 'New Kresh'."

We coasted away from the other destroyer and watched it go, back towards the sun for maximum acceleration to the outer reaches. Sub-space messages were already reaching out to the Toarvak type destroyers to tell of its coming. My new Kresh and I were in tune to each other and down on Daedalus Two were a considerable number of human boy-children, each with a silver ball in his brain. These improved human beings would grow up to become the new Kresh that would crew the other Toarvak destroyers. On Daedalus One, the Gnathe would decide amongst themselves who would join this band of the fortunate improved and also breed accordingly. In the meantime other human and apes would need to be absorbed into the gestalt and await the servants of the Kresh. We had a lot to do in the mean time and I needed to speak with the nannites Sharn and Minns.

We could see the mountains that divided the American lands as we approached from orbit. The Cheyenne complex lay below us and the silver dome of the nannite science labs shone in the morning sun.

CHAPTER SEVENTEEN

The first time that Alexander switched off the time stasis field, Jennet/Link found a world placed on a war footing. The Gnathe had established bases on the larger icy moons of Saturn, Uranus and Neptune. Even on Pluto, because of its orbit, a listening post had been established. Outside of the orbits of the planets lay the vast Kuiper belt with its many moonlets and planetesimals. These had been seeded with crystals as well, by flying the giant gourds out there, piloted by the Gnathe.

On the surface of the solid moons the nannites had constructed detection devices all facing out to the unfriendly dark reaches of interstellar space. The only metals that the Jupiter based society possessed, were the ones that had been traded for with old Earth and they were used sparingly.

Here among the vacuum of space the rescued nannites maintained the detection devices. This was their natural element as they required no air or food, only the weak sunlight was sufficient and when energy stocks became low there were plenty of ice moonlets to convert. From time to time Kamiel-637 had up-dated reports from the other namesakes of the ceaseless watch that yielded nothing. Meanwhile Hannah and her new team of research scientists worked ceaselessly to perfect better long-range scanners.

Nannites are by their nature patient and as long as the situation had not changed, a diligent watch would be maintained. All the Nano-ships and their crews that Link had rescued were more than happy to patrol the empty reaches of the furthest orbits of the icy bodies endlessly circling around the red sun. As time went by they mined the occasional metal rich moonlet that had become trapped out here from the birth of the system. Some, they used the science of Nano-technology on, to reproduce more of their own kind and blended minds to make them different personalities. The over-riding program that was instilled into the newcomers was always the same, to protect the flesh and blood members of their society.

The moment that the time stasis field closed down Jennet and Trann made their way to the wormhole controls and Jennet strapped herself into place gripping the bottom two crystals with her feet and clenching down onto the top two with her hands. This time her mind was joined with Trann's for extra power and she extended its awareness into the matrix. All around the system, spreading far out into the Kuiper belt she was aware of thousands of tiny beacons shining in the night. The only clue she had about the physical whereabouts of the sun and planets she needed to find was that it was closer to the galactic centre than Jupiter. She began to search for a mental signature that would be an echo of Trann's.

Nothing! Nothing that she could get a grip on, but something was there. Something that told her that her daughter lived even though she could not be contacted! The double mind became aware of a third that intruded into their world. It was Alexander!

"Lady Jennet and Trann! Come out! Come out now! You have been in there for more than a day. Sharn has been monitoring your vital signs and they are showing too much stress. You need water and food. Let go and return," the human commanded. "Enough! You must rest and we will try again in another fifty years from now."

Link returned to her body with an awareness of muscle ache, thirst and hunger.

Alexander led the way to a more comfortable perch and seated area where flasks of water were placed on a table.

Plenty of food both hot and cold lay on plates and in bowls for the two time travellers to replace their energy levels. The two Brood-mothers began to eat and drink ravenously as they had started their one-way journey through time without first feeding themselves. The immediate dip into the cosmos searching for the Three Worlds had proved harder than they had thought. The frustrating feelings of disappointment did little to make them feel any better.

Once her appetite had waned, Link/Jennet opened her mind to Alexander and passed over her poor results, but including her feeling that her daughter had survived. There was nothing that she could be sure of, except that she knew as all Gnathe knew whether or not a close family member had died.

"What do we do now, Lady Jennet?" asked Alexander as he looked into the face of his once sworn enemy.

"I for one will get some sleep after you have updated me on what has transpired on this world while I and my daughter have been switched out of it," she said and drank another flask of water. "By the way, Alexander, how has Hannah adapted to being part of the great scheme of things after her death and rebirth?"

"Surprisingly well, all things considered. At least she feels needed by all of the community and Fredrick has adjusted to the reality of her need for him, being the reason he is here. She is trying to develop a better early warning system so that we cannot be crept up to, like the Three Worlds must have been!"

"Yes, I was aware of the expansion far out amongst the scattered and frozen comets. There is crystal everywhere out there. More than enough to construct a box around any invader and cast it into the sun," she said and yawned. "Enough Alex! We must sleep for a while, before we try fifty years more into the future."

Twice more they were brought back into the normal space-time without success. Alexander had travelled with them with Hannah and Fredrick, leaving instructions with his deputies as to when to bring them back. This time the Gnathe decided to eat well before scanning the interstellar reaches. The human part of the time travelling crew decided to take a little time revisiting the rest of the defence commitments and find out what progress had been made. They parted their separate ways and agreed that Link should start a sweep tomorrow.

During the meal, Link/Jennet turned to her daughter and said, "I think you should visit my Egg-sister, Chang and spend a little time with her. Look around at the homestead and enjoy a well-earned rest for a while. She will be pleased to see you after all this time and you can tell her that I will come to visit her very soon. I will come before I travel onwards into the future. Go after this meal and surprise her. I will stay here and rest for a bit."

"Are you sure mother? I must admit I would enjoy seeing Chang again. It would make a change to be fussed over by someone!"

"Trann! You know that I do not make a great deal of emotive nonsense towards you, but you are my daughter and I have a great love for you. I value your mind!"

Trann stood up and laughed at her Brood-mother perched indignantly on the other side of the table and said, "You are so much fun to tease!"

"You spend too much time with humans! Now go and I will scc you tomorrow!"

The Lady Jennet-soo-shang, once Link-soo-shan the Ultimate Ruler and one time Tyrant watched her daughter disappear with pride. Although not quite genius level, she was a lot more intelligent than most of the Gnathe, as was her sister Suzzan. Some genetic secrets she had kept from the masses for herself. She walked over to the building that housed the wormhole machine, to see what extra refinements had been added in the last fifty years. The nannite constructed four-sided open pyramid had been rebuilt with refinements in her absence. She could see extra crystals inserted into the silver sided system. The conical construction still faced horizontally so that the open end had a flat floor to walk on, but the sides were studded with extra command crystals all connected to more telekinetic types. In the last fifty years someone had increased the power and range of the wormhole creator, beyond anything that Link/Jennet had envisioned.

Her inquisitive mind was alight with curiosity. She just had to try it. The whole place was quiet and there wasn't a technician or Gnathe anywhere to be seen. She stepped onto the perch and gripped the four command crystals with fingers and toes to try out the feel of the device and un-expectantly tripped the power switch with her weight on the perch.

This was the very time frame that Toarvak 6 had oozed out of a fault in the side of the mountain. There would still be some time to pass before the reality of the Kresh machines would be solved after Suzzan was released from the time stasis experiment being carried out on Daedalus One.

The powerful mind of the one time Ultimate Ruler stretched out into the matrix and was aware of every single beacon in the interstellar darkness. The sharpness and the clarity almost overwhelmed her. She was even surer that her daughter was still alive, even though she could not contact her. She looked deeply into the galactic centre for some sign of mental activity and found a whisper of Gnathe and human minds. She decided to wait until tomorrow before she concentrated her will in that direction again. She would need the extra strength of her daughter's mind to increase the power and maybe she would build a greater group mind to fish in this direction. Before she stepped off the weight activated perch she sent her questing mind out into the opposite direction and became abruptly aware of an ancient evil.

Her mind was filled with a hunger that set her teeth on edge and filled with alien memories.

The mind was ancient and made of millions of creatures bonded together without free will. It was old, so very old that its years were measured in billions. It had come into being when this sun was first shining on a world that had yet to live. It had used many species of creature to host its parasites. Its home world had eventually become a planetary mind composed of every living thing's consciousness all bound to the propagation of the symbiotic parasite. The first sentient beings that had landed on the Goss's planet had soon succumbed to the spores and had increased the intelligence level exponentially. They had unwillingly taken the infection back with them. Now the spores had a means to spread beyond its home world.

Civilization after civilization fell to the parasite. Every new world found, spread the spores and became part of the Goss. The mind of this abomination was wracked by a constant hunger to propagate. All those who carried the spores retained their individual minds, but no free will. Breeding programs were set up to increase the populations, so that more spores could find an unwilling home. Genetic improvements were made to enable the hosts to carry more of the spores and spread them when the carrier died. This could be at any time whenever the spores would trigger off a ripening. The hosts' body would die, but the spores could keep the host from final dissolution and the only retreat of the captive mind was madness, until the body decayed to the point that it could not move and the spores left it. The cities of the Goss were minimal life support places so that the maximum amount of flesh could be stacked together to give the greatest number of hosts. All life existed to give the Goss a home in living flesh.

There could be no resistance and no cure for the fungal spore infection until the Empire of the Goss met the Kresh. The Kresh were partially immune and it had exploring ships away from the planetary home. These they alerted and the Toarvak exploring ships became destroyers. They fought the Goss from system to system destroying all infected worlds wherever they found them, driving the abomination back. At last the home world was found of the Goss and sterilised. The Kresh fed their own world to their sun rather than allow the Goss to infest it any more than it had and take the results of their science. Bit by bit they destroyed the empire of the Goss, seeking out its arks in the outer darkness and hurling them into the nearest star. Still the search went on and the Goss hid away from the last ships of the Kresh.

All of this flooded into Link-soo-shan's mind in the instant she made contact. Desperately she constructed barriers in her mind to shut it out. The Goss dug in and removed Kamiel's conditioning to make her its puppet.

The ancient voice roared in her head, "**There was one Ark left, little one and I survived. I am even now building a fleet of ships to search for you. Your use of wormholes alerted me and from your thoughts, I can see that you can do this with your minds! You will be welcome inside the Goss. I have a world that has sentient life. I have plundered it for metal and fuel. These people are mine and easy to control. Join me and I will give you dominion over all that lives on your world and you shall have immortality!**"

Each thought drove into her mind like a white-hot spike.

Link-soo-shan was filled with an old hatred that sang through every nerve-end. The loss of her original egg-sister Chang and her Empire throbbed in her mind. The humiliation of her new station in life filled her mouth with acid. She was Gnathe and these humans and apes were dross beneath her talons. This world belonged to the Gnathe as once it had belonged to her, from the mountains to the sea.

The seductive offers began! The false promises etched out how it could be!

It could be hers again!

She would build wormholes for the Goss, helping it spread and spread until it infested every world in this galaxy and still it would not be enough!

It promised that the spores would not feast upon her flesh and she would never die! All of her old enemies would scream out her name in agony and terror, unable to defend themselves from her pleasures and the pain she could inflict.

As she frothed at the mouth, twitching spasmodically in the thrall of the Goss, it spoke again, **"Do this for me little one and live for ever! Show me where you live and be my ally. You shall have something of mine a piece of my gestalt to be with you so that you will not forget my offer!"**

A hungry rat-mind wriggled and bit in her consciousness burrowing into her mind. It was a cunning animal intellect that mentally stung and fed off her memories making a copy of all she knew. Even in her bitter hatred she could not snuff it out. It was looking for her knowledge of where she was!

"Where are you, little one? Ah! Somewhere in that direction! A little more --------"

Link-soo-shan wrenched herself from off the scaffold and

released her hold on the crystals. She lay on the floor in a pool of her own vomit gasping for breath, all the time conscious of the rat-mind ferreting about in her memories. She concentrated her mind to the two small command crystals she carried in her wrist pouches and brought them into contact with the telekinetic one at her throat and sought for the location of Alexander.

There was a distinct 'pop' of expanded air as she materialised in Alex's sleeping area next to his bed. The leader of the humans and apes slept soundly on his side facing away from her. His breathing was regular and slow. Link-soo-shan imagined the joy she would feel by breaking his neck and stretched out her hands towards her old foe. From the smallest of the three fingers to her thumb, her hand was twice the size of any human's and she clearly remembered the pleasure she had throwing his body against the wall when she had brought him back from the Citadel.

The rat-thing's bloodlust was swelling in her mind as her hand reached the shoulder of the sleeping man. She abruptly walled it off behind a block she had just constructed in her mind.

She gently shook the Mayor awake; - fighting the almost overwhelming urge to choke him to death and said, "Wake up Alexander. Wake up before I kill you!"

Alexander was out of the bed and across the room by reflex action, ducking under her arm. He stood behind a chair, while he hit the communication button, putting him in contact with the ever-watchful Kamiel. He stared up at the massive form of the Brood-mother twitching and shaking before him. She was clenching and unclenching her hands into fists. Flecks of spittle coated her chin and vomit stains coated her fur down the front of her chest. Her eyes looked as if she had seen the bottom of Hell. They were wide and staring with the split pupils opened to the maximum capacity.

"Keep me constrained," she pleaded, "before I rip your head off!"

Kamiel and Asue appeared and immediately welded her arms and upper torso to the wall with strips of nannite, in machine time, so that all Alex could see were two, silver blurs.

"Do not attempt to go into my mind without backup. Get my daughter Trann. Find Azander, Marren and Ender-whann-soo with more adepts if you can. I have something in my mind! I cast my mind out to find any traces of the Three Worlds using the new apparatus. I think I found faint traces and let go until tomorrow. I foolishly sent my mind into the other direction and contacted an ancient evil. In an instant it turned me back to how I was."

Alexander had known Jennet/Link a long time and knew not to question her until her conditions had been met. He did as he was asked and soon was joined by his old friend Ender and a number of other older Gnathe.

Ender and her daughters faced the one time Empress, who had her limbs broken and was left on the 'Killing Stones' to die of thirst for disobeying her laws.

"Lady Jennet," she said, "tell us as much as you can before we go into your mind."

"I have memories of an abomination that has ruled an Empire for millions of years, spreading along this galactic arm. It is something that will sicken you to the roots of your being and it wants to come here! It needs us! We would become its puppets! It left me with a terrible gift, the mind of something vicious that mentally bites! Get it out before I lose my control. Please!"

Ender built a group mind, taking Alexander with her and leaving one of the Gnathe behind as an anchor.

The raw emotion of boiling hatred roasted the first probe that the group mind sent in and they recoiled trying again. The gestalt reached behind the block that Link had imprisoned the alien thing and tore the rat-mind apart. Now it probed the well of hatred that Link was sinking inside and one by one they excised the repressed emotions that the Brood-mother had long held at bay. The long years spent in the company of Kamiel's mind, waiting for Alexander McBald to age and take control of the Genesis project began to exert influence. Alexander had spent a great deal of time with the altered Link-soo-shan, sharing Kamiel's mind when they had both waited for the years to pass on the space station, until they at last were able to return without altering the time-lines. They had got to know and even like each other during the passing years, becoming friends. Alexander lent some of his mental strength to his old enemy to give her support.

Link's genius level mind had been able to overcome the penetration of her mind by the Goss. Her ruthless logic had held sway and she could see through the alien's offers of dominance as a sham, besides which she had outgrown all of those early enmities. This was her world and she would fight for it to the last breath. This society was entirely due to her actions and reactions many years ago. Without her none of this reality would exist. These were her people! Her healed mine joined the gestalt and opened up the alien memories to their inspection. Once all details had been shared amongst the group mind they returned to their own bodies to think about the spread of the Goss.

"Listen to me my friends," Link/Jennet said to them all. "This thing is ancient beyond belief, but is only as immortal as its hosts. Now that I am free of its conditioning I can view its history without fear. It knows of my existence and what we can do with group minds and wormholes. It will

235

seek out my mind again as it now understands my mental signature. This thing knows me! The Goss will try anything to infect us here on this world. We have lived in the most virulent atmosphere of any life form. The nannites could not design Nano probes to destroy every infection at once, but one by one Sharn has tailored nannites to form screens that prevented any of our microorganisms from travelling through the gates. She needs to work on a system of delivering self-replicating nannites programmed to destroy one thing only. We need to take a prisoner or two to keep for testing. My mind will be like a magnet to this thing. Put me in stasis for ten years and I will direct my mind back to the Three Worlds when the time has passed. I felt a faint echo of Gnathe and human life when I looked in that direction. Let it alone and I will see if it has grown stronger when I am reactivated. In the meantime work on a way to find the Goss before it finds us! Make sure that nothing can get through from any direction!"

Alexander turned to the rest of the Gnathe and said, "I cannot think of a better idea than the Lady Jennet has given us. We need to put her mind where this abomination cannot find her. Kamiel and Asue we need you to work on this possibility to eradicate the spores for all time. Tell Hannah what we have found out this day. Trann will also be travelling forwards with Jennet for twenty or more years and then we shall see if her senses were playing tricks on her. No one is to use the wormhole apparatus to focus their minds anywhere until Jennet returns. In the meantime there is much for us to do, regarding defending this world against the Goss.

Ten years after the 'gathering' all nine of the Toarvak ships were crewed by 'new Kresh' and were busy building an impenetrable defence around the Three Worlds.

On Earth, Sharn and Minns had brought forth real Kresh from the samples given over by the Toarvak ships. The aliens had been a mixture of exact clones of the crew with a successful attempt to produce a combination of the genetic patterns to create new individuals. All of the immature Kresh were born as fully functioning hermaphrodites and as they reached a certain point in their development, became sexually aware. The Kresh stood upright on two legs that were jointed the same as a human with large splayed feet. The arms were different however and had two elbows and a wrist terminating in a three-fingered hand with two opposable thumbs. The head had two eyes facing forwards bright blue in colour with a split iris like the Gnathe. They were able to see into the infrared end of the spectrum, so they could see in the dark. The muzzle jutted forwards to a single hole, with a large bulge on each side that sprouted whiskers as wide as the outsides of its face. The crowning glory were the ears that could swivel around to face any noise. They stood upright and were shaped like a long ellipse that was twice as long as their heads and slightly cupped. There were masses of whiskery hairs around the edges. From top to toe they were covered in velvety fur of different colours. Some were pie-balled and some were the same colour all over. The sounds that they made were ultra-sonic squeaks that only they could hear. Fortunately they were all born telepathic and because of the Toarvak ships extensive memory banks they could be raised, as they would by their own kind. Some of the nannites that had arrived from the moon had adopted the Kresh shape, spending their time with the young as role models and nursemaids.

The only things different in their lives, was that they grew up knowing the alien world of their re-creators all around them. The Gnathe found their minds a delight in complexity and monitored their progress as they grew. When the sex change began the aggressiveness of the changelings waned and a different mindset took over. Those that felt predominately female formed groups that became a family, each with a male-minded Kresh or two as a central pivot. The males after breeding would change sex to female and a female-minded Kresh would become male if she were not carrying young.

As time went by one of the Kresh would begin to put on weight and become the dominant member, thickening up his/her arms and legs to become a possible formidable fighter. They were referred to as 'First and whatever Clan he/she headed plus the colour that her fur pattern became.

The names became too unwieldy for human, ape and Gnathe to be sure of, so they were all called by their rank as 'First'. All of the clans were created on the basis of the most easily formed group minds amongst the individuals. Those who had captained the Toarvak ships were all complete Clans or families. They had been picked for exploration not combat, but had adapted very quickly. The newborn Kresh had all been taught the history of their coming into existence and were eager to resume the hunt for the remains of the Goss. Before all of the alien species got to that stage a blending of science and psychic abilities needed to happen. Without crystal, this was not possible, so Toarvak 6 and 7 were going crystal mining on the surface of the gas giant, Icarus with their crew of New Kresh.

CHAPTER EIGHTEEN

We lifted from the surface of Daedalus One as a complete unit. The over-mind took over as identities merged and Toarvak 6 went out of phase. Next to me the company of Toarvak 7 rose in tandem and then began to fall towards the seething gas giant below us. We both were on board an independent group of Gnathe in each ship. Each group had 'borrowed' the activating telekinetic crystals from the wormhole station at the Cheyenne complex. Without them the wormhole was shut down and no traffic could be actioned between the Three Worlds. New Kresh and Toarvak worked as one mind, as it had been designed to be. In the Kresh language Toarvak meant collective and in the losing of my individuality I gained the awareness of the gestalt mind. The over-mind commanded and my systems obeyed. The clarity of purpose coupled with the extent of intellect that the group mind possessed, made the entire Toarvak move and think like a living organism. This is how it was to be Toarvak! I was completely alive again for the second time in hundreds of thousands of years.

For several seconds we went back into phase and allowed the massive world beneath us reach out to the substance of the ship with its gravitational pull. Immediately both Toarvak ships began to drop towards the orange and red planet below. Bright, white cloud formations stayed separate from the orange swirls and danced in slow motion around the upper bands. The view of the gas-giant filled the observation screens to the point that we seemed suspended over an endless swirling horizon of bright colours. Storms the size of the planet sized moons reached out for us as we continued to drop.

Once again we went out of phase and entered the first

cloud layers. Violent disruptions exploded around us as turbulence from deep beneath, caused the clouds to swirl and eddy. Lightning flashed and forked in and around my surface. We were suspended in a void of bright orange and deep brown smoky pillars that darkened as we dropped.

We needed to go much deeper into the maelstrom. Under instruction from the Toarvak mind I allowed a small amount of my substance to return to the universe and felt the gravitational pull of 2.5 gravities exert itself on that bubble. Outside, the pressure was rapidly climbing to twenty atmospheres and the temperature ascending from minus one hundred and fifty Celsius to the upper thousands the deeper we went. This region became an inky darkness the deeper we dropped. After some time we entered the region of liquid metallic hydrogen and the outside temperature exceeded thirty thousand degrees Celsius. The pressure outside had climbed to twenty thousand times the atmospheric level of Earth before we entered this region. Now it climbed to several million times, as we entered the sea of metallic hydrogen and approached solid ground. Under this mantle of super condensed material lay the rocky, silicate core. It was inside this outer crust that the crystals formed. Down here the pressure went off the scale and squeezed anything of a crystalline nature into bizarre compounds under the heat. Some of the crystals exuded into other dimensions under this pressure and could distort time itself when channelled. They all needed tuning to be of any use.

The Gnathe had become sensitive to the psychic enhancing qualities of these immensely hard gemstones and had altered their genetic balance to be able to use them. Whatever natural telepathic abilities were inherent in the Gnathe, the crystals increased them exponentially.

Other qualities were also enhanced by contact with the crystals, depending what abilities they improved. They had colonised a world that had started off as a gas giant and had its deep mantle of gas stripped away by the expanding sun when it changed sequence from being a yellow star to a red giant.

We were looking for crystal under very different conditions. I felt the outer layer of my substance lower into the interface of silicate rock until the small piece of me that existed in the outside universe ground into it and stopped my downwards movement. Now the Gnathe adepts grouped their minds into a tightly held collective and sent their telekinetic grasp outside the Toarvak. They were sat inside the bubble that remained in this universe, protected by my outer shell, but resisting two and a half gravities and millions of atmospheres of pressure.

Halfway around this world Toarvak 7 was doing the same as we were. Both group minds were aware of each other as they sought for the crystal reefs. In the pitch-blackness the group mind felt along a rift in the silicate rocks that was glowing dull cherry red under the intense heat. Here jutting into the metallic hydrogen was what we had came for. A spur of crystalline growth had been squeezed out of the bedrock of this world. Welded into this slab of rock were imbedded all types of raw crystal.

The group mind indicated to the Toarvak and I obeyed. The surface of my substance sank into the ground and contained the entire mass. Once all of the crystalline growth had been encapsulated I put the entire piece out of phase with the universe. We nipped the prize out of the bedrock and stored it away to cool, when we returned to the higher levels. The Gnathen power of five reached out again with her telekinetic sense and found more of the rift. Once again Toarvak and Suzzan's group mind worked in tandem to remove and store the crystalline growths. The seventh Toarvak and its Gnathen crew were achieving a similar rate of success around the other side of the world. By now however the Gnathe were beginning to feel the strain of working under two and a half gravities in their bubble of the outside universe.

The Toarvak heard the command, "**Up and away from here. Enough!**"

I obeyed my group mind and separated our ship from the universe and put us all out ofphase. Immediately the pull lessened on the Gnathe and they began to feel better and we drifted out of the gas-giant's grasp. As we rose into the frigid layers of the outer clouds I allowed the area around the crystals to benefit from the cooling effect by partially re-phasing the hold of the ship. As there was now no need to remain as a Toarvak the individual minds returned to each body and enjoyed the view from the observation deck.

Larse, Samuel, Jon, Jaffin and Sing-mace-khann gathered together and just stared through the wide port at the world beneath them. Stood with them also was Suzzan and her four partners who had directed the telekinetic fishing expedition. To these flesh and blood creatures the vision of the gas giant rotating beneath us was a wonder to behold. Through my long association with humans I to could appreciate what we had accomplished. To all the Toarvak ships the way we operated was not a mystery, as it was what we were designed to do, but it was the first time we had fished inside a gas giant! The Kresh had no reason to do what we had just accomplished. This was a spin-off from a different point of view, using a science that belonged to someone else.

Larse pointed at the swirling vortex beneath us and

said, "That area down there could swallow our home moon without touching the sides! I can hardly believe what we have just done!"

Suzzan gave a short laugh and replied, "Just you wait and see what we can achieve with almost unlimited crystal. I will have to re-activate Khann-link-sool's mind that is stored in my crystal case to help tune these untouched gems. We need her to work with us. Some time ago I asked Sharn if they could grow a clone of her descendant, Shan-khann-soo and keep it mindless. That Gnathe has now reached maturity in the life-vat and is ready for implantation. Her mind is far too valuable to allow to go to waste."

I directed the Toarvak vessel towards the ancient planet Earth and spoke to the assembled minds, *"Approach do we to the Cheyenne complex soon. Ready you must be to disembark. The crystalline rocks excavated from Icarus have been cooled. Broken them apart have I, so that you may examine the crystals without delay."*

Beneath us two large flat-bedded trucks had been parked away from the entrance waiting for our precious cargo. Toarvak 7 had positioned itself above the nearest to the entrance and extended a tube to the open container. Like eggs slipping down an ovipositor the crystals were passed into the truck's storage place. Never had so many crystals been seen in one place and I had my load to deliver also. Both ships had sorted and cleaned the silicate fragments from the crystals so that only pure un-tuned crystal was delivered. These had yet to be sorted into types and the shaping of these would have to wait for the re-activation of Khann.

On Daedalus Two the growing of the gourds for use in space had reached harvesting time. It would soon be time to manufacture glass from the abundant sand deposits. Already a number of nannites from the moon had taken up residence with the Gnathe and were offering their skills for the benefit of the transplanted colonists. The 'Silver Ones' as they were known amongst the Gnathe, had built a furnace and had taught some of the kindred how to smelt iron and turn it into steel on a small scale. The original Carriers and the Zanth had been transported as young, centuries ago when the genetically altered Gnathe had arrived on Daedalus Two. They had done very well on the new world under the yellow sun and had soon returned from the wild after Toarvak 6 's attack, to the control of the Gnathe. Now with steel at their disposal the kindred soon learned how to make carts and harness them to the carriers to increase their load carrying abilities. All the gourds needed, were to be fitted with the crystals harvested from Icarus, so that they could be teleported into, without damaging the outsides other than the window aperture. The glass observation windows were put in from the inside so that air pressure sealed them against the outer shell. Nannite expertise kept them in place and Nano-technology kept them clean. Soon the teams of five would take them into orbit to test them once the crystals were tuned.

The host world to the Goss had been developed by the parasite driven Bazantii for more than two hundred years since its arrival. Spoil heaps spread across once green pastures. The air was foul and rank around the foundries that were producing the metals necessary to the manufacture of the armada that the Goss was building. Wherever oil could be found the Bazantii had been forced to drill for it and processing plants had been built as close as possible. The Goss had infected every living thing that breathed on this world. Animals toiled side by side with the cat-people and when hunger from those that endlessly worked could no longer be endured, the weakest was offered up to fill the empty bellies of the carnivores. The Goss was very efficient with its life supporting hosts. The rat-things from its home world it allowed to spread and breed and feed off the leavings and rotting food left over by the Bazantii. All were host to the spores of the Goss, but there were never enough warm living things for the Goss to breed inside. Fresh meat, fruit and vegetables were lifted regularly up to the ark to supplement its supplies.

The mind link had shut down too soon for the intelligence to know exactly from where the mind of the creature called Link-soo-shan had originated. This was the first time it had made contact with an independently psychic minded being, that was familiar with telepathy. What it had picked up was the fact that these creatures could open wormholes with their minds! Once it had them in its collective, the whole of this galaxy would be open for its use and spreading. Only one creature had stood against it and nearly obliterated its spread. All it knew about them was that they called themselves Kresh and now there were no more. It had them in its grasp for a short time before those so far unaffected had destroyed their world, rather than letting it blend their science with all the other sentient creatures it had assimilated.

This was its greatest problem with the cultures it took over; no original work of any kind was ever done again. These latest additions to its collective mind had no technology of their own, so the Goss had to implant the knowledge that it had gained from the others. It had to keep up the breeding rate amongst these quite short-lived creatures, or its own mind would begin to fail. There were a few thousands of the builders of the Ark still alive, but their breeding rate was falling and it needed new minds to control. Already the Bazantii had matted coats and flabby muscles where poor diet and lack of proper exercise were taking its toll. The cities that the Goss built were minimal life support, comprising of shelters to keep out the cold and wet, with communal sleeping quarters where the Goss would encourage the Bazantii to breed. It provided nurseries for the young to wean from their mothers and as soon as they were able to work under its command, work they did. There was no love on this world or any tenderness and care. This was a Goss dominated world and it existed to do its bidding.

Once, the Goss had dominated five star systems and its mind had been a vast thing full of knowledge stolen from its hosts. Great Arks had been constructed and sent to find new life bearing planets. One had found the Kresh and infected their world. The Kresh had proved to be partially resistant to the spores and had sent messages to their own exploring ships warning them of the home world's peril. Their science had been the most advanced that the Goss had ever seen, at its cost. Rather than allow the Goss to steal their secrets, they had torn their world out of orbit and sent it into the sun to cleanse it of the infecting spores. The exploration ships had modified themselves to become offensive destroyers and had hunted down and totally cleansed each planetary stronghold of every air-breathing, living creature that the Goss had infected. They then set out to find and destroy all the Arks, each the size of Earth's moon, scattered throughout space. Long after the last Kresh died the Toarvak destroyers still hunted for the infestation obeying the last order.

It took them more than a hundred thousand years to achieve this success, but they still were not able to know that they had found all of the infected worlds and Arks.

One Ark had not been found and had left all the others to be hunted down as sacrifices. The Goss was as ruthless as it was resourceful and very, very patient.

The Goss had hidden from the search by voyaging far out on the edge of the galactic arm where the stars were sparse, leaving all the infected behind. It had survived by raiding the poor worlds orbiting the red dwarfs and feeding the Ark's needs. As each of the infected worlds were cleansed and the Arks found and destroyed the Goss diminished. In between journeys the majority of the life forms were put into suspended animation until the Goss parked the Ark in orbit around a star. Whilst the sentient people slept, the parasite went into a lower state of consciousness. Each time it awoke fully, more of the units that gave it its mind's power had died. It was desperate for fresh hosts when it found the Bazantii world.

The inside of the Ark was laid out as a composite world to provide life support for the myriad life forms collected from all the worlds that the Goss had touched with its infection. A central artificial sun provided light and warmth deriving its power from the sun they orbited.

Intelligent people were bred to provide a host for the mind of the Goss to thrive. There were thousands of each species all providing the collective mind for the parasite to be and control. Many of the occupants had never seen the outside of the Ark's environment and lived and died inside the artificial world. The only time that they went outside would to gather and mine whatever minerals the Ark needed to sustain life. Breed, eat and die was all any of the sentients could hope for and to provide the Goss with a warm living host. There were five different intelligent species of alien people, all living together on the inside of the moon-sized ark. The spherical vessel spun rapidly to provide artificial gravity to the inhabitants. The closer to the poles the life inside spread, so those who lived there felt a lesser gravity. Those that had evolved in the highest gravity lived and farmed around the false equator. Bands of settlement spread out from there towards the poles. The Goss did not interfere with the lives of its collective mind and allowed them to exist where they wished. When it needed an outside work force to gather minerals and metal ores, then it directed those it selected to the numerous spacecraft stored away.

The Ark itself was controlled from a centre at the 'North' pole that did not rotate with the rest of the vessel. It was here that the Goss kept an assorted crew that it used to direct the giant ship to operate the drive and weapons systems. None of the aliens could communicate with each other on a personal nature, all obeyed the Goss who did their thinking for them.

The insectoids were happy in the lighter gravity so had little problems with being in free-fall. The queens and their attendant males were settled in the highest region of the spinning moon, leaving the sterile females to do the Goss's bidding elsewhere. They were the size of a large dog and made up in numbers for their size. The bottom of the insectoids resembled a large egg with the blunt end facing forwards. They ran around on six legs jointed from this bottom section. On top of this was fixed a globe with four equal-spaced arms that carried a mixture of pinchers and tendrils. The heads rose from this body on a short neck and were covered in cilia that waved in an intricate dance around the eight eyes spaced around the top of the head. The mouthparts ended in a pair of powerful mandibles capable of severing a human leg. Evolution on their world had produced intelligence in these creatures and a telepathic link so that individual minds could link up to solve greater problems. The main intelligence resided in the queens and the flying males provided the creative insights that drove them. All of them could group together to form a complete unit and so they made excellent servants for the Goss.

Around the central section lived the reptilians that were used to a higher gravity than the other life forms. The Lagdoo resembled the Raptors of prehistoric Earth, only with six digit hands and slender prehensile tails. They were omnivores and had a totally logical mind. These were the people that had discovered the Goss and had been mastered by the infestation and forced to spread it to the other worlds. They had discovered how to force wormholes into existence by using 'black hole' gravitational warping. Now they were the only ones left of their kind and yearned to wander under a natural sun. Some had been sent down to the Bazantii world to over-see the toiling six-legged cats.

The other spaces of the inside of the Ark were occupied by the Conics. These people were shaped like a double inverted cone. From the bottom, there were a series of eight donut shaped rings, gradually reducing in size towards the head, forming the first truncated cone. On top of this were two more of the same size, forming a neck and three more rings opened up again to form a head.

The top donut housed the mouth at the top and was surrounded by six eyestalks that gave them an all around view. Just below the double ringed 'neck' a set of six tendrils sprouted, followed by another six more powerful, four rings down. Underneath the bottom ring a set of sturdy, short jointed legs ended in squat feet that could send the Conic in any direction. Their method of communication was by varying the colours of the top ring, while the rest of the Conic remained any colour it wished depending on its mood. Their speciality had been electronics driven by their abilities to channel stored electricity within their own bodies. Primitive Conics had hunted their prey and stunned them with an electric shock carried within one of its lower tendrils. They had not yet developed space flight when the Goss enslaved them, but had added their science to enhance the collective once taken.

The other race of beings, that were held to be another host to the Goss were known as the Thipdar. They were trip'o-dal creatures with two legs at the front and a single leg at the back ending in ball-shaped pads. With the legs locked the Thipdar could stand perfectly motionless for any length of time. From the shoulders were two large arms with two smaller ones underneath. At the ends of the wrists were three fingered hands with opposable thumbs. The hands on the heavy arms had fingers that came to bony points. The smaller arms had delicate hands with touch sensitive pads on the fingers.

The head was shaped like a globe with a flattened surface. Two round eyes that shut sideways stared out of the alien's face below a broad forehead. Its ears were pointed at both top and bottom and stood out from the creature's head facing to the front. Some way under the eyes was positioned the mouth, hidden by a row of tendrils that hung down over its chin. The skin was smooth and a golden colour with sprays of dark spots curling over it. They like the Lagdoo were also a space faring race and had welcomed the infected ship to land on their world. They had just started to explore the system of planets and moons of their home system when the Goss put an end to all that.

In orbit around the Bazantii world the Goss waited for another sign from the mind of the creature it had tantalised with the offer of immortality and almost limitless power. It understood the need for revenge and the sweet feeling of winning. It was time to avenge its demise by the Kresh. The Goss wasn't fussy and any warm living thing would do, but preferably intelligent hosts were to be preferred. The parasite needed to increase its intellect from the remnants that it possessed at the moment and the Gnathe would do very well! It dreamt of spreading from star to star until it filled this Galaxy. What then?

The body in the growing vat stirred in its mindless sleep. The muscles had been stimulated throughout the long process from the moment that Shan-khann-soo divided her egg into two and gave one up to Sharn's tender care. An accelerated growth rate had been applied so that adulthood had been obtained at a more rapid pace. Shan was still carrying the single Brood-mother young in her pouch and marvelled at the progress of the clone.

Suzzan-link-khann nodded to Sharn as she opened the battered case with her crystals set into their separate niches. She reached for the one that carried Khann-link-sool's memories and personality, plucking it out. She rested it in the palm of her hand and wondered to herself of the consequences of what she was about to do. The liquid had all but drained down to the bottom of the vat and the mindless hulk settled into its harness when she pressed the crystal to the dent in the Brood-mother's forehead and bound it in place. A mild shock was given to induce the sleeping body to breath and waken.

The chest gave a shuddering gasp and inflated. The hands clenched and unclenched. Underneath the feet the last of the liquid drained away and the glass sides slid down into the floor leaving the Gnathe stood.

The eyes opened and stared at Suzzan, while Khann cleared her mouth and spat the viscous fluid upon the floor.

"What have you done?" She said.

"You are needed. Do you think I would do this lightly? Remember that you said to me when we activated the crystals, that I should not be afraid to waken you again. That time has come. We have more crystal than you have ever seen in your previous life, all of it un-tuned," Suzzan replied to the stunned Gnathe.

"This body has no mind! I have been given another lifetime," she exclaimed in wonder. "Give me mental contact with you. I need to be aware of all that has happened since I was last awake."

Suzzan told her again of the Goss and all of the implications and their progress up to this moment.

Many light years away Link-soo-shan had once again returned to the outside world from the stasis field of the time distorter. She had demanded all the news and a good meal before she tried to focus her mind onto the direction of the Three Worlds. This time she made sure that she would not alert the Goss to her presence by weaving a mind shield around the wormhole apparatus. Ender-whann-soo and her daughters had travelled forward in time, leaving their kindred to tend their homestead without them, under the eye of the lady Jennet's egg sister, Chang, who was now beginning to show her age. She was carrying Brood-mother young with the intent that they would take over her affairs when she died. Jennet/Link had time hopped a great deal of time and was still in her prime with possibly at least a thousand years ahead of her.

The nannites she had saved from the empty reaches of the galactic arm had built a civilization of their own far out from the red sun that warmed Jupiter. All they needed was the location of the Goss and they could exact the cure. But first there were other plans to bring to fruition.

Link-soo-shan tried the wormhole apparatus with her daughter linked with her, this time with Alexander as an anchor. Ender and her daughters concentrated on the mind-shield to keep her safe. Now when she directed her mind towards the Three Worlds, a number of beacons shone out in the darkness of the Matrix. This time she could feel short gates in constant use and the overwhelming identity of her other daughter, Suzzan. Now she reached out for the main gate at the Cheyenne complex and made the connection. Immediately Alexander ordered the trickle charge to be powered into the grid to hold the wormhole in place.

CHAPTER NINETEEN

Without any warning, the gate on Earth's wormhole section opened and a number of Gnathe and humans walked through, all dressed in form-fitted silver suits.

The leading Gnathe surveyed the astonished group, moving crates of foodstuffs into storage and said, "Who is in charge here? Do any of you know how we can be put in touch with Suzzan-link-khann? Tell her that her Brood-mother is here! That should get her attention!"

Simon DeBret left the company of men and apes and approached the silver-suited figures, after instructing one of the apes to fetch Suzzan and the crewmembers of Toarvak 6. Others of the ruling council made their way to the wormhole chamber to greet the visitors. At the front of the group now stood a grey haired, basically human figure. He was tall and well built, but his body shape was more like a Neanderthal than modern man. Prominent bony ridges rose over his eyebrows and his skull was wider than normal at his forehead. He wore darkened lenses over his eyes to combat the brighter sun.

"My name is Alexander Mc Bald, leader of Jupiter's human and ape civilisation that brought you here. We really do need to talk to whoever is in control of the Three Worlds or the closest representative. We have brought our Kamiel with us to help you to prepare for the problems we have uncovered."

Simon laughed and said, "Do you mean the Goss?"

Link-soo-shan stared hard at the human and asked, "How do you know about the Parasite?"

"There would seem to be an awful lot of information that we need to share," replied Simon. "Your nannite should blend minds with our Kamiel 97 so that both of them know what has transpired. The person you need to make telepathic contact with is this man stood here. He is called Larse and is part of a Toarvak. That too needs to be explained. Follow me and we can go somewhere far more comfortable than here. My office is only a short way from here so we can use the conference hall next door."

Kamiel-637 made contact with his counterpart and the two exchanged personal memories and details as the mixed group made their way to the hall next to Simon's office.

Some hours later, after the different histories of both cultures had been updated to cover the events that had lead up to this very moment in time and space, Simon introduced the original Gnathe to the Kresh representative.

'First of Clan; -WBS, (white with black stripes)' was the elected leader of all the newly recreated Kresh. He/she had now become a fully developed Kresh leader with the muscular frame and status of an adult master. The Kresh stood a clear head taller than Larse and with the upright ears swivelled towards the gathering he/she was an imposing sight. The whiskers stood out as wide as the creature's shoulders, from the two large bulges each side of the prominent nose. First's bright blue eyes stared hard at the gathering as he/she reached out to the alien minds.

The mind of the Kresh had a musical quality about it and had a contralto sound as the Kresh made contact, projecting, "I am First of the Clan - WBS (their minds were filled with a dappled pattern of black stripes on a mottled white background) and the elected leader of the Kresh. The clone I am of he/she that commanded the Toarvak ships, long, long ago. Hunted down we did, every Goss world and infected Ark we could find, before we died. Know our history you do! From your account it would seem that we missed one! Even after our deaths the artificial intelligences continued the search with some success. Gave to the Toarvak ships the last order I did. Senile and confused at the time my original self had become somewhat. My sorrow you have, that the command was not more specific. Never the less, the past is how it was and cannot be changed, so to the future we must look. Re-created by the nannites, Sharn and Minns, my people, the Kresh, have been. Now hunting for the last Ark we must begin before the Goss once more spreads. Seeking your home and technology as you have found out, infected another world the Parasite has and is to add to its store. Stopped it must be, but how do we find it before an armada of infected ships it unleashes?"

"It has been inside my mind," replied Link-soo-shan. "It is a greedy thing and to be feared, but it holds as hosts a number of alien peoples. All that I know at the moment, is that it lives on a world much further out on the galactic arm towards the rim. Our world is lethal to others because of the many microorganisms that thrive there. We wear these suits to protect you all from them. Our nannites have experience with dealing with deadly organisms. I propose that we set a trap, capture one ship and study the organism of the Goss and seek a cure."

Lord Samovar had crossed over from Daedalus One to Earth to be here as the represented leader of that world. Jondar had similarly used the short wormhole to journey from the other planet-sized moon. Both of the Kamiel nannites had made fleshly contact with a human to be able to share the telepathic bond. Kamiel 637 had joined with Alexander while Kamiel 96 had bonded to Larse who in turn carried the mind of Toarvak 6 with the rest of the crew.

Lord Francisco Samovar leant forwards in his chair and studied the imposing Gnathe across the table and said, "What do you have in mind? The fact that you have put that proposal forward means that you have considered something."

Link-soo-shan stretched her arms and shifted on her perch and said, "Very astute Lord Samovar. Yes, I do have a plan of sorts that needs to be honed by all that are here. It came to me after I understood more fully that the Toarvak ships can 'go out of phase' with the rest of the universe. What I propose, is for me to act as bait on board one ship and attract the Goss's attention by seeking its mind again to consider its offer, but not here. We need to find a world barren of intelligence, orbiting another star and place me there. Call the sun, Trap and the planet Bait! Next we need to produce a mind screen of a multitude of life to draw the ship and the Goss. This creature has never come across the power of the group mind except for the Toarvak operated by the Kresh. In orbit we will need, out of phase, at least two other ships that will carry our nannites. They will disable the Goss warship when it comes, penetrating the hull taking whatever is controlling the ship prisoner and study the parasite. Using Nano-technology they will design a hunter-killer that will bind the Goss and render it inoperative. We will also jump the captured ship to another location by surrounding it with the Gourd ships, so that the Goss cannot send reinforcements. Once we know the nature of the enemy then we can go to the next stage and that is the elimination of this abomination forever."

Both of her children stared at their Brood-mother in horror as the risk to Link's mind and sanity sunk in.

The rest of the assembly considered her proposal and the older Ender-whann-soo imprinted on their minds, "The plan is right! It has to be considered by all of us here as the only way to stop the re-spreading of this creature. I will add one proviso however. To produce the mind screen we will need to transport a great deal of Gnathe from Jupiter who in turn will carry lethal microorganisms. We need another ship to carry them, isolated from the Toarvak crew and to gather as many nannites as we can from the civilisation they have been building at the outer reaches of the system. Send one of the Toarvaks now to Jupiter while I return and explain the situation, using the new star-gate.

With the agreement I contacted Toarvak 9, relayed the order and sent them on their way to the Gnathe home world.

"I shall go with you to the world you have called Bait," came another strong thought from a Gnathe. "Hello Tyrant! It is I Khann-link-sool, reborn from my memory crystal into a young new body. It would appear that we all have much to thank you for. I have studied our history, since re-awakening."

"You were once my adversary," Link replied. "I hope that we can become friends in this time frame. We will have much to do together to defeat this abomination."

Khann laughed and answered, "You have my word that I shall do all I can. I have spent a great deal of time tuning the crystals that the mining ships keep bringing back from Icarus. We have an abundance at our disposal, have no fear of that!"

Ender's mind made fleeting contact with her grand-Brood-mothers mind, "We also have much to discuss when we have time!"

Link turned to face Larse and considered him.

"I am told that you are part of a Toarvak. Explain this to me and show me this 'out of phase' ability of your ship!"

Through Larse I communicated to all of those present, *"Designed by Kresh was I, to be able to change from this universe to others. Untouched am I by the forces of this continuum when out of phase. Through the energy of a sun can I pass and ignore the forces outside my substance. Travel with me you could on the next crystal mining expedition and experience the power of Toarvak!"*

I waited for the reply from this Gnathe from another age. Her mind was powerful beyond those I had melded with in the past. I also felt the power of the strange human by her side. He too was mentally enhanced beyond even the members of my crew. I wondered what I could do if allowed to enter his brain? Could I improve him further?

Into my mind came the cold analytical mind of the new nannite Kamiel 637 with a resounding, "No!"

First, thoughtfully gestured to all of the silver suited group and projected his/her mind, "All of you would benefit from experiencing the Toarvak in action. It will help you to plan accordingly. Toarvak 6, collect your crew and take us to the crystal reefs on Icarus."

Hovering above the complex, I extended myself into the conference room and enveloped all the living matter into a pseudopod and took us out of phase. My crew linked up and became the gestalt mind that controlled the ship.

"I will take you safely to the very surface of Icarus. This will demonstrate just what I am capable of, in what would seem to be impossible conditions for survival. Watch the cloud layers change through the observation port as we approach."

Some days later, shipments of tuned crystals had been sent to all the four worlds and were busily being shared out. The Gnathe of Daedalus Two had installed them in the new space going gourds and had crewed them with compatible group minds. The same thing was happening on Jupiter as the armada of tiny ships were put together. Now the search began through the memory banks of the Toarvak ships to find a suitable world to set the trap and one to transfer to.

Finally, in orbit around a red giant, they found an almost barren world locked in ice with warm-blooded life about the equator. With the abundance of crystal at our disposal and Kamiel's expertise, it did not take long to make a copy of the equipment based at Jupiter. Hannah had insisted on coming with Link-soo-shan to fine-tune the electronics that gave the wormhole its stability once opened. Fredrick would not agree to stay on the home world while she came, so accompanied her with his old friend Minnis. The nannite had renewed her symbiotic relationship with the giant as soon as he arrived on Earth and had astonished the Kresh with the abilities that she conferred on the human while he was encased in her envelope. I still carried a part of the mind of this extraordinary nannite that Kamiel had designed and built. She was the only nannite to have complete free will without any inhibiting programming. It was the blending of her mind with mine that gave me a greater adaptability than the other Toarvak artificial intelligences. It was this that enabled me to recognise the humans and Gnathe as possible 'New Kresh' and show the others of my kind what could be achieved.

I, Toarvak 6 had been chosen to carry the wormhole gate to the bait location. The sun was remote from the area that we called home and had no name given, so we called it as agreed, Trap and the planet, Bait. Orbiting the semi-frozen world were two moons half the size of Earth's satellite, but ideal for what we wanted. Inside each moon, out of phase, would be Toarvak 1 and 2 each carrying a fleet of gourd ships, loaded with their own command and telekinetic crystals, impossible to detect by radar or any other sensing equipment. Riding the outside of each of these Gnathen vessels would be the nannite contingent that would be launched at the Goss ship after it materialised from its wormhole. It would be their task to immobilise the ship while the Gnathe transported it to another location in orbit around a brown dwarf star. Here another Toarvak ship lay in waiting, with a set of Gnathe crystals on its surface that had been expanded as a lattice to the size of a hollow moon with the control centre a globe at the bottom. Once inside the Toarvak ship's envelope, the ship would shrink to fit and go out of phase taking the Goss ship out of this universe all together. This would take it out of communication with the main intelligence. Once inside, the nannites would set about capturing and restraining the crew while they studied the infection of the Goss.

The idea of curing the alien hosts had never occurred to my masters, as we did not have the science of Nano-technology linked to the re-creation of DNA patterns. This science could be applied in reverse. The Kresh had not felt the necessity to create independently operating nannites with personalities beyond our own kind. Again the blending of Human, Gnathe and Kresh science proved to be greater than the sum. Once they had reached maturity my original masters, the Kresh, had settled on the Southern Continent of Daedalus Two and began to selectively breed and build their own integrated civilisation with the help of the Gnathe. From the nine ships that had been built originally, they had managed to commandeer two of them to process materials mined from barren worlds and reproduce more Toarvak ships. The combined civilisation now had fifteen at its disposal with more to come, controlled by a mixture of all the intelligent races. These were true co-operatives or Toarvaks.

Larse and my operating crew came on board and eased themselves into the command positions and I flowed over them leaving just their faces open to the air. Also with us came Link-soo-shan, her daughters Suzzan and Trann with the newly re-created Khann-link-sool. The aging Ender-whann-soo and her daughters, Azander and Marren were also with the company. Alexander, Hannah and Fredrick had accompanied the wormhole equipment with Kamiel 634. All of the Jupiter bred had been cleansed of the virulent microorganisms that they had grown up with and could now mix with the others of the Three Worlds. These were all in the command section of my Toarvak, while much deeper inside, separated from them were several hundred, mixed Gnathe and their kindred. With them were humans and apes to make up the mind strength as bait. Ender and her brood-daughters were to establish a false babble of minds multiplying the number in the ship to feel like many hundreds of thousands living on the planet we called Bait.

Link-soo-shan dredged up from her memories the false persona of the Lady Jennet-soo-shang that she had used before during the time of her seeked revenge. She worked on the identity, altering and adding to it until she produced a copy of her old personality, dominated by the lust for power and revenge. To this personality she added false memories of the world they had named Bait. Link transferred the façade of the living world of Jupiter to the frozen and barren world they had decided to use. The Brood-mother from another time allowed me to enter the false mind, so that I would know this maddened creature from the controlling personality. Should the false mind take control of her body and not be able to be expunged, I was to put Link-soo-shan out of phase in my substance. The old mind was a fearsome identity and of a kind quite new to me. In all the many thousands of years I had existed I had never encountered such ferocity, rage and cunning. Should the great Lady Link not be able to expunge this maddened creature from her brain, I would have no hesitation to do as she wished. My respect for this Gnathe grew as I had got to know her and her history. She was willing to risk her sanity and with it her life to keep her people safe from this abomination.

To try to make sure that this did not happen, the Gnathe would form a group mind to anchor Link-soo-shan with reality. Khann would join Link in controlling the puppet personality that would confront the Goss, while her two brood daughters added their power to the mind-link, with Alexander the blending force containing the gestalt.

There were enough Gnathe and human telepaths to build a very large group mind to oversee the transference of the Goss ship to the brown dwarf location, using the multiple crystals carried on the gourd ships. All it needed now was to put the plan into action. As we merged minds to become Toarvak I surrendered my consciousness to the gestalt and control of all my functions. A mind within a greater mind I flipped us out of phase, twisted the fabric of the ship into a wormhole and sped towards the giant red sun we had named Trap. During the length of the journey I maintained the life signs of my crew, fed them and removed their wastes. Whilst moving through the empty void I could sense the other two ships falling through null space with me. Time stood still in real time, as we passed through the vortex of the unreal existence of being out of phase with the rest of the universe. The rest of the travellers seemed frozen in time as we sped on through the twisted skeins of the underlying fabric of space. Only the members of the Toarvak experienced subjective passing as they reached out for the exit of the wormhole at Trap and passed through travelling towards the sun.

From here a dark, cold world orbited, with one face locked to a giant red sun that dominated the sky, eclipsing the view of the two moons that were on the other sunlit side of this life-bearing world. My two companions entered the space behind me and made for the orbit that would intersect the two small satellites, made brief contact and left me to intersect the world below. The Toarvak mind opened up the mass of my substance to the universe again and we plummeted down towards the surface of Bait. Once imminent impact had been sensed, we once more phased out and entered the surface of this lonely world, passing through its molten core. After some time we were released from the rocky embrace and once more emerged into the frigid air. With precision timing the Toarvak switched us back into the universes' clasp and we floated down to sit on the bedrock amongst the tree-like organisms that competed for the watery light. My substance began immediately to spread out and cover as much of the ground as we could. I began to build extended quarters for all the passengers who would become the enticing magnet to the Goss's senses. Now was the time for the members of my crew to be released from the ship's embrace and become separate identities. Deep beneath us there was still an amount of thermal warmth and I delved down towards it to conduct it into the base of the sprawling community. The energy from the sun would not be enough to keep everything going without this as well. I gauged the temperature to be no more than ten degrees Celsius above freezing. On the other side of the permanently dark side it would fall far below. I set the 'passengers' the task of gathering as much organic material as they could find and to fill the bins that I extended from my outside walls. The entire workforce wore suits that I had previously constructed to allow them to breath and stay warm. Filling the bins would require effort and this activity the Gnathe adepts would multiply to give the allusion that many hundreds of thousands of them were here. I would reassign the molecular content to be processed as food for the multitude. After several 'days' had passed and Ender was ready to produce the false mental readings, Link-soo-shan decided that the time had come to lure a Goss ship within range. Inside both moons the other Toarvak ships 'One' and 'Two' with their crews, were also ready. The Gnathe and the nannites had taken their places inside and outside the life-pods. The human called Fredrick had taken passage on Toarvak One with his companion, Minnis. He was intent on gaining access into the Goss ship along with the nannite forces.

Hannah checked and rechecked the power supply to the new apparatus that Link would be using. She had added to the design of the cage. All around the four sided, flat-ended open pyramid, was a second cage insulated from the seeking frame. The eight points of the cube carried a shielding crystal connected to a parallel wiring system. This would be operated by the diminutive scientist the moment that she caught any feed back from Khann, Link and Alexander operating the false personality of the puppet creature; - Link-soo-shan's alter ego. At the same time both of the Kamiel designated nannites, made sure that the generators that were using the thermal energy deep beneath the surface of this world, were running smoothly. One generator was dedicated to the wormhole sensing device's new shields, while the others that the nannites had constructed, continued to feed hundreds of imitation power outlets to give a false sense, of a power using civilisation spread over this world. There were transmitters and receivers scattered all over this world to fool the Goss ship into thinking that this was the home world of the Gnathe.

Ender-whann-soo and her brood daughters, Azander and Marren had spread out within the settlement that was part of my substance, into a triangular position. Each one of them was as far apart from the other as was possible. They began to open up their minds to the Gnathe, human and apes that were within their field of operation until they had a new thing. They constructed a vast group mind composed of individuals that they began to duplicate over and over again. As each set of minds budded off from the centre, they would offset them and anchor the duplicate at another position. When they had a hexagon built of the triangles, they multiplied the hexagons until the false minds had spread over the sunlit area of the world they had named Bait, in the liveable band around the equator. They left gaps from time to time so that it would not look too regular and artificial. Once the false minds had become set in their consciousness, Ender began to remove some of them on a variable basis until the balance of minds became unsettled and the population over the area was more of a natural mix. The construction became firm and now she induced as many of the Gnathe that were in this artificial population to bond together in a group mind to bind it all together. Leaving Azander and Marren in control she stepped out of the gestalt and oversaw the created mind-set she had built. From where she probed from, this world was populated by a spreading civilisation all around the temperate part of the planet. The Goss would sense a world ripe for assimilating and should be fooled. For one thing it would not be expecting such a ploy to be sprung!

Ender-whann-soo once the victim of the Empress of the Gnathe reached out to her old tormentor and entered her mind and said, "It is ready my Lady. You can show the Goss that we live here and set the trap!"

Link-soo-shan approached the framework with some apprehension and stood for a moment readying herself for the ordeal to come.

Alexander and Khann each placed a hand on her

266

shoulder sending her thoughts of encouragement, while Suzzan and Khann added their support.

"You once were part of moving a world and saving a civilisation old friend," Alexander projected to the Gnathe. "I know that you can do it."

"Be prepared all of you, for when I make contact, it will be as if your mind has been plunged into Carrier shit. This thing is so old it reeks of the grave and it will expect the mind of our puppet to crumble. Form your group mind and add Ender to it as well as yourselves and again, I warn you to hide as you have never hidden before. It is time," she said and walked onto the frame.

Carefully she made contact with the command crystals with her feet and hands and sent her mind questing into the matrix, out towards the rim of her galaxy.

CHAPTER TWENTY

Once again Link-soo-shan allowed her mind to flow from her body, outwards towards the rim where the stars were sparse. Behind the strongest mind block that she could manufacture lay quietly the strength and knitted group mind of her companions reinforcing it. Rising into consciousness and restrained only by her will, emerged the ruthless, maddened, revenge hungry re-creation of her original warped mentality. The Tyrant lived again to serve another purpose and like a sentient puppet, raged against the controlling strings. Link fed its hunger for revenge and opened up its false memories that had so carefully been crafted by her companions and herself.

Onwards she sent the maddened alter ego, fishing for the greedy, super-mind of the parasite known as the Goss. She became aware of being noticed by an interlocking mind of enormous strength.

"Little One, you have returned!"
"You promised revenge, power and immortality! I have considered your offer and I accept. I have so very many enemies that I want to see suffer under your rule," the alter ego of the deposed Tyrant and Empress of the mighty Gnathen lands replied.

Behind the blocks set up in her mind the other members of the group mind felt the stench of the mental corruption and the sickening, disgusting odour of a gaping grave left open far too long. Knowing that they were no match for this ancient parasitic life form, they concentrated on keeping the block intact, so that not a whisper of their presence would alert the creature. The gestalt reached out and included Hannah to increase their strength.

"Where are you, my willing partner? Show me your planet and its sun's position and I will send you one of my ships."

"Here I am, mighty Goss. Look into my mind and see my world and all of its people. Use my mind as a channel for your abilities, to sense the Gnathe and human creatures that live here," Link offered.

Greedily the Goss entered the alter ego's puppet mind and sensed the false, rich pickings that Ender and her brood-daughters had spun around the world. This world was not as populated as the Goss had hoped, but the Gnathe had control of wormholes by the power of their minds and a technology that the Goss could not understand. It knew that it would when it got here and seeded the creatures with its spores. What these creatures knew, the Goss would understand and use. With these aliens under its control the whole of this galaxy would eventually belong to the parasite.

Suspecting nothing, the Goss rejoined the false Link-soo-shan and I too became part of this gestalt and we created a massive Toarvak. I reached out and gathered in my nearest two companions partially hidden inside the two moons, to strengthen this link even further. We now had the power and range of three independent Toarvaks added into the gestalt and the block held firm! At all costs we had to keep the abomination ignorant of our presence and unsuspecting.

The Goss reached out like a corrosive whip and dug into the helpless mind before it and searched for answers.

"What is the position of your sun relative to the star charts of this area? Show me so that I can send a seeding ship full of spores. I promise that you shall have everything you want.

I will see that your enemies will suffer and you shall have power beyond your wildest dreams, Little One. Wait! Where is the rattoid mind I sent to burrow into your mind and find my answers?"

"I destroyed it," spat the false mind in angry defiance, attempting to block off the bitter strength of the opposing identity. "If you do that to me again, I will help you no more," and the counterfeit mind oozed a raging resentment back at the parasitical over-mind. "Just give me what you promised so that I will serve you well and rule them all!"

The essence of the Goss wrapped itself around the now captive mind in a vice-like grip and answered, **"Little mind of inferiority, do not tell me what to do! I have no use for you any more. It would be better that you should die this moment, now that I know where you are. Let me see how you deal with a host of rattoid minds released into your poorly defended consciousness. I must now go, as I have preparations to make. I will not hear your mind again, arrogant, puny mind of rage. Its time for you to die!"**

The Goss withdrew, leaving the minds of the rat-like things behind to ravage the alter ego. The group mind swooped upon the bloodthirsty creatures that tried to fasten upon the mind and ego of Link-soo-shan. With an ill matched set of antagonists there could only be one outcome. Khann, Suzzan, Trann, Ender and Alexander bonded together with Link-soo-shan, hunted down and destroyed each rattoid mind. At the same time Hannah switched on the shielding crystals to totally cut them off from the Goss. We Toarvaks had withdrawn as unnecessary, after lending them our strength and did not interfere with the hunt.

Now all they had to deal with was the false mentality of the old Tyrant, which was fighting to retain control of Link-soo-shan's body. The combined mind pulled the false identity back from the forefront of Link-soo-shan's consciousness and allowed the real personality to retake control. Without pity, they walled it in and blocked it off, deaf to the mental screams of frustration and rage that erupted from the constructed personality. Safely hemmed in by the group mind and unable to make neurological contact with the brain that briefly carried it, they set themselves the task of dissembling the false Tyrant. Ruthlessly they expunged its memories and extinguished the hatred and the rage until all that was left was the ghost of the once Ultimate Ruler of the Gnathe.

Shakily Link picked herself up from the floor where she had dropped, twitching and vomiting what she could from her empty stomach. Alexander reached forward to help with Khann and Link motioned him away accepting the hands of the others.

"Keep your distance Alexander," she weakly asked. "I can't guarantee your safety. I made this counterfeit too well and struggle to believe I am free of its warped madness. There could be an uncontrollable reflex action. We have not come this far together for me to twist your head off! I need some water and a little time. Hannah keep the shielding crystals powered for a few moments longer in case that abomination comes back looking to see if I have survived!"

Khann helped her old enemy to her feet and declared, "We have all done extremely well. The trap is sprung and the Goss believes that this is the home world. All we have to do is wait for its ship to open a wormhole into our space for the next part of our plan to take action."

"I will return to my daughters and assist them in maintaining the false life signs for this world," said Ender-whann-soo and returned her mind to the task.

"I know where the planetary system is, where the Goss

has placed the Ark. I have found the Bazantii world! We know where to go after we have captured the infected ship," Azander cried out to the tired company. "I harvested gently on the outskirts of its mind and it was so arrogant that it never knew that I was there. Here is where it is, Toarvak 6. Can you recognise this position on your star charts?"

"I know exactly where this planetary system is located. I have sent the co-ordinates to all the other Toarvaks and now we wait for the Goss ship to emerge. I do not feel we will have long to wait. The Goss is greedy and we know it well!"

****

Some days later a rupture appeared in space/time near to the world they had named Bait and a large metal cylinder emerged into existence, rotating steadily, carrying an extension of the Goss mind. Greedily the entity reached out for the rich pickings of a virgin world and picked up the false indications of a new civilisation to assimilate. The cylinder was almost a mile in length and a good half-mile in diameter. The Goss ship eagerly made for the planet below and braked to go into orbit.

The other two Toarvak ships were mainly hidden inside the two small moons, each with a small observation post in phase, jutting out of the moons surface, monitoring events. With a surge of power the Kresh ships rose out of the moons interior and swiftly approached the Goss seeding ship, flipping in and out of phase, they cast off the armada of Gourd Ships to encircle the vessel. Undetected by any metal sensing devices, the giant Life Pods were telekinetically driven to touch the skin of the alien ship where the nannite crew tethered them securely. Soon they were fixed to the outside and rotating with it. They rapidly transferred themselves to the surface of the Goss intruder and began to seep into the interior and disappear from view. Only Fredrick remained outside, waiting for them to activate the airlock to let him in.

The brief view of the Kresh vessels as they phased into the same universe and abruptly disappeared, shocked the Goss into a state of fearful apprehension. It had not done battle with these destroying agents of destruction for over a hundred thousand years. It had always lost! Frantically the guiding intelligence tried to engineer a wormhole back to the Bazantii system, but it was too close to a planetary body for this type to work.

The group mind consisting of every Gnathe on board the Gourd Ships, reached out and warped space, to hurl themselves and the Goss ship through the Gnathen built wormhole. They transported into the space created for them, inside the expanded Toarvak, in orbit around the brown dwarf star.

In the unexpected darkness, the Goss Ship found itself abruptly inside the crystal-encrusted lattice, shaped like a globe that was the expanded Toarvak, waiting patently for its arrival. Immediately Toarvak 9 shrunk around the cylinder until it covered every single square inch of the surface and went out of phase. Three more Toarvak ships materialised at the location and joined the sister ship inside the out of phase, miniature universe and waited for results.

Suddenly the Goss mind controlling the ship became separated from the vast mind of its whole consciousness.

The immense mind of the parasite felt the Goss seeding

ship disappear from its awareness. The parasitic entity sent its attention away from the shipyards of the Bazantii world and searched for its missing element. It focussed on the location of the foolish identity that called itself Link-soo-shan, that had been destroyed and cast off. There was nothing there! Not one intelligent life sign could be sensed. For the first time in the billions of years it had existed, the Goss knew fear and became uneasy! The part of its mind that ran the seeding ship had recognised Kresh destroyers that had appeared for only a second or two. Where had they gone? What had happened?

Toarvak 9 now looked like a huge cylinder with a pronounced bump at one end where the crew and the power of the Toarvak ship was situated. The Kamiel type nannites had immediately sought out the engines and power systems, neutralising them and quickly operated the air lock to allow Fredrick to enter the vessel. The rest of the Sharn and Minns category, biogenetic engineers had gone hunting the crew. Asue and others of her kind sought out the computers and made copies of all the relevant information, putting them on standby and locked the internal doors.

The Toarvak gestalt linked to me, relaying all that Fredrick could see inside the alien ship and I fed it back to Alexander, Hannah and the Gnathe.

Fredrick and Minnis were busily keeping themselves out of reach of the many life forms teeming inside the vessel. There were thousands of piglet-sized, rat-like creatures all throwing themselves uselessly against the nannite invaders. Something similar to a pile of conically shaped donuts with an inverted cone as a head was flailing around with a tentacle that carried an electric charge and trying to seize hold of the silver beings with its other tendrils. The nannites just drained it of power and immobilised it while they penetrated its body, seeking the controlling force. At the same time a number of six limbed cat creatures similar to the mythical centaur were trying to bite and overpower a greater number of Sharn and Minns who were unhurriedly connecting to their nervous systems and rendering them paralysed. Everywhere there were silver blurs as the nannites phased in and out of computer time.

Everywhere Fredrick and Minnis looked, a variety of different creatures were all trying to ward off the attentions of the nannites. A large lizard type creature wearing a harness of tools crashed into a Sharn and was stopped where it stood by her immediately flowing over it and binding its arms. The scaly head abruptly drooped as the nannite penetrated the nervous system and began its search for the parasite. It was impossible to work out whether some of the life that endlessly surged against them was intelligent or not. Everything that was alive inside the vessel was motivated by one purpose and that was to stop the silver coloured creatures from invading further.

Something like a cross between a spider and a huge ant began to flood into the chamber that Fredrick found himself. They were as large as big dogs and were equipped with powerful mandibles and jointed arms, some ending in pinchers, others in tendrils. The spin of the ship gave an artificial gravity that kept the creatures on the 'floor'. Minnis hurled herself upwards and Fredrick dug the nannite-covered fingers into the bulkhead ceiling and tethered himself there to watch the endless battle surging over the non-responding nannites.

"Alex, this is incredible," Fredrick projected through the crystal provided by the Gnathe. "Look through my eyes all of you. The ship appears to be run by a multi alien crew and things I cannot guess the purpose of. Some of the rat creatures have exploded and a fine mist of threads is floating in the air. I am sure glad that I have my own air supply!"

Minnis interrupted the human, " Sharn and Minns have managed to locate a single organism that inhabits all of the life in here and is wound around their nervous systems. They are releasing the Nano-tech hunter killers into the bloodstreams of the aliens they are attached to. Also they are releasing them into the air in their billions! This should be interesting!"

The part of the Goss cut off from the rest of its vast intellect, felt real fear for the first time in its existence and was terrified. It could not contact the rest of its mind and could not understand what was happening. For the very first time in its long life, it felt itself begin to die! The silver creatures were not alive and would not succumb to the spores released into the air. It could feel its iron grip on its hosts slipping away and with it mindlessness! As more of the spores were destroyed, the darkness began to rush in. Its last thoughts began to gutter out like a candle flame running out of wick.

The effect was instantaneous as the intelligent life turned on the animals, particularly the rat-creatures! It soon became obvious amongst the alien creatures who were sentient and what was an animal. By now Fredrick had released himself from the ceiling bulkhead and was walking around the corridors and rooms of the ship observing the carnage. The human watched fascinated, as the aliens began to group together and systematically wipe out the rattoid infestation and several other dangerous animals. The conical creatures were catching the rat-things with their top tendrils, stunning them with their electrified one and stuffing the creatures down through the mouth on the tops of their inverted conical heads. The six legged cat people were similarly scrunching the madly scuttling things between their jaws and swallowing them whole. Everywhere Fredrick looked, the sentient aliens were enjoying a feast. It was then that he noticed the emaciated state of the alien life forms that were similar to his basic shape. An alien pressed past him on three legs and reached down to an unlucky rattoid with its four arms and tore it apart. The creature paused as it caught sight of Fredrick and pushed the pieces of bloody meat into its fringe-covered mouth and then rapidly spat the bones on the floor. The nannites joined in the hunt and silver blurs flashed from place to place as Asue opened the doors to allow the hunter-killer Nano-tech constructs to make their way through the ship. She also increased the airflow through the vents to carry the air-born microscopic spore killers to spread.

Minnis contacted her friend and one time killing partner with the words, "All clear Fred. The others have confirmed that all the spores are dead and you can remove the main part of your helmet. The air is fine and it will do you no harm to have your own set of spore killers in your system."

Fredrick did so as he walked into a large antechamber and became the focus of attention of the sentient aliens, when they could see that he was flesh and blood like them and very different.

The human relayed the information back to Toarvak 6, "All is OK. They seem to be interested in me and I am not the telepath that Alex is or Link-soo-shan and the other Gnathe. I suggest that you all come over and make contact with these curious people. They are waiting for the first move and I don't quite know what to do!"

There was a load pop as Link-soo-shan twisted space and ferried Alexander through with Khann, Ender's brood-daughters and her own. Suddenly the aliens became even more interested in the new arrivals. Because the Goss had telepathically linked them all to each other it was not difficult for the rescuers to make contact with the freed minds.

As I was no longer Toarvak with my crew, my mind was filled with the question; - "Could all these become New Kresh? Would it be possible that sometime in the future more of my kind would roam the stars containing and controlled by these alien species?"

Suddenly the future looked very interesting. I continued to 'eavesdrop' on the exchange of information between the rescuers and the aliens. My people quickly formed a group mind and downloaded the situation to all the alien races controlling the cylinder. We learnt that the reptilians were the first contact with the Goss and were the race that built the cylinder shaped interstellar vessels and referred to themselves as the Lagdoo. The three legged aliens with the four arms were known as the Thipdar and had reached the stage of just beginning to explore their own system with rocket propelled space ships when the Goss dominated Lagdoo arrived with the insectoids also under its control. The other life forms infected by the Goss were the conics as we referred to them. Their own name for their species was a combination of multicoloured lights flashed across the top ring of the inverted cone shaped head. Only the nannites had any chance of being able to decipher their visual language, but fortunately they could respond to telepathic communication. Neither the conics nor the insectoids had reached the point in their development of considering space flight.

The big, six-limbed cats were the Bazantii and we learned they were the latest sentient creatures to be inducted by the Goss parasite. The memories these once magnificent creatures had of their world, was a paradise turned into a polluted hell as the Goss removed the metals and minerals from the planet by open cast mining and smelting plants.

These people had been adjusting from hunter/gatherers to limited agriculture when the Ark of the Goss came to their world. All the Bazantii looked undernourished and their fur matted with filth showing myriad sores where the bones stood out from the skin and had broken through. This also explained the hunting down of the rattoid creatures and the communal feast that had ensued when the controlling influence of the separated Goss mind was cancelled by its death.

The insectoids developed miniature group minds so that any number of the sterile females would be controlled by a 'queen' and assisted by a number of males. Each group mind could link up with the next one and pass control over to a specified leader of a larger group. It would be possible for thousands of the insectoids to be controlled by a single multi-group mind. It was this ability that the Goss put to use and it used them in construction and mass production projects such as the building of the cylinder ships.

Because of the loss of creativity, nothing had been improved upon in any of the aliens' science or technology. The cylinder ships were exactly as they had first been built millenniums ago. The weapons on board were of original Thipdar design and the electronics that controlled everything had been adapted from the Conic's own systems. The only innovations were in linking all the different alien technology together. This was the one aspect that the Goss could do and having no basic mind of its own, it assimilated the fresh minds into its selfish gestalt. It was driven by the need to reproduce and spread. I now had a much better understanding of our common foe and fed this knowledge to the other Toarvak ships.

Link-soo-shan reached a decision and with the agreement of the others passed around enough command crystals to the other aliens so that each species had sufficient, to be able to telepathically connect to the Gnathe, apes and humans. She then indicated to them that it was time to move the ship to the Three Worlds' location.

Once again I released my consciousness to the group mind of the Toarvak and the over-mind took over. The four Toarvak ships filled with 'The Will and The Way' twisted space/time and brought the precious cargo into orbit around Icarus.

⁜⁜⁜⁜⁜⁜⁜⁜⁜⁜⁜⁜⁜⁜⁜⁜⁜⁜⁜⁜⁜⁜⁜⁜⁜⁜⁜⁜⁜⁜⁜⁜⁜

The Gnathe had determined that the rescued aliens would be downloaded to Daedalus Two in the vicinity of 'Sings sweetly in the Evening'; so that the Gnathe could make sure that all was well with them. The aliens took some time to adjust as none of them except the Bazantii, had ever set foot on a planet's surface before. The nannites built acceptable shelters quickly for each type of alien to live in. a variety of foodstuffs were presented to them all, to see what would be agreeable to the various digestive systems. As it seemed that the hated rattoid creatures were acceptable to them all, through the long years of domination by the Goss then those that had escaped the mass slaughter were kept in breeding pens as a staple diet. To the pleasure of the Gnathe it soon became apparent that the Pod Vine fruits were a universally digested food. Soon the insectoids had ploughed and planted an area sufficient to help sustain the new arrivals and proved willing harvesters for the Gnathen crops. Once shown by the kindred how to plant the young vines, the extensions of the 'Queen's mind and will, began to clear new land.

The conics developed an amazing ability for fishing, by entering the sea and floating with their v shaped heads above the waves. Bobbing about in this position they were able to stun the fish with their electrically charged tendril and gather them up with the others. Considering that they had never seen water as extensive as the sea around the coast of the south continent, they amazed themselves and came to the conclusion that they had evolved by a sea on their own long lost world. Soon the Gnathe developed a taste for fish as well as everyone else, smoked, cooked or raw!

Bazantii hunting skills soon began to add a varied diet of meat to the growing table of assorted foodstuffs. Once the nannites had tested the compatibility of the alien creatures to the Earth and Gnathen wildlife that thrived on the continent, the Bazantii gathered them in.

It soon became apparent that the Thipdar were brilliant toolmakers with the ability to use four hands at once. A group of them took up residence on the Northern continent and settled amongst the apes leaving some of their number behind. It was obvious that when the Goss became defeated it would not be long before they would become settled on all three worlds.

The Lagdoo had transferred to the Cheyenne complex to add their knowledge of the cylinder shaped vessels to the ruling council. There were not so many of them on board the Goss ship as they were the ones who ran most of the systems under the domination of the Goss. There were only two males and six females as crew. All of them were determined that when the fleet took off for the Bazantii world they would be going as well. Their minds were coldly logical and helped considerably in the planning of the coming assault. Once they understood the role of the nannites better it was they that thought of the chink in the armour, in the Goss's use of the cylinder ships and its infestation of the planet.

A massive debriefing of all the aliens took place and the captured cylinder shaped interstellar vessel was studied by the nannites.

****

Soon it would be time to gather in all the necessary parts of the plan and make way towards the world of the Bazantii and the Ark of the Goss. At last the 'Will and the Way' of the Kresh would be coming to call and I, Toarvak 6 would be the prime mover of the end of the Goss.

CHAPTER TWENTY-ONE

More than twenty circuits of the sun had the Three Worlds orbited and at last nearly all preparations had been made, now that the location of the Goss was known, a watch had been placed upon the world of the Bazantii. The polluted and gutted world had become an even busier hive of industry as more of the cylindrical vessels of the Lagdoo were manufactured and fitted out with weapons. The last Ark of the Goss remained in orbit, surrounded by the newly built ships, crewed by the old captive aliens and the new Bazantii.

Toarvak 9 remained out of phase, its crew in stasis, invisible to all sensors, waiting for our arrival and observing the situation. So far no cylindrical ships had left to spread the infection to other star systems. Should any do so, then other Toarvak ships planted at the edge of the Bazantii system would engulf them and go out of phase, taking them out of our universe. Each Toarvak had nannites on board, programmed with the Nano-tech hunter/killer, ready to penetrate each vessel and sterilise the infection. The ships of the Kresh did not have to lay waste to planets and civilisations, now that there was a cure that left the host empty of the Goss.

As a precaution all three worlds had been seeded with the Nano-tech hunter/killers and also the home world of the Gnathe. Jupiter had been sprayed with the microscopic machines from orbit from the space station, which had also been effectively sterilised. If the deadly parasite did make its way to the combined civilisation then it would soon perish. The spreading patterns of the minuscule nannites were studied, by placing markers in the clouds of the dumped nanoparticles. They showed that the particles did not make their way to the ground fast enough to affect the hosts and needed to drop a lot quicker to do the job they were designed to do. After some nannite deep thinking Kamiel realised that the dandelion seed construction with a smaller fluffy head would be perfect. All they had to do was to increase the size of the seed head that contained the nanoparticles in their millions, to a heavier weight. Once down at ground level the heads could explode and the hunter/killers drift with the breeze. When they were inhaled, or touched any wet area such as the eyes, mouth or excretory organs the atomic sized nannites spread throughout the host's system. They would even penetrate bare skin and burrow into the bloodstream. Imprinted into each hunter/killer was the atomic structure of the spores of the Goss. It was at this level that the nanoparticles took the spores apart and shredded their construction, using the freed atoms to reassemble themselves and add more of their number. Once all the spores were destroyed, they were programmed to go onto standby alert, to watch for any stray spores that might re-infect the cleared hosts.

There were millions of probes stored into the Toarvak ships and each dart shaped probe carried in turn, millions of the nanoparticles. The entire force of the Kresh ships now numbered more than a two hundred as empty moons and barren worlds were torn apart to build them. Kresh, Gnathe, Humans, Apes, Lagdoo, Thipdar and the Conics all were suitable as mixed Toarvak crews. The insectoids being basically a group mind anyway, found that they could meld with the Toarvak artificial mind quite easily and crewed with a Gnathe interpreter, so that there would be no problems with identifying instructions. The Gnathe found that the insectoids were exceedingly logical, even more so than the reptilian Lagdoo. As a non-technical race that specialised in genetic engineering of themselves and their creatures, they found that they had a lot in common with the Gnathe. Our new alien friends continued to prosper and spread out over the Southern continent of Daedalus Two and were helped to diversify with the limited genetic pool that they had, by the intervention of the nannites, Minns and Sharn who 'tweaked' the genes at their disposal.

The years had gone by and the Goss collective mind continued to plunder the Bazantii world, while we were careful not to alert it to our constant observation. After some time the uneasiness of the parasite abated as the Three Worlds continued to stay hidden from view and no more mental probing took place from Jupiter. The nannite community at the edges of the old solar system continued to grow and exploit the rich pickings of the Kuiper belt. The population of the nannites continued to increase here as well at Earth's moon, in line with the planned attack of the Goss stronghold. Soon we would be ready.

Larse had settled down on his planet of origin and had fallen in love with one of the daughter's of Francisco's younger 'wife', Yolanda. They had produced several boys amongst his children. All of them carried a small silver ball, tucked into the base of their brain stems. The eldest of them, Johan, was aged fifteen the same age as Larse was when we first met and about to enter the great adventures of puberty. I had carried out the same improvements that I had engineered in his father, with the same results. All across the settlements the boy children had been 'improved' by other Toarvaks imparting a small part of their substance into the children. A few of the girls were able to travel the same path as the boys and develop into the same type of augmented human. It was a beginning that would alter the human race as fundamentally, as the genetic engineering done by the Gnathe.

Part of me still lived inside my human companion and

would only be reclaimed by me on his death. This was something to my surprise that I found difficult to contemplate and deal with. It was very strange to me, as I had so many different Kresh as hosts over the years.

I have been the mind inside the host of many, but the one I remember the most, will always be the boy who carried me when I had no memories of my proud and mighty past. Larse taught me to feel the emotions of a warm-bloodied creature of flesh and rather than my master, he became my friend.

****

The time had come and I had been sent to find Larse to tell him the news; - the last preparations had been done. Everything was ready and it was time to leave.

My alter ego dropped out of orbit, spiralling down to the farm where my human partner now lived and hovered above it.

I reached out to Larse and connected to his mind, *"Larse my friend ready the time has come to leave this world and once again become Toarvak. The final time of the Goss has come and we are to once again to play our part."*

Larse rose from his chair combed his greying hair from off his forehead with his fingers. He walked slowly over to the open door where he could watch Emelia picking fruit from the raspberry canes for the evening meal. His youngest daughter, Esmeralda, stood holding the bowl at her side. They looked up as they had suddenly become darkened by the shadow of my presence in the sky above them. He sighed and stepped outside into setting sunshine and deep shadow, to place his hand upon her shoulder.

She jumped at his touch and swung round to stare him in the eyes and wilted a little under his honest gaze.

"It's time," she said.

"Yes my little flower, it's time. At last we are ready to remove the abomination from our lives. I am Toarvak and must play my part in the plan, laid down by the Gnathe. I will come back, my love. I will come back," he said and kissed her gently.

"I know you will, but will I still be here? How many subjective years will you be gone? Time will stop for you once you enter the wormhole, but not for us! Will your own children still recognise you when you return," she sobbed, "still relatively young and unchanged?

"I do this for them and you," Larse replied. "I must go and play my part. You knew that I was in at the beginning and I must be there at the end."

I could not miss the emotion of this moment and my neural circuits cringed as I dealt with the flood of the emotions pouring out of my friend. The pain that these humans suffered in their relationships was compensated by the joys, but one paid a heavy price for the other. Among my fellow Toarvaks I was unique in the ability to understand and share in the welter of emotions that my hosts brought with them. Part of my persona was imbued with the nannite Minnis, who had risked her unique personality to bring me down, when I was hell bent on destroying these three worlds. The time I had wandered these three worlds with Larse had also had its effect. I like to think that the blending together produced a better Toarvak.

When the other Kresh ships found my way of thought difficult to understand. I reminded them that if it were not for the changed way that I thought, there would be no resurrected Kresh and as I called them, New Kresh. They found me too emotional and felt that I had lost the logical approach. Again I reminded them that when they went **Toarvak** with their crew, the combined mind was of mainly flesh and blood, not cold circuits.

I interrupted the departure with the news that the part of me that was the ship was still overhead and spoke to the mind of Larse, *"Our position we will have to take in the wormhole queue. Going we must my friend and soon."*

"Demon! Give me time," replied Larse.

"To go, we must. Sorry am I that this day should come with so much pain. I am Toarvak 6 now, not Demon," I gently reminded him. *"Tell her to wait in a stasis field for our return, with the children."*

"Emelia, I have to go. I have to go now! Contact my friends at central office or your father and ask to be put in stasis until I return with the children. Your father will help you," Larse pleaded.

"If we go into time stasis, everyone that we all know will be changed by the lost years. No, Larse I could not do that to our children. It is a sacrifice we both knew that one day we would have to bear," Emelia stoically answered, holding in the turmoil that she knew her husband would read from her mind if she let go. "Take this bowl of raspberries with you. They will remind you of me and our time together."

With those words ringing in his ears and holding the bowl, Larse watched his wife and daughter turn and run into the house and shut the door. I extended a pseudopod down to my friend and whisked him into the ship hovering above him.

Inside the ship were the rest of my Toarvak crew and stored away were the nannite invaders of the Goss's realm. Also Alexander and his friends were also on board. The Gnathe were calm and resigned to the journey, for it would be a long one. The Bazantii world was far out towards the rim at the very edge of the stars. Once again Larse, Samuel, Jon with the two egg sisters Jaffin and Sing-mace-khann were united in Toarvak. All were leaving family behind. I gave up control of my identity and merged with the collective. I surged up and over the bodies of my gestalt consciousness, leaving their faces clear of my substance and surrendered completely.

Hannah and Kamiel 637 were adjusting the mind reaching apparatus and wormhole connector to serve a slightly different purpose. The male personality nannite had come up with a potentially, sensational and dangerous idea. All the controlling Gnathe had been consulted with Alexander and Hannah involved.

As Kamiel had once remarked to the surprised Link-soo-shan when she found that her personality had survived her second 'death'; - "We artificial intelligences never waste anything that we can salvage."

Not all of the Goss spores had been destroyed when they had been studied to design the hunter/killer Nano-probes. A similar type of Nano-probe to serve a different purpose had genetically altered some of them. It had been programmed to alter the excessive, reproductive drive of the mindless spore to something entirely at odds with its false ego.

This would only be tried after the world of the Bazantii had been freed of the Goss's influence and also the last Ark. The cylindrical vessels would be targeted en mass with the exception of one vessel that would be put into storage, phased out of the universe and still infected.

In the state of Toarvak under the group mind's control, we entered the first wormhole and sped through the timeless state inside its boundaries. We exited at a distant trajectory, of a lonely blue-white star that had roasted what planets orbited the sun, by repeated wide-ranging flares. As we swung out of reach of the star's grasp another wormhole opened up and once again we hurtled through it heading towards the Bazantii world. Out of phase at the moment of exit almost the entire fleet of Kresh Toarvak ships swooped out of the hole in space-time and spread out to the co-ordinates that Toarvak 9 had supplied.

Beneath them, orbiting a yellow sun was the world of the Bazantii. It was once a beautiful planet untouched by the poisons of industrial usage. Now clouds of polluting yellow smog obscured areas of countryside where the iron ore was being extracted from the earth and processed by vast furnaces. There were still places of clean forest and croplands to enable the toiling millions food, at a minimal level. One of the nannites main tasks would be the reversal of Goss's attentions and the return of the native population to a more pleasant lifestyle. Although they could not return to being hunter/gathers a more adaptable civilisation would be theirs under the guidance of the Guardians.

The Goss had been waiting for its sense of active wormholes to alert its consciousness to any attack and unleashed an ancient weapon from a long dead host. The wormhole became a one-way system, letting the arriving ships come through until the far end of the hole in space-time evaporated and closed over. Again and again the Goss's senses reached out to try and detect the minds of those who had come through the wormhole. There was nothing and yet the hole in space-time had definitely been used! It knew that something had come through as it frantically searched, broadening its telepathic receptors.

Unseen, fifty of the fully loaded Toarvaks dropped down onto the world below and released the deadly cargo of probes. Billions of nannite designed, hunter/killers exploded from the carriers and were spread by the wind across those areas of industrial pollution heavily populated. Also from a port rendered in phase for the time it took, thousands of nannite dropped out in their familiar thistle down configuration. Theirs would be the task of re-organisation of the alien peoples freed from the infestation of the Goss. They would be permanent guests on this world until they were sure that all of the lethal spores were eradicated. This could take many, many years until the quarantine could be lifted and also depended on Kamiel's offer to the Goss.

The Toarvak ships each targeted a cylindrical vessel of the Lagdoo and released a mist of hunter/killer Nano-probes shepherded by a group of nannites to their destination. Working with the known design of the Lagdoo ships it did not take long for the nannites to make their way inside and corrupt the computers into silence. All drive systems were rendered inoperative.

The last Ark of the Goss presented a different set of problems. Because the freed aliens from the first cylindrical vessel had lived inside the Ark, the Gnathe, Humans and Kresh had a reasonably good working knowledge of the inside. They already knew its weak spots and entry points. The launch tubes that the rattoid creatures had been delivered, down to the planet below, became an ideal way for the nannites to invade. The ark became surrounded by an invisible swarm of Toarvaks, all synchronised to go into phase together while some of them would enter the inside of the Ark and attack from the interior. I with my special cargo of people had been picked to go with them. As we approached the moon's surface I could see many airtight building scattered about its surface. Still out of phase we dived through the moon's crust and entered the interior. I cast out anchor lines in phase with the molecular signature of this miniature world. High above us shone the artificial sun and its attending shields that gave night and day to the inhabitants that lived on the moon's inner surface. I released my cargo of Nano-probes in a set down pattern in synchronisation with the other Toarvaks. I solidified the anchor lines into ridged legs and we waited for the effects to spread throughout the captive aliens. It did not take long for the Goss infected creatures to lose interest in the new visitors straddling their world.

The next part of the plan took action a little later.

Inside the control centre, a group of nannites connected to the flesh of sterile suited Gnathen adepts would be teleported in, leaving the nannites in control while they teleported back out. Moving at machine speed the Guardians soon bound the infected Lagdoo to the walls of the chamber and waited for the next action to be carried out. The returning suited Gnathe would enter a chamber containing the hunter/killer Nano-probes to prevent any infestation by untreated spores.

One of the cylindrical ships abruptly disappeared from this universe as a Toarvak Kresh ship took it out of phase and its own nannites disabled the drive, taking it out action. They also froze the computers leaving only life support.

Over the next couple of days, the Goss began to feel itself rapidly diminish. The mind that was spread out over the world of the Bazantii began to dim, while cylindrical ship after ship vanished from its shrinking mind in a matter of several hours.

Its stronghold, 'The Last Ark of the Goss', began to go silent to the parasites' mind. The combined knowledge of the different species began to dwindle until all it was left with, were a group of the Lagdoo that were imprisoned in the control centre. Inside the hollowed out moon, the same hatreds had flared up and a mass slaughter of the rattoid creatures was taking place, as the aliens that had existed on the brink of starvation, killed and ate whatever they needed. Once their collective stomachs were full and an uneasy peace reigned they began to recognise that the silver forms of their benefactors were new. At this point the Gnathe began to teleport inside the moon with a member of each race to explain the situation and their plans for the future.

Link-soo-shan climbed onto the mind enhancing structure that was a repeat of the equipment that she had used on Jupiter. She gripped the control crystals with her feet and hands and sent her questing mind out into the matrix and searched for the remnants of the Goss over-mind. She did not have far to seek.

"Remember me?" questioned the mind of Link-soo-shan.

"You were the one I called Little One!" replied the Goss in surprise and fear. "You should be dead!"

"You were meant to think that. I can feel that your mind is not so powerful now and can do little in the way of damage to anyone ever again," she replied.

"What do you want?" the Goss enquired directly. "Have you come to gloat? Am I about to die completely? Is this your revenge?"

Link ignored the fear-laden entreaties and let the Goss drown in its terror and uncertainties. When she felt that the Goss was more than ready to listen to Kamiel's proposition, she continued.

"We will give you back a little of your mind. There is one cylindrical ship still crewed by Goss dominated aliens. My friends will bring it back into this universe and you will feel strengthened, but not too much. They are the last part of your combined intelligence and we need to speak to all of your present mind," Link explained. "Remember you have nowhere that you can go and can do no more damage. You are contained like smoke in a bottle."

The Kresh Toarvak warped back into the universe and the Goss mind reached out to all its units, increasing in intelligence. It also realised that it was no match for the intelligence of the Gnathe mind that held it still in a vice-like grip. The Goss gestalt reached out to the mind of Link-soo-shan with its original question.

Link-soo-shan was quite blunt and answered, "We have a use for you and an offer. For the first time in your immense existence you have been studied by some of the strangest minds in the existence of this universe. A group of artificial machine intelligences with integrated personalities of once flesh and blood personalities. They are totally incorruptible and will never waste a useful resource, no matter what! The humans call them Guardians and they are constructed beings. Let me introduce you to Kamiel 637."

At Link's nod, Kamiel walked forwards and merged his nannite hand with the flesh of the Gnathe. Once linked the nannite could use Link-soo-shan as a conduit to speak with the Goss.

"Listen carefully to me," the cold and logical mind instructed the parasite. "I am going to make you an offer. I have at my command, atomic sized programmed machines that have been used to totally destroy any of your spores they come into contact with. We can control matter at the atomic level. It is a science that has passed out of the control of living beings and now belongs to nannite minds. Using the genetic engineering expertise of the Gnathe, joined to our minds in a symbiotic manner, we have studied the spore that gives you an ego and control of your hosts. It also gives you a telepathic link to every sentient alien species that you have used. Our science can remove the control without erasing your identity, or the memories you carry of long dead sentient peoples. We can genetically alter the structure of the spores so that the Goss can live, but never control a sentient being again. You would be a universal conduit to all sentient beings, cohabiting their bodies and conferring the gift of interspecies telepathy. Alone, the spores are mindless and can only exist at the level of the creature that they inhabit. We will give you your continued existence at the price of your being no longer able to control your host. Should that ever happen then Nano-probes carried by the host, will seek out and destroy you. Think about the terrible state of the worlds that you have dominated and the inability to advance with any new ideas or research. We will take care of your reproductive needs and harvest the spores when needed. I guarantee that we will spread your life form throughout the varied species that are willing to join the federation that the future offers. Think about what we could all achieve working in partnership! The choice is yours."

There never was an alternative for the parasite to choose from and it became a symbiont instead. The mind proved to be a treasure trove of information of forgotten civilisations and some odd and incredible sciences from eons ago. The symbiont had re-spread throughout the sentient species of its one time domination and into the Kresh, Gnathe and the Human crews of the Toarvak ships. Infection by the new Goss spores made it possible for all sentient creatures to converse with each other no matter how different, without the use of the command crystals. These were now to be used as an integral part of the wormhole connecting Stargates that the new civilisation would be planting on every world they required. The Conic's poems of scintillating colours were incredible to see and the music and songs of the Thipdar were an entertainment in its own right. The insectoids' logical approach and expertise in genetic engineering rivalled the Gnathe. The insectoids had also become expert chess players once introduced to the game and a challenging opponent to anyone. Each race had an enormous input of knowledge to offer to the others. There would be plenty of room on the Three Worlds for all the different races of the rescued sentient beings to settle until empty liveable worlds became available. This would be sorted out when we returned and now all we had to do was go home. Daedalus Two was already home to those we had liberated from the first cylindrical vessel of Lagdoo and would welcome the rest of the Goss's once subjugated peoples.

The unfortunate fact was, because the ancient Goss weapon had closed and evaporated the wormhole, there was no direct way back. We would have to travel sideways and find a connecting route back from wherever the end of the wormhole materialised. It took quite some time and a lot of travelling until at last we received a heroes' welcome when we finally returned to the Three Worlds, with the last Ark of the Goss and the fleet of cylindrical ships. Unfortunately more than two centuries had passed by, in the time that we had taken in travelling to the Bazantii world and back again. Everything had changed. The alien races we had left behind had prospered and the wormholes were busy with constant trade between all four worlds. Once the now symbiotic Goss had been introduced to all those living there, a new dawn of co-operation began. The Kresh made plans to snatch their world back, just before it was torn out of orbit using the same technique that the Gnathe had used to remove the Earth from the expanding sun. After this they would eradicate the Goss from their old world, replacing the parasite with the new symbiotic spores using the Nano-probes.

****

AFTERWORD

Larse had kept his raspberries in a stasis chamber to bring back to Emelia as a token returning present, but for Larse however there was nothing to come home for at all. To his great, great, great grandchildren he was a figure out of history, commanding great respect, but not love. His love was long gone from this place and time, Emelia had eventually died of old age more than a hundred years ago, the matriarch of his family.

Larse lived for a while longer, but one day decided he had had enough and called to me to come for him. He let himself die, on board the greatest weapon ever made by the Kresh. I held him in my mental embrace in Toarvak, as he willed himself to stop. When his mind ceased to be, I found the ultimate grief beyond anything I could bear. I surrounded his wasted frame with my substance and drifted up above Daedalus One's clouds until I entered the cold vacuum of space. There was only one place to go.

I took him to the heart of a star, out of phase with the universe and here I rest. I am the only one of my kind to develop a soul and emotions. At long last I have realised that I have a female mind and that I loved this human being too. He was my son.

Outside roar the nuclear energies of a white sun while I make up my mind to join him in oblivion.

My task is done. I released my control of phasing out of this universe to embrace the destructive power of the sun and welcome the peace to be.

End.

Epilogue

A thousand Toarvaks surrounded me putting me out of phase and out of reach of the fires of this sun.

A voice spoke, ***"Your task is not done. It is just beginning!"***

ABOUT THE AUTHOR.

Barry Woodham was born in 1943 and has lived in Swindon, Wiltshire in England all of his life.

He spent his working life as a design engineer/draughtsman and worked on the nuclear fusion project for thirteen years. Finding himself with nothing to read one lunchtime, he began to write the saga of the Gnathe and the Genesis Project. The thought occurred to him that any life form evolved to live in this world would not be able to cope with the micro-organisms of another eco-system on an alien planet. After many of his colleagues began to read the chapters as quickly as he could finish them he continued on and finished the first book. The alien Gnathe are instinctive genetic engineers and alter living creatures to be their tools by the use of their brooding pouches controlled by the third sex. This first book is set millions of years after the sun has entered its red giant stage and is set on a vastly altered Jupiter. Humanity and intelligent Pan-chimpanzees are recreated by four Guardians made of nano-technology sent towards the stars from the dying Earth, to bring back mankind. One ship is stuck in the Kuiper Belt until it begins to fall towards the new sun and the crew are activated.

He was able to take early retirement through a legacy and continued to write the next book following on from Genesis 2, called The Genesis Debt. These have both been self published on Amazon.

He has now put the final touches to 'Weapon', the third book in the series that has been self edited and printed in a spiral bound condition.

While writing Weapon he decided to link all the books

together as 'The Genesis Project' and write all the books into a series. He is now written a forth; - 'The Genesis Search' set hundreds of thousands of years after the events that occurred in Weapon. This part of the saga concerns the deliberate collision of the Andromeda Galaxy with ours in the distant future. What kind of entity could cause this to happen and why? This book attempts to settle those questions and concerns building a hunter/killer group from the ones who defeated the 'Goss' in Book Three by going back in time to remove their DNA and clone them, restoring their stored minds into young healthy bodies. At the same time whole solar systems are being rebuilt and moved by wormhole technology to the other side of our galaxy to be launched as a globular cluster towards the Greater Magellanic Clouds and safety.

Whilst writing this forth book the idea came to be, that my group of mixed human and aliens would find themselves having to deal with the abandoned machine intelligence of Von-Neumann probes left behind by the events produced by the 'Harvester' and this would be worth considering as the fifth Book;– Genesis 3, A New Beginning.

The complete range of 'Genesis Project' books by Barry E Woodham are available in hard copy and eBook file formats and include:-

Book 1. 'Genesis 2'
Hard copy	ISBN 978-1-909020-79-5
eBook for Kindle	ISBN 978-1-909020-81-8
eBook for all other readers	ISBN 978-1-909020-80-1

Book 2. 'Genesis Debt'
Hard copy	ISBN 978-1-909020-82-5
eBook for Kindle	ISBN 978-1-909020-84-9
eBook for all other readers	ISBN 978-1-909020-83-2

Book 3. 'Genesis Weapon'
Hard copy	ISBN 978-1-909020-85-6
eBook for Kindle	ISBN 978-1-909020-87-0
eBook for all other readers	ISBN 978-1-909020-86-3

Book 4. 'Genesis Search'
Hard copy	ISBN 978-1-909020-88-7
eBook for Kindle	ISBN 978-1-909020-90-0
eBook for all other readers	ISBN 978-1-909020-89-4

Book 5. 'Genesis 3 A New Beginning'
Hard copy	ISBN 978-1-909020-91-7
eBook for Kindle	ISBN 978-1-909020-93-1
eBook for all other readers	ISBN 978-1-909020-92-4

Also a new fantasy book 'The Elf-War'
Hard copy	ISBN 978-1-909020-94-8
eBook for Kindle	ISBN 978-1-909020-96-2
eBook for all other readers	ISBN 978-1-909020-95-5